DIPLOMA

By the same author:
DIPLOMATIC PLEASURES
DIPLOMATIC SECRETS

*Also available*

Anne-Marie Villefranche
PLAISIR D'AMOUR
JOIE D'AMOUR
SECRETS D'AMOUR
FOLIES D'AMOUR
SOUVENIR D'AMOUR
MYSTÈRE D'AMOUR

Margarete von Falkensee
BLUE ANGEL NIGHTS
BLUE ANGEL DAYS
BLUE ANGEL SECRETS

Anonymous
CONFESSIONS OF AN ENGLISH MAID
BEATRICE
BLANCHE
LAURA MIDDLETON
ADVENTURES OF A SCHOOLBOY
MANDOLINE
THE BOUDOIR
THE NEW STORY OF O
CHAMPIONS OF PLEASURE
CHAMPIONS OF LOVE
CHAMPIONS OF DESIRE
CAROUSEL
SABINE

# DIPLOMATIC DIVERSIONS

*Antoine Lelouche*

Nexus

First published in Great Britain in 1992 by
Nexus
338 Ladbroke Grove
London W10 5AH

Copyright © Antoine Lelouche 1992

Typeset by Phoenix Photosetting, Chatham, Kent
Printed and bound in Great Britain by
Cox & Wyman, Reading, Berks

ISBN 0 352 325305

This book is sold subject to the condition that it shall not, by way of trade or otherwise, be lent, re-sold, hired out or otherwise circulated without the publisher's prior consent in any form of binding or cover other than that in which it is published and without a similar condition including this condition being imposed on the subsequent purchaser.

## Contents

| | | |
|---|---|---|
| | *The Author Clears Up A Misunderstanding* | 6 |
| 1. | First Impressions Should Be Distrusted As Too Generous | 7 |
| 2. | The Pleasures Of Love Require An Accomplice | 24 |
| 3. | Interesting Discoveries In The Dark | 42 |
| 4. | A Day Of Scholarship And Culture | 60 |
| 5. | An Alarming Ultimatum Is Delivered | 79 |
| 6. | Some Secrets Are Not Secrets At All | 96 |
| 7. | A Reputation For Generosity Can Be Bought Cheaply | 115 |
| 8. | At Times The Poor Have Their Uses | 133 |
| 9. | Unauthorised Disclosures | 152 |
| 10. | A Taste of Rural Pleasures | 172 |
| 11. | Politics Is Mediocrity Of The Highest Order | 193 |
| 12. | Life Being As It Is, One Dreams Of Revenge | 214 |
| 13. | They Are Confusing, Lovers' Goodbyes | 234 |

# *The Author Clears Up A Misunderstanding*

A Paris newspaper reported not long ago that I had been offered two million francs by the French government as an inducement to surrender my foreign diaries and publish no more. That was soon after the publication of *Diplomatic Secrets*, the second volume of my adventures in the Diplomatic Service, written in the form of a novel and with the names changed, but based on the diaries.

Publication of the first volume, *Diplomatic Pleasures*, was met by threats, not offers, threats to take legal action by some of those who recognised themselves and their inglorious actions in the novel. Naturally, I was not deterred from writing a second volume, which caught the attention of officials who dislike to be shown for what they are.

It is with regret I reveal that no offer of two million francs was made to me. There were certain discussions, yes, but no sum of money was named that was impressive enough to persuade me to abandon the pleasures of authorship. Therefore, I have written this third volume – for those who are amused by the only too human frailties of men who are inclined towards a pompous view of themselves.

During the course of relating the curious events of my years abroad in the service of France, certain high officials, it has to be said, appear in a comic or even a dishonourable light. So be it – I am not responsible for the follies of others, only for revealing them.

Antoine Lelouche
Paris 1991

# 1

## *First Impressions Should Be Distrusted As Too Generous*

By eleven in the morning the temperature had risen above 35°C and Marcel Lamont was sweating lightly in his white suit as he sauntered very slowly along the stone quayside. He was hoping for a refreshing breeze from the sea, but the air was clammy and still, much like a steam bath. Perhaps countries could be found elsewhere in the world that had a climate even more oppressive than the island Republic of Santa Sabina – but it had never so far been Marcel's misfortune to visit them.

Three years' service at the French Embassy here had done little to acclimatise him to the tropical heat and humidity. Nor to reconcile him to his lack of prospects for advancement – to be posted to Santa Sabina was the equivalent of being sentenced to Devil's Island. The entire personnel of the Embassy were there because they had offended against the unwritten rules of the Diplomatic Service. Some transgression or other of theirs had been found out, not quite serious enough to warrant dismissal or worse, but of the kind that brings down official wrath and punishment.

In the case of Marcel it was, to be sure, a mere peccadillo of no significance to anyone of sense, and in transferring him to the Embassy at Santa Sabina a serious act of injustice had been perpetrated, in his opinion. The whole affair consisted of a pompous idiot of a politician drinking too much one lunchtime in Paris and going home to sleep it off. His return early in the day had taken his pretty young wife by surprise, and he too was surprised to discover her in bed in the afternoon, clad only in expensive perfume. He became sober and very wide awake on finding Marcel with her, equally naked though without the perfume.

Naturally, it was not the first time that Marcel had enjoyed the honour of making love to Madame X. He had been her devoted lover for almost two months, and in that time she had found it possible to visit his apartment several times a week, and this in addition to his visits to her apartment when the coast was clear. When Monsieur X the important politician reeled into his own bedroom half drunk, he was too late by only five minutes to observe with his own eyes his wife's third act of love with the stranger. And this was just as well, for Marcel had made of his third time a veritable *coup de théâtre*, which if Monsieur X had seen, would have enraged him even more than discovering his cherished Veronique naked and lying in contented exhaustion in the arms of another man.

Their passion had been so furious that while Veronique lay on her back to receive him Marcel had knelt between her thighs and lifted her legs up into the air, holding them to his chest with one arm, her graceful feet up above his head. She sighed and wriggled her charming bottom on the bed while Marcel grasped her slender ankles and amused himself by opening and closing her legs slowly, as if they were a pair of scissors! From her beautiful face, flushed with emotion, he turned his admiring gaze to the dark brown thatch between her thighs and the long pink lips within it.

'*Ah, chéri* – do not keep me in this delicious torment – let me feel you plunging inside me,' she murmured, her eyes filled with a look of yearning desire.

'Have a little patience,' Marcel coaxed her, and made use of one hand to slide his stiff part between her smooth thighs from behind, so that it lay on the moist lips they hid. Then, as if performing a conjuring trick, he took hold of her ankles again and opened her legs wide to disclose his jutting part in all its pride and strength.

'Marcel – give it to me,' she sighed.

He held her legs very wide apart, the position pulling open the thin lips between them, and by pushing his bent knees under her bottom and leaning forward, it became possible to slide the head of his jerking part into her. At once Veronique uttered a thin shriek of delight and begged him to continue. Very willing to oblige her, he hooked her legs over his shoulders and pushed out his own legs straight behind, all the weight of his body now supported on his arms, his hands planted firmly either side of Veronique's head.

'In, in!' she moaned, and with a long hard thrust he pierced her to the very limit of his fifteen centimetres. He seesawed backwards and forwards in her slippery split, turning his head to press eager lips to the satin flesh of her inner thigh, and then to lick his wet tongue up and down it.

'*Ah, que je t'aime*, Marcel!' she moaned, her excitement at a frantic height as his hot belly pressed closer between her legs and his penetrating length plunged still deeper into her. He gasped out her name repeatedly as his body shook to the force of his stabbing.

'*Ah mon Dieu!*' Veronique screamed shrilly, her eyes closing and ecstatic convulsions shaking her body. Marcel jabbed faster and spurted his rapture into her, his teeth sinking into the soft flesh of her calf in a love bite that left her with a red mark for a week afterwards.

It was fortunate that her husband missed all of this. When he entered the bedroom fifteen minutes afterwards all was calm and content. Veronique lay naked on her back with parted legs, her beautiful breasts and belly shiny with perspiration. An unknown naked man lay on the bed beside her, his eyes closed as if he slept after strenuous efforts, his cheek resting on Veronique's bare thigh.

He was a man with influence, this politician, and he had gone with his absurd complaint to the very top so that instead of the posting he expected daily to London, Marcel was informed by his superior that he was to be sent at once to Santa Sabina – a country of which he had never until that moment heard. He could have resigned from the Diplomatic Service, naturally, but he felt himself ill trained for any other occupation.

The docks at Santa Sabina were not impressive. To be candid, nothing in the whole of Santa Sabina was impressive. The long stone quay on which he was strolling could accommodate no more than four ships, but that was sufficient. Three ships arriving within a week was the record. On this particular day there were two in dock, both of them scruffy tramp steamers with rust-streaked hulls and soot-stained funnels. Big passenger liners never came here – for one thing there was no reason to do so, and apart from that, the water wasn't deep enough round the island for any vessel over 1000 tonnes to approach.

Marcel ambled along sweating past the tied-up ships, one of them Portuguese and the other Egyptian. A surly-looking sailor stood at the top of each gangplank as lookout, not to prevent locals slipping on board to steal, for the Santa Sabinans were noted for their honesty. What happened as soon as a ship tied up was that fifteen or twenty young women dashed aboard to provide the crew with the consolations of female company they had missed at sea. The duty of the deck-watch was to count them aboard and count them ashore afterwards, to make sure none tried to take up permanent residence on board. The reason for the surly expression of the watch was that he was having to wait until his shipmates below had been properly solaced, and came up on deck to relieve him and let him go below for a turn with a girl or two.

Halfway down the quayside stood the Customs House, and round it were stacked bales and boxes and crates that were waiting to be examined. Clearing Customs for incoming goods – and people – was a long and leisurely affair here. Some of the stacked wares looked as if they might have stood there for years. As Marcel passed by a higgledy-piggledy pile of bales, a girl glanced up at him from where she sat on one of them. She smiled in the most friendly manner and he wondered why she was not on board a ship earning cash. And seeing a good-looking and well-dressed man, her smile grew broader. To Santa Sabinans foreigners were all rich.

She was sixteen or seventeen, he guessed, an island delight. They were to be seen everywhere, young girls like her – in the city squares, in the cafes, and in the countryside. They were always available for casual lovemaking, these charming dark-haired, olive-skinned, round-bosomed and big-bottomed girls who smiled so amicably. Some were prettier than others, but all had the broad-faced, snub-nosed and mop-headed Santa Sabina look. To Marcel they were flowers for the plucking.

This one wore a button-front white cotton blouse and a bright red skirt that ended halfway down her bare brown thighs. Beside her on the sacking bale lay a white plastic handbag and a pair of red shoes she had taken off to ease her feet. Except for the upper classes who had learned European ways, shoes were not much worn by Santa Sabinans other than on formal occasions, and a pair of woven straw soles kept on by a thong were the normal footwear. That this girl had shoes with her showed that she was on a mission of some importance, not merely servicing foreign sailors on tramp steamers.

She smiled her very friendly smile again and suggested that Marcel might wish to join her for a while in a private gap she had found in between the bales, where for only a hundred *tikkoos* she would allow him to take the fullest advantage of her. The sum was trifling – hardly ten francs – almost everything local being astonishingly cheap by European rates. But Marcel had not come to the docks in search of what he could easily find in town for nothing. Yet at the same time, he was the politest of men, with a fond and properly Parisian regard for young women.

'I regret, Mademoiselle, that I am unable to accept your very charming suggestion,' he said. 'I am here waiting for a ship to arrive that is overdue already by two or three hours.'

'My name is Carmelita,' said the girl.

She smiled again and lifted her short skirt to show more of her thighs. Marcel glanced down by reflex action, knowing quite well what he would see. Only the very wealthy in Santa Sabina wore underwear. Carmelita was exposing for his interest a patch of thick black curls where her thighs met.

'That's very pretty,' he said, returning her smile, 'but as I have already told you, Mademoiselle Carmelita, I am waiting for a ship to arrive. I am here to meet someone from it.'

'The ship from Djibouti,' she said, her skirt still held up. 'I am waiting for it too. It has been reported off Selvas and is sailing along the coast. It will be here in another hour.'

'How do you know that?'

'I have a friend in the Harbour Master's office. You must not think I am just a fifty-*tikkoo* woman who goes with any foreigner on a ship. I have important friends everywhere.'

'And also on the ship we are waiting for – the *St Fiacre*?'

'The captain is my special friend. Every time his ship comes here I go to him and stay with him in his cabin until he sails again. Sometimes three days, once when his ship had breakdowns in the pumps, almost a week. Captain Bertran could hardly stand on his feet when he got out of his bunk afterwards. Two sailors carried him up to the bridge when it was time for the ship to depart. He is a fine man.'

'But if your Captain will be here within the hour, why do you invite me to go behind the bales with you?' Marcel asked with a wide grin.

'Ah, Monsieur – we Santa Sabina girls can never have too much love. If Captain Bertran's ship came in on time, I would be in his bunk with him now. But he is late, and I am lonely. You are young and you look strong enough to please a woman well. There is no need to pay me a hundred *tikkoos* if you think I am not worth it afterwards. Have me first and then decide how much.'

Who could resist Carmelita's charming offer? Certainly

not Marcel, on a dull morning with time to spare. He had been sent for the previous day by the Ambassador, and instructed to meet the *St Fiacre* and welcome the celebrated ethnographer, Madame Nanette Jarre, who was about to visit Santa Sabina on behalf of UNESCO.

'Certainly,' Marcel had said, very well aware that he got all the jobs no one else at the Embassy wanted, 'but one small point – what is an ethnographer, if I may ask?'

His Excellency had talked at some length and evasively about the exactness of scientific disciplines and studies, from which it had become apparent that he too was as ignorant as Marcel as to what ethnography might be. Evidently it had some importance, if the Government of France and UNESCO were prepared to pay for sending an ethnographer to the remote island of Santa Sabina.

Further information on ethnography had been hard to find. The first three volumes of the Embassy encyclopaedia had vanished long ago – no one remembered when. Eaten by termites in an abnormally wet winter, one person had said. No, destroyed by Monsieur Boyes, the Second Secretary, to make pipe-lighters, according to another. Torn up page by page when the loss of a freighter in a monsoon caused a most inconvenient shortage of toilet paper, said a third. What disaster was responsible might be the subject for disagreement, but it was undeniable that the relevant volume was missing.

Recourse to the office dictionary had been disappointing, for the brief definition had been far from informative. *Ethnography*, it had said, *the branch of anthropology pertaining to the scientific description of the races of the earth*.

Marcel shrugged and accepted Carmelita's suggestion. After a quick glance left and right along the quayside to see if he was observed, he turned sideways and slipped in with her between the bales. They were stacked three high, reaching to well over two metres, and had a faintly vegetable smell through the sewn sacking. It was impossible even to guess at what might be shipped in this way other than cotton, which was neither grown on the island nor imported raw.

With a grin on her round face Carmelita tugged his sleeve to lead him deeper into the hideaway, then placed herself with her back to the bales, unbuttoned her blouse and pulled it out of the waistband of her red skirt. A moment later she undid that too and let it slide down to her feet, then kicked it off and stood with her legs apart to let him see her. Marcel noted with delight that her body was well proportioned, with breasts that were big soft handfuls of pleasure. Her belly was smooth and broad, her skin coffee coloured, gleaming and unblemished. As was usual with her people, the tips of her breasts were not pink or russet, but a rich copper-brown.

'Do you like me?' she asked.

'You are enchanting, Carmelita,' he replied, and he felt her busy fingers tugging open his trousers. In Santa Sabina there was no shyness, no modesty, no hesitation, no reserve about lovemaking. It was as natural as breathing, and no one thought twice about doing it anywhere, anytime, with anyone who caught their fancy. To the European way of thinking, this made Santa Sabina a second Garden of Eden, a paradise of earthly delights, where a man could enjoy five or six different pretty women a day for the asking – for as long as his stamina held out.

But as is well known, the original Garden of Eden contained certain problems, and so did this tropical one. Early on in his three years on the island Marcel had been forced to accept the sad truth that lovemaking with the hot-blooded women of Santa Sabina usually proved to be a disappointment. They snatched at pleasure as if the world was about to come to an end. Lucky was the man who succeeded in penetrating a dark-haired beauty for more than thirty seconds before the violence of her movements brought matters to a premature ending.

In this, the traditions of the country favoured the women and put them in control. The European way of a man mounting a woman was thought bizarre – the Santa Sabina system was for a man to lie on his back while his woman knelt over him and pleasured herself on his body. The European usage of language was wrong here, for in no way could she be said to be *his* woman. To state the position precisely, she was no one's woman, but the male beneath her was *her* man, in the sense that she was making temporary use of him. How this female dominance had come about, no one could say, and perhaps there was scope for anthropological research, though Marcel doubted whether that was what would interest Madame Jarre.

For himself, Marcel was without prejudices in matters of love and he had no objection to the local reversal of positions. But intellectual approval was not the same as practical preference – and for a good reason. The regrettable truth was that when a Santa Sabina woman spiked herself on a man's advantage, she was transformed into a sexual dynamo. She bounced up and down with a furious enthusiasm that brought herself and her partner to a climax in seconds.

Fortunately, this could not happen with Carmelita, for there was not enough space between the stacked bales to lie down and give her the upper hand, so to speak. There was no choice but to stand facing each other, bellies touching and backs against the rough sacking walls while Marcel handled her bared breasts with keen pleasure. In her busy fingers his male pride was at full stretch, and she made use of it as a handgrip to pull him even closer to her.

'Be patient for only a moment or two, Carmelita,' he said, a smile on his face.

She was standing with well-parted thighs, steady on her feet and braced against the bales, ready for his grand entrance. He dropped a hand down to her thick mat of curls and stroked the protruding wet lips he found there.

'Is it true what they say about you foreigners?' she asked, her hips jerking to the caress of his fingers. 'You never do it properly with your women – you make them lie down on their back and crush them under you with your weight. Is this true?'

'Is that what Captain Bertran does to you?' Marcel enquired, his fingers moving gently in her slippery warmth.

'No – he has travelled much and knows the ways of many lands. With me, he lies down and we do it in the proper way.'

'An obliging man, your Captain.'

'I suppose that when his ship sails to Yokohama he does it in the Japanese way,' said Carmelita with a thoughtful smile, 'and when he returns to his own country, then perhaps he crushes his woman underneath him until she collapses with fear . . .'

During this brief excursion into the talents and capabilities of her seafaring friend, Camelita's voice had become ever more shaky as her emotions were stirred by Marcel's fingers between her parted legs. As he well knew from experience with scores of Santa Sabina women, their climax came very easily. Carmelita's dark brown eyes stared glassily into his smiling face and then rolled upwards, showing the clear whites, as her body went into spasm against him.

Easy come, easy go, as the saying has it . . . and Carmelita's pleasure was quickly over. She stared at him with a questioning look on her face.

'Why you do that to me?' she asked, her clasped hand round his hardness rubbing its swollen head up and down against the wet lips between her legs where his fingers had been.

'Ah, but we have our strange little games, we foreigners,' he said, grinning at her obvious puzzlement. 'It amused me to see your pretty face in your moments of pleasure.'

Carmelita said nothing to this new evidence of the stupidity of all foreigners. With her free hand she held herself open and guided his stiff shaft to her entrance. 'Push!' she ordered him. Marcel bent his knees and straightened them again, penetrating up inside her, his hands clenched on the cheeks of her bottom. He thrust in and out vigorously, knowing she would complain unless he rammed hard, and he felt her bare belly thumping back at him – like two goats butting their heads together, as they described it locally. Carmelita put her hands on his shoulders, held on tight and sighed continuously, her head back against the bales and rolling from side to side.

'Faster!' she gasped, and her belly beat against him. Marcel gripped her bare bottom harder, his fingers sinking deep into her soft flesh as he accommodated her with short rapid stabs. A wailing cry signalled the onset of her second climax, her eyes rolling upwards again. She squeezed her body so tightly against Marcel that he was instantly overwhelmed – his desire erupted in hot throbs. Carmelita gasped and moaned and clung tightly to him, long after her brief pleasure was finished. She waited for his tremors to fade away before she giggled and asked him if he thought she was worth a hundred *tikkoos*?

'But of course,' he said, releasing his clutching grip on her bottom. 'I hope that your Captain gives you more than that when you stay in his cabin with him. He is a fortunate man to have a very charming girl devote herself to him for days on end. Where does he come from – is he French?'

'Yes, he is from Zeebrugge, he told me.'

By the time Marcel had explained that Belgium was not a part of France, his softening part had slipped from Carmelita's warm nest. She made no move to put on her clothes, but stayed as she was, leaning comfortably against the bales with her legs apart and her breasts bare and pleasing to the eye.

'I keep my shoes on when I do it with the Captain,' she said proudly, playing the ultimate status card. 'He likes me to walk on him first before I straddle him. It makes him hot for me. Do you want me to put my shoes on for you?'

While she was volunteering this interesting information about Captain Bertran and his bunkside preferences, she held Marcel's relaxed implement in the palm of her hand.

'But your *zimbriq* is soft!' she complained, using the local word for his most important male part. 'It is useless!'

'By no means, Mademoiselle,' Marcel answered, grinning at her eagerness to repeat the climax she experienced only a minute or two before – the characteristic insatiability of the females of the island. 'My *zimbriq* is as well able to serve you as any you will come across in Santa Sabina. But we have a small fault, we foreigners – between one bout and the next we require a little pause to recover our breath.'

'But that is soon remedied, Monsieur,' said Carmelita with a smile. She sank down slowly into a squatting position, her back propped against the bales behind her and her knees spread wide. Marcel looked down with delight at her brown-skinned breasts, fully exposed by her unbuttoned blouse. They were much bigger and rounder – softer and plumper – than might be expected in a girl as young as this one. But it was a racial characteristic of Santa Sabina females, he knew, and one that he personally found charming.

Carmelita rolled his soft part between the palms of her hands to encourage it, and when it began to stiffen and lengthen, she bowed her dark-haired head and put out her tongue to lick over the purple head. Marcel gave a long sigh as her fingers grasped his dangling pompoms with a light and sure touch. She broke off her licking to look up at him and grin.

'Now it is almost ready again, your *zimbriq*,' she said.

He stared with wordless admiration down her naked body, past her chubby breasts to her splayed thighs and the thicket of jet black hair that was also an island characteristic – and another that he invariably thought charming.

'Do you like my *gublas*?' she enquired, using the vernacular Santa Sabina word for breasts, and when he nodded, she cupped them in her hands, lifting them to make them look bigger still. At once Marcel reached down to take a firm hold of them himself and when she removed her own hands, he thrust his belly forward to lay his upright part between them and squeezed the pliable flesh round it.

'Another foreign trick?' Carmelita asked, her black eyebrows arching upwards. 'But it is impossible – you cannot make love to my *gublas*, Monsieur.'

He showed her how very wrong she was by pressing them closely together round his straining part while he thrust briskly into the fleshy pouch they formed. Carmelita stared up open-mouthed at his flushed face, astonished by what was being done to her. Then she shrugged in acceptance, for it was known to all that foreigners were mad. She unbuckled his belt to pull his trousers and underwear down to his knees, then grasped the cheeks of his bottom tightly to urge him on.

'Is that the way of it?' she asked, grinning up at him.

'That's it, *ma petite Carmelita!*' he sighed, sliding up and down the satiny skin in the cleft of her breasts.

She glanced down at the unhooded purple head that emerged and disappeared swiftly between her soft fleshy *gublas*.

'Just like a tortoise putting his head out of his shell,' she said with a giggle. Marcel's hands on her breasts grasped with cruel force as he gasped loudly and shook frenziedly on knees that were suddenly shaky as his hot torrent spurted up her warm brown chest to her throat. He leaned back against the bales to recover, watching the proof of his satisfaction trickling down between Carmelita's breasts to her belly.

'You like me a lot, I can see that,' she said. 'You will give me a hundred *tikkoos* when we've finished.'

'But I think we have finished,' Marcel suggested. 'As you can see, Mademoiselle, my *zimbriq* is soft and small now.'

Carmelita was not listening to him. Her fingers tugged at the part under discussion, and her fingernails sank into his flesh to arouse it, evidently in the belief that she was owed another bout in return for her amiability in allowing her breasts to be used for a curious foreign custom.

'That's better!' she said after a moment or two, sliding her hand rapidly up and down his fast-stiffening shaft. She rose to her feet and came closer to Marcel, and he felt her insert his reawakened part once more between the warm and slippery lips between her legs. He was about to bend his knees and push into her when Carmelita assumed the control of the situation which came naturally to the island women.

She pushed hard against his chest with a flat hand to tip him off balance. The stacked bales behind his back held him upright and prevented him from falling – and in a flash Carmelita had impaled herself on him with a fierce thrust of her belly.

She grasped his hips and rammed hard against him, and Marcel grinned wryly at the thought that, even though squeezed between goods piled on a quayside, she had found a way of reverting to type – he was as helpless under her onslaught as if she had him on his back on the ground and was sitting over him. Now she was in this mode, it was merely a question of how quickly she could slide herself up and down his shaft. As if to confirm the truth of his conclusion, she slammed against him with such violence that he feared she would ruin and destroy his cherished part.

His ordeal did not last long. In moments her head lolled back until she was staring straight up at the strip of sky showing between the bales. Her loins bucked hard against him, while she shook and moaned in a crisis of sensation. For Marcel also the moment had come – the fury with which she ravished him brought a torrent of passion spurting into her.

'The ship!' she was gasping. 'The ship!'

It was some little time before Marcel recovered sufficient of his tranquillity to pay any attention to her words. When he was breathing normally again, he turned his head to stare over his shoulder, out along the narrow canyon between the bales, to see a ship nosing into the harbour past the breakwater, its stubby funnel trailing thick black smoke behind it.

'Captain Bertran has arrived,' said Carmelita, and jerked her body away from Marcel, making him gasp as his sticky part was rudely dragged from its soft haven.

'Gently, gently!' he reproved her mildly. 'The ship is only entering the harbour and is not yet tied up. You cannot be very desperate for your Captain's embraces after what you and I have just done together.'

'Give me the hundred *tikkoos*,' she replied, 'you said I was worth that,' and she turned away to retrieve her red skirt from where it lay on the grey flagstones of the quay.

Marcel was outraged by this instantaneous change of mood when she thought her regular lover close at hand. He was well aware that Santa Sabinans had other views on the conduct of relations between men and women – for them lovemaking had no sentimental attachments, it was an entertainment to be enjoyed as often as possible, without guilt, yet also without affection. But even though he understood that, he was offended and annoyed at being dismissed by a seventeen-year-old with a request for cash.

Hemmed in on either side by the stacked bales, Carmelita bent over to pick up her skirt, revealing to him the *café-au-lait* cheeks of her bare bottom.

'Ah no! It is too much!' Marcel exclaimed. 'I refuse to be sent packing by a girl in this manner! Me – Marcel Lamont! It is atrocious!'

Her removal of herself from him had been so very rapid that his *zimbriq* still stood stiffly out of his trousers. With one fast step he was close behind her, his hand on the nape of her neck to keep her head down, and his other hand parting her hot cheeks with fierce fingers.

'No more!' she shrieked. 'My Captain is waiting for me!'

In the dimness down between the bales, where the sun did not reach, Marcel caught a glimpse of black curls and pouting lips. He bent over the girl and held her tightly while he rubbed the swollen head of his *zimbriq* between the cheeks of her bottom, as if about to plunge into her rear entrance. The instant that Carmelita understood the threat to the natural order of things, she uttered a shriek and sank to her hands and knees to escape. Marcel went down with her, keeping a tight grip, and as soon as he found the right way in, he pushed hard. The smooth and soft clasp of her flesh was so exciting that he butted her like a wild goat and she screeched and struggled to break away.

'Carmelita – you are a bad girl to behave with such lack

of consideration,' Marcel gasped as he butted away.

Her indignation did not last long – no Santa Sabina woman could ever resist the feel of a hard *zimbriq* inside her without succumbing to its vigorous blandishments. She braced herself on straight arms to withstand his assault, her protests turning to gasps of encouragement. And though Marcel was too lost in the joys of revenge to notice it, his victim was taking charge. She was completely open to him, her soft bottom jerking against his belly to draw him in deeper, as if her hot flesh would swallow him up. The overwhelming sensations which he felt did not last for long before his nervous system threw the safety switch. His belly convulsed against Carmelita's bare bottom, his whole body bucked in release, and his rapture jetted into her.

As before, his ecstasy lasted longer than hers. Before his final wet throb, she had escaped from his slackening grasp. The Captain was waiting for her, she insisted, and he was a man of importance, not to be kept waiting. Marcel pushed himself back on his heels and sank down slowly, his back on the bales, until he was sitting on the flagstones, his legs stretched out and his wet *zimbriq* softening visibly. Carmelita pulled her red skirt up her legs, tucked in her blouse, and held her hand out towards him. Marcel dug into his trouser back pocket to find a 100-*tikkoo* note for her.

'No, no, no, Monsieur,' she said, waving a finger at him, 'you must give me five hundred, after using me without my consent. If you do not, I shall go to the harbour police.'

'And I shall explain to the harbour police that you asked me for a hundred, but only if I thought you worth it,' Marcel retorted, 'but, alas, after three times with you, my judgment is that you are not worth that much. But I am a kind-hearted man, and so I offer the price you asked.'

'Monsieur, that is a very cruel thing to say to me. And it is also a lie, as you very well know. My body is very nice and you liked me enough to do it to my *gublas*, and I let you, though it is a strange sort of thing to do. But if you prefer to distort the truth and shame me instead of giving me what is due, then I spit on your feet in contempt.'

'What you say is perfectly true, Carmelita,' Marcel confessed with a grin. 'I was angry because you were so eager to run away when you saw the ship. Here are two hundred and fifty *tikkoos* – more than twice what you asked when we met, and half what you ask now. I think that should resolve our differences.'

She took the money and put it in her white plastic handbag.

'*Au'voir*, Monsieur,' she said, stepping carefully over his outflung legs, and neither thanking him nor spitting on him.

She disappeared round the corner of the stacked bales. Marcel shrugged and climbed to his feet, fastened up his trousers and brushed off his jacket with his hands. It was time to look for Madame Jarre coming ashore.

# 2

## *The Pleasures Of Love Require An Accomplice*

One of the very many inconveniences of Santa Sabina was that it possessed no airport. For those who desired to visit the small tropical republic there was no choice other than to voyage by sea – and that was not easy. No large steamship companies had a regular service calling there, there being too few travellers to make it profitable.

In consequence, those whose diplomatic or commercial interest compelled them to make the journey found it necessary to fly to the nearest point of convenience – Djibouti, Goa, Madagascar or Bombay, and wait there for a tramp steamer sailing with cargo for Santa Sabina. These voyages were unscheduled, and depended on the age of the ship and the reliability of its engines.

There was an interesting reason for this curiously backward state of affairs. Though Santa Sabina had been a republic for a century or more and held regular elections, the presidency was not contested. It was handed down in unbroken line from father to son in the da Cunha family, the largest landowners. As head of state, the current President da Cunha, eighth of his line in office, was able to veto any development he considered a threat to the traditional Santa Sabina way of life.

High on the President's list of undesirable developments were foreign tourists, and the lack of an airport was an effective way of keeping them out. Not that any but the hardiest and most senseless of tourists would have chosen Santa Sabina for their vacation, its climate being murderously hot and humid all year round. But it was better to be safe than sorry – in addition to cash, which was welcome, tourists brought ideas with them which were not welcome at all. Lavish spending by them could rouse in the minds of Santa Sabinans questions about why they were poor and foreigners were rich. Since there were no realistic answers to questions of that type, they were better not asked, in case thoughts of revolution followed in their train.

In truth, the island Republic of Santa Sabina was so poor and backward that no government in the world had thought it worth while to maintain any kind of diplomatic representation there until a few years ago. What brought about the sudden change was an extensive survey carried out by the World Bank, or some such meddling institution in far-off and insanely rich America. The survey findings suggested the possibility of oil fields off the west coast of Santa Sabina, and massive quantities of gold and rare minerals, including uranium ore, in the mountains of the interior.

At much the same time it was realised by the nuclear powers and the would-be nuclear powers that Santa Sabina was extremely well placed as a base for submarine and long-range ballistic missiles. But for that permission would have to be obtained and treaties signed with President da Cunha. In a great scurry of diplomatic activity a score of nations raced against each other to offer Santa Sabina aid and assistance, development loans and favourable trade terms, technical back-up, cultural exchanges – much as, in centuries gone by, intrepid explorers offered glass beads and steel knives to backward tribes in exchange for land and women.

President da Cunha was not a simple tribal chieftain with an antelope bone through his nose and zigzag tattoos on his sexual organ. He took whatever was offered free by the Americans, the Germans, the British, the Japanese and all of the others vying for his favour – and gave them nothing in return. He signed no treaties, and entered into no binding agreements, he allowed no foreign investment. In short, he kept Santa Sabina as it had always been and put the aid grants and development loans into a numbered Swiss bank account.

All of which goes some way to explain why it was that Marcel Lamont of the French Embassy in Santa Sabina stood on the quay watching a lamentably ancient steamship manoeuvre its way into the harbour and come gingerly alongside. From nowhere appeared two Santa Sabina Customs officials, bare-chested and barefoot in the heat, but wearing their uniform trousers and peaked caps as they waited for the gangway to be lowered. Their interest was not in examining the ship's freight, but in drinking a bottle or two of the Captain's whisky, a beverage every sea captain was well supplied with, but which Customs officials could never afford on their pay.

Marcel had expected pretty Carmelita to be first up the gangway to greet her Captain, and in this he was not disappointed. Hardly had a rickety gangplank been set up between stone quay and ship's side than she went flying up it, calling out at the top of her voice *'Mon capitaine, mon capitaine!'* and brandishing her white plastic handbag as if it were a flag. Not for even an instant had Marcel thought he had blunted her appetite for love – the very idea was too flattering. He knew from three years of experience that the island females, from twelve years upwards into late middle age, were insatiable. Captain Bertran was surely about to indulge his ardour for female consolation after his voyage from Djibouti.

There, up at the top of the rickety gangway, looking around her curiously, stood Madame Nanette Jarre. Marcel's heart gave a little leap in his chest at this first glimpse of her. That she was a Parisienne was obvious to him at once, for in spite of the tropical heat she had chosen to dress with style and chic. She was wearing a pale yellow blouse under a smartly cut white suit, white kid gloves held in her hand and a little pill-box hat on her head of a colour that matched her blouse. She was wearing stockings, Marcel noted as she began to descend the gangway

– something which European ladies in Santa Sabina rarely did.

Marcel hastened to the foot of the gangway and held out his hand to assist her ashore.

'I welcome you to Santa Sabina, Madame,' he said with a bow and his charming smile, 'on behalf of His Excellency the French Ambassador, and myself. I am Marcel Lamont.'

Nanette Jarre, the celebrated ethnographer sent by UNESCO was no dried-out scholar without style or make-up. She was perhaps two years older than Marcel, who was only a few months short of his thirtieth birthday. She stood as tall as he did, and she was slender, with walnut-brown hair worn short and in a froth of curls. Her eyes were a very dark brown, her nose bold, her mouth generously wide – in all, a most attractive woman, particularly to a young man of Marcel's fervent inclinations, who was restricted by a cruel fate to the wives of diplomats on the island, apart from the ever-eager Santa Sabina girls.

But it was evident to Marcel, as he conveyed his greetings, that Nanette Jarre was in considerable discomfort. She swayed a little as she attempted to reply and she was having difficulty in breathing.

'But this atrocious heat, Monsieur Lamont . . .' she murmured faintly, 'it is killing me . . .'

A burly and unshaven sailor in canvas trousers and dirty vest had followed her down the gangway carrying her luggage as if it weighed nothing – two leather suitcases with straps round them, a briefcase, a hat-box and a portable typewriter.

'Madame Jarre is unwell,' said Marcel to the sailor. 'Fetch a taxi quickly – they stand just outside the dock gates. I must get her to a doctor at once.'

The man nodded, dropped the luggage where he stood, and set off at a lope along the quay.

'Take my arm, Madame,' said Marcel, 'allow me to support you until the taxi arrives. Have no fear, I shall take good care of you and get you the best medical attention available.'

Nanette took his arm thankfully, for her legs were unsure and she was experiencing some difficulty in remaining upright. The curls over her forehead were stuck to it with perspiration, and her pretty face was pale.

'Is the climate here always so insufferable?' she gasped.

'Alas, I must inform you there are no proper seasons here in Santa Sabina,' he said. 'The temperature remains uncomfortably high throughout the year, though for the month of July it drops a few degrees when the annual rains start.'

Nanette gazed at him in horror, much too far gone to comment on his meteorological information. She swayed giddily, at which Marcel passed an arm round her waist to keep her from falling. He was relieved to hear the clop-clop of hooves on the flagging and into sight round the stack of bales where he had, not more than half an hour ago, enjoyed the facilities of Carmelita for a small cash consideration, there appeared one of the ancient carriages which passed as taxis in Santa Sabina.

It was an open four-wheeler of the antiquated type the locals called a *barossa*. Elsewhere in the world it would have been horse-drawn, but horses were expensive in Santa Sabina, and the public conveyances were hauled by mules. Marcel had almost to lift Nanette up into the carriage, for her strength had drained away. The sailor heaved in the luggage and was rewarded with a suitable tip.

'The Grand Hotel Orient – as fast as you can,' said Marcel to the driver, a thickset man the colour of cocoa, wearing on his head a battered old British-style black bowler hat in which he had stuck a long turquoise peacock feather.

This was the hotel where Marcel had lived ever since he came to Santa Sabina. By any reasonable standard it was fourth rate, but in the island's capital it passed for a luxury hotel, most of its rooms having a private shower. Living there freed Marcel from the many problems of renting an apartment or even a villa outside the city and hiring servants, which was what diplomats stationed here normally did.

He was well aware that his colleagues at the French Embassy regarded his choice of hotel as deliberately perverse, for they thought the Grand Hotel Orient was, at best, dubious – a place where unreliable men took women who were not their wives for an afternoon. In the normal way of things the celebrated visiting ethnographer would *not* have had a room reserved for her there.

But circumstances were irregular at the time of her arrival. The New Excelsior Palace Hotel was temporarily closed because of a plague of tiny pink water-scorpions lodged in the tanks to emerge through the bathtaps, a condition difficult to rectify. The Versailles Majestic was in the throes of redecoration, made necessary by the destructive abilities of white termites, which had consumed much of the ground-floor woodwork in secret before being discovered when a ceiling collapsed. The Splendide-Ritz had benefited by the closure of the two other hotels and was totally full. Only the Grand Orient could provide a suitable room for Madame Jarre.

These grandiloquent names belied the premises, of course. All had cockroaches and the local species of albino mice throughout their unreliable structure. None would have received even a one-star rating anywhere else in the world – but what of it? Style is relative. The Grand Hotel Orient was on fashionable San Feliz Square, close to the city centre, and it was there that the *barossa* was carrying Marcel and the lady at a stately trot, that being the maximum speed any Santa Sabina mule would condescend to go.

Nanette lay back on the cracked leather seat, her pillbox hat clinging to her head, her face turned up towards the over-clouded sky. The jacket of her smart white suit was undone, and through her silk blouse Marcel observed that her breasts were provocatively shaped, round and small and set high on her body. He also took note of the white-gold wedding ring on her hand and wondered who Monsieur Jarre might be, and where.

The faint breeze of the carriage's moderate speed through the streets seemed to revive Nanette a little. Her head rolled on the seat-back so that she could stare with troubled brown eyes at Marcel sitting beside her.

'It is too stupid to give you so much trouble,' she murmured faintly.

'Think nothing of it,' he said with an encouraging smile. 'I well remember what effect the climate had on me when first I arrived here. Happily the organism accustoms itself speedily to our local conditions.'

'Impossible . . .' she whispered, her eyes closing again.

Outside the Grand Hotel Orient the driver got down from his seat to unload the luggage. Marcel half carried Nanette inside, her feet moving uncertainly. The hotel was owned by Baltazar Costa, with whom Marcel had made himself well acquainted. The oldest of the proprietor's eight daughters, Concepcion, was in charge of the reception desk that afternoon. During his lengthy stay in the hotel Marcel had become very well acquainted indeed with nineteen-year-old Concepcion, but of that her father knew nothing.

Concepcion stared with round black eyes at the pretty French lady half fainting in Marcel's arms.

'It is Madame Jarre,' he said quickly, 'she is ill – I think it is the heat, but who can say? Please telephone urgently for Dr La Paz to come to see her, while I get her to her room where she can lie down.'

'Room number 416,' said Concepcion, handing him a key with a carved wooden number-tag attached. 'I will call the doctor and then come up to assist you. She looks very unwell, poor lady – will she live? My father will be very displeased if she dies in the hotel.'

Naturally, the Grand Orient had no lift. Only one hotel in the whole of Santa Sabina could boast of so modern a device – the New Excelsior Palace – and few made use of it since the day it had jammed between floors, trapping the occupants for seven hours until the mechanism was freed, whereupon the wooden lift fell down the shaft and shattered to firewood in the basement. No one was killed, happily, but three guests had broken ankles and an unmarried lady from the American Embassy claimed damages on the grounds that the furious descent and dreadful stop had caused her bust to sag prematurely, as could be seen.

Nevertheless, like the magnificent names of the local hotels, the room numbers were deceptive. The Grand Orient had no more than nineteen rooms in all, spread over three floors. As Marcel knew very well, rooms with numbers beginning with 3 and 4 were to be found one floor up, at the top of the grand staircase. A number beginning with 5 or 6, which included his own, was up on the floor above that. The cheapest rooms of all, located on the top floor under the roof, had numbers starting with 7, 8 and 9, for the sake of appearance. No one was deceived.

But on the other hand, there was no possibility that Nanette could climb even one flight of stairs. Her eyes were closed and her breathing ragged. Only the support of Marcel's arm held her upright, and as she leaned against him, right through her thin clothes he could feel the unnatural heat of her body. There was nothing for it but to scoop her up in his arms and carry her up the grand staircase!

So slender a woman could not be said to be heavy, not in any real sense, but the climb and the ambient temperature in the hotel combined to half kill Marcel. The final few steps to the landing were almost beyond him, so shaky were his knees, but wheezing and puffing badly he reached the top step at last and staggered along the passage looking for a door with 416 on it.

It was, as he expected, a large and pleasant room with a high ceiling and double glass doors giving on to a balcony over San Feliz Square. The floor was done in pink tiles, only a few of them cracked, and the bedhead was of bamboo. He sat Nanette down on the edge of the bed and at least she remained upright, although it seemed to him that her breathing was becoming more irregular yet. There was only one thing to do – her body temperature must be lowered at once!

Marcel flung off his jacket and tie and kicked off his shoes. Nanette looked at him vaguely, too distressed to understand his actions, and she made no resistance when he took off her jacket and unbuttoned her pale yellow blouse, tugging it out of her skirt and off. Under the blouse she wore only the flimsiest of transparent brassières, which he did not touch. He went down on one knee to remove her white patent-leather shoes, then stood and hoisted her to her feet to unfasten her skirt at the waist and let it slide down her stockinged legs to the tiled floor.

Her knickers were small and close fitting, made of black silk with a pattern of tiny white daisies in a line down the front, beginning at the waist and vanishing out of sight between her thighs. There was no time to undo her garter-belt and roll down her silk stockings – Marcel picked her up again and carried her into the bathroom.

Though so-called, the room contained no bath, only a shower fixture in one corner, without curtain or basin to stand in – merely a small drain set in the tiled floor to carry off the water. Marcel turned on the cold water and with Nanette in his arms stood beneath the spray. Shirt and trousers were soaked through in seconds, but most of the water was falling on her – on her face and the front of her body, cascading down between her breasts in their transparent little brassière, down her bare belly and between her thighs.

The water was not really cold at all, only tepid, but it was very much cooler than Nanette's body and before long it brought refreshment to her hot flesh. Her face turned upward toward the source of the water, and it streamed through her hair, turning its natural dark brown yet darker – and it was only then Marcel realised he had not removed her little pill-box hat. Whatever held it to her head was loosened by the falling water, and the hat fell to the tiles and rolled into a corner, its pale yellow now a saturated black.

Five minutes or so of the shower had some effect – Nanette's eyes opened again and she stared up at Marcel in surprise and, he hoped, gratitude. His arms were aching, and judging that she had recovered sufficiently to stand on her own feet – with some support – he set her upright with her back to the tiled wall.

'Your clothes,' she whispered, 'you have ruined them.'

Marcel shrugged and told her not to trouble herself. What was important was whether she felt a little better now. She assured him that she did, and would have thanked him profusely, but he suggested she conserve her strength and let the water continue to reduce her temperature.

This was how Concepcion Costa found them ten minutes later when she arrived with a large bowl of ice cubes from the bar – Nanette in soaked-through underwear and stockings, supporting herself by leaning back against the wall of the shower. But not only the wall held her upright – Marcel in shirt and trousers held her by her narrow hips, as wet as she was, his curly black hair plastered over his forehead.

'The doctor is on his way and will be here soon,' Concepcion announced. 'Here is ice, Monsieur Marcel.'

'Excellent,' he said, reaching for a handful from the offered bowl. He rubbed the ice gently down Nanette's body, from under her chin, over her throat and down between her breasts, round and round her bare belly, then slipped the cubes into the front of her tiny knickers. Nanette gave a little cry, but let him do as he thought best.

He put two or three ice cubes in each of her armpits and made her cross her arms to keep them in place. Concepcion stood silent and watched him while he applied more ice to the back of Nanette's long neck and held it there.

'I think Madame has been cooled enough now,' said Concepcion after a while. 'Let us dry her a little so that the doctor may examine her properly.'

Indeed, the treatment was having the desired effect – Nanette was more alert and was breathing almost normally. With only a little help she moved from under the shower and Concepcion took charge while Marcel turned off the water and removed his soaked and clinging trousers and socks. While he was thus engaged, he missed the pleasure of helping Concepcion take off Nanette's brassière and knickers and stockings and wrap her loosely in a thin white bath towel. By the time he caught up, Concepcion had Nanette lying on the bed, her hair wound in a smaller towel as if in a turban, and an ice pack on her forehead.

It was not long before Manoel La Paz arrived, an old friend of Marcel's and the most fashionable doctor in the city. He was a man of forty or so, completely bald but with a thick black moustache that drooped over the corners of his mouth in bandit style. He glanced at Marcel standing by the open window in only his underpants, almost dry on him already, and then at Nanette prostrate on the bed and wrapped in a towel.

'My dear friend,' he said to Marcel with a knowing smile, 'it is much too hot in the afternoon to make love to foreign ladies – they are not as accustomed to our climate as charming young ladies like Mademoiselle Costa here. I fear that the orgasm is more than their overheated bodies can tolerate – you have been here long enough to understand that it is better to wait until after dark with European ladies.'

'Manoel, my friend, you jump to conclusions and misunderstand the situation here,' said Marcel firmly. 'Mademoiselle Costa will support my contention . . .'

'Ah!' exclaimed La Paz, taking Nanette's wrist between his fingers to find her pulse, 'I understand now – you were in the midst of a threesome, you and Mademoiselle Costa and this lady, when she collapsed. My congratulations on your initiative and imagination, but the time of day was badly chosen.'

'Monsieur La Paz – we were not doing anything at all,' said Concepcion. 'Madame Jarre fainted even before Monsieur Marcel brought her up to her room.'

'No need for excuses, Mademoiselle, we doctors have seen all this before, many times,' said La Paz airily.

He sat on the side of the bed and uncovered Nanette's breasts to listen to her heart with his stethoscope. She herself said nothing, though it was evident that she was conscious and able to hear the conversation.

Marcel made no further attempt to set the doctor right – long experience of Santa Sabina had convinced him that it was quite futile to try to correct local opinion on sexual myth. Not that it was of much importance to him if La Paz went about gossiping to his friends that he had been summoned to attend a lady who had collapsed during a three-way love bout with a distinguished member of the Diplomatic Corps and one of Baltazar Costa's many daughters. Perhaps Nanette would be annoyed if she found out – but that was unlikely. As for Concepcion, the island girls were utterly without modesty or shame.

'You did the right thing, cooling her under the shower,' said La Paz. 'She must rest now and not exert herself. Make sure she drinks plenty of fluid – water with fruit squeezed in it, but no alcohol. I shall leave some salt tablets for her.'

He shook hands with Marcel before leaving, enquiring to whom he should send his account. Marcel suggested the Embassy, since Madame Jarre was in some sense an official guest.

'Very well,' he said, 'but do not attempt to make love to her for the next two or three days, my friend, until she has become more accustomed to our climate.'

Marcel shrugged and said nothing. While Concepcion was gone to find a chambermaid to sit with Nanette and put ice packs on her forehead and make her drink a litre of water every hour, he put on his wet trousers again. Jacket folded over his arm and his shoes in his hand, he said *Au revoir* to Nanette and saw her lips move, though her murmur was too faint to hear.

Back in his own room he stripped off his wet and clammy shirt and trousers and his socks, which had left a squelching trail of footprints along the passage from door to door. The trousers would require the attention of the hotel staff, to dry and iron before the suit could be worn again.

He was in the process of removing his underpants when there was a tap at the door and in came Concepcion Costa without waiting to be asked. Doors in the Grand Hotel Orient were not self-locking – unless the occupant remembered to slide a small bolt across, anyone could stroll in.

There was no point in being modest with Concepcion – she and Marcel had made love casually many times. With a smile at her, he completed the removal of his final garment and sat naked on the side of his bed.

'All goes well with Madame Jarre?' he asked.

'She will sleep, I think,' said the girl. 'I have left Sofia to attend to her. May I speak with you, Monsieur Marcel?'

'But certainly. What is it – I see questions in your eyes?'

'It is what Dr La Paz said about the three of us making love together. You did not deny it, though it was not true.'

'He would not have believed me – and it does no harm.'

'Is that the only reason?' Concepcion asked.

'But what other reason could there be?' he said, failing to understand the direction of her questioning.

'When I saw you holding the lady under the shower without her clothes on, you were looking at her with a strange expression,' said Concepcion. 'The water had soaked through your trousers and they were clinging to you – and I could see a long bulge where your *zimbriq* was standing up stiff. It seemed to me that if I had not interrupted at that instant, you would have removed the strange and unnecessary knickers Madame was wearing and propped her up against the bathroom wall while you did it to her. Am I not right, Monsieur Marcel?'

He grinned at her, standing so boldly in front of him with an accusation that was not perhaps entirely without an element of truth.

'Dear Concepcion,' he said, 'I cannot deny that the sight of Madame's unclothed body aroused me, but I do not think I would have so far forgot my responsibilities to have her in her state of semi-consciousness.'

'For that I have only your word,' she replied, nonchalantly, 'and I know you to be a hot-natured man. I think you would have not been able to resist the temptation of taking those knickers off to see her *kuft* – and then you would have wanted to feel it, and from there it is a short step to making full use of it.'

Marcel smiled to hear the local word for the soft-lipped

slit between a woman's thighs. His smile broadened when Concepcion kicked off her shoes and pulled her pink-striped frock over her head. As was customary with all Santa Sabina women but the very rich, she wore nothing at all underneath it. She was almost twenty, which was reckoned mature by island standards, and her breasts were deliciously round. Her skin was an attractive *café au lait* colour, her belly smooth and just slightly curved, with a round button set in it like an eye.

The feature that drew the eye and held the attention was the luxuriant black fleece between her thighs – the curls so thick that her *kuft* was completely hidden.

'Who can say?' said he, humouring her as he had humoured La Paz. 'The sight of a pretty woman's body has a powerful effect on me, as you have good reason to know.'

'Yes,' she said with a small grin, 'the proof of that stands very plainly before me.'

And indeed it did – Marcel's ever-eager part had reared up to its full height between his thighs and was nodding rhythmically as if in agreement with her statement. He held out his arms to her and she moved close in between his knees to let him squeeze the cheeks of her bottom in his hands and kiss her belly.

He knew she would be disappointed and offended if he failed her expectations, even though he had already that day devoted much of his stamina to little Carmelita out on the quayside. He slid the tip of his tongue up Concepcion's belly and licked at the coppery-brown buds of her breasts.

'I think the real reason why you did not contradict Dr La Paz was because you had a great desire to do what he said you did – to make love to Madame Jarre and me together at the same time,' said Concepcion. 'Isn't that so?'

The thought had not previously occurred to Marcel, and it was not without interest. But certainly he had more than once been with two women together, usually two Santa Sabina women friends who liked to share. Nanette Jarre and Concepcion Costa together was a new concept, the slender pale body and small high breasts of one contrasting with the rich skin tones and full breasts of the other. The merest suggestion of it caused his standing part to jerk sharply.

'Would you like that, Concepcion – the three of us naked on a bed together?' he asked.

'I have often wondered how foreign women make love,' said she with a certain curiosity in her voice, 'and in that way I would find out everything. She has small *gublas*, Madame Jarre, not as big as mine, but when I took off her knickers I saw the curly hair between her legs is almost as dark and thick as mine – and that seemed to me strange.'

'Really?' Marcel said, his tongue still busy with the buds of Concepcion's breasts.

She giggled and pushed at his shoulders, forcing him over on his back on the bed. In another moment she was sitting across his loins in true Santa Sabina style. His *zimbriq* was already at full stretch, but she held it between her flat dry palms and rolled it to make sure.

While Marcel watched, the fingertips of his left hand combed up through her thick patch of curls to make a parting and bare the dark brown lips. She held them open, displaying her wetly pink interior, while her other hand gripped his stiff shaft and guided it into place. She raised herself a little and sank down again to push him deep inside her.

'Today you have *me*!' she informed him. 'Tomorrow you have Madame Jarre. Then perhaps you arrange it to have both of us at the same time – yes?'

'That I cannot promise,' Marcel sighed, losing himself in the sensations of Concepcion's warm and slippery flesh round his *zimbriq*. 'European ladies are not so easily persuaded to taste new pleasures as the charming young women of Santa Sabina.'

'You have persuaded many European ladies while you have been here,' she answered, smiling down at him, 'including the wife of His Excellency the French Ambassador, who used to come here to this room to make love with you.'

She slid herself up and down his impaling shaft with vigorous speed, her soft breasts bouncing to the rhythm. Marcel lay at ease on the bedcover, pleased for once that the Santa Sabina way required very little effort of the island men. All that was asked of them was to lie on their backs and let the women have their way. While his *zimbriq* would stand up straight, a man was able to gratify his woman any number of times.

Concepcion cried out loudly, her back arching and her head thrown back. For Marcel the moment had come – her bouncing had brought him to the edge of ecstasy and her sudden climax took him over it with her, his hot essence gushing up into her belly in furious spasms.

As he had soon discovered some years ago, when he started to explore the pleasurable possibilities of Santa Sabina, young men and women alike thought of little else but making love. He had been told by more than one local that it was only natural for boys and girls to play 'Snakes and Turtles' with each other from an early age, and to be experienced in the full act of love by the time they were eleven – and this they repeated many times a day.

Perhaps it was this precocity that accounted for the failure of Santa Sabina males to be able to satisfy their girls after a few years. The boys were said to be at their best at eighteen, after which their natural abilities waned until they were able to perform no more than once a day. When they were thirty they were considered useless by the women, who looked to younger men for the satisfaction they required so very frequently.

Concepcion sat with hunched shoulders, staring down between her thighs, to where Marcel's now limp part would have slipped away from her, but for her restraining hand.

'Do foreign ladies always lie down on their backs for you and let you lie on top of them?' she asked, a thoughtful look on her pretty face.

'Not always,' Marcel answered, 'there are other ways.'

'Then show me one of them,' she said at once.

As the afternoon had advanced, the heat seemed to have grown more intense and debilitating still. Even lying on his back for Concepcion to make love to him – she expending all the energy – had caused Marcel to perspire all over his body. Nevertheless, to disappoint the girl in this would have struck a devastating blow at his male Gallic pride. To relieve himself of any excess depletion of his stamina, he arranged her on hands and knees on the sagging bed.

'Like goats!' she said with a giggle. 'At the convent school the good sisters said it was a sin to do it like this!'

'How would they know?' asked Marcel, amused and surprised to learn that the nuns of the Convent of the Precious Blood gave instruction to schoolgirls on the postures of lovemaking.

By this time the sight of Concepcion on all fours, bare rump at his disposal, had proved to be pleasantly arousing to him. Her full round breasts dangled beneath her and the curve of her belly was a delight to see. Marcel knelt on the bed behind her and put a hand between her thighs – and at once she parted her knees to display her dark-curled *kuft*.

'What else did the good sisters at the convent teach you?' he enquired. 'Were any other positions forbidden?'

'They told us the right way is man under and woman over,' she answered, 'or if there is nowhere to lie down, then standing up belly to belly. Everything else is foreign and sinful.'

Marcel was playing slowly with Concepcion's wet *kuft* while he listened, sliding his fingertips up along the long fleshy lips between dark curls. She turned her head to stare at him over a bare brown shoulder, a grin on her face.

'Make me sin, Monsieur Marcel,' she said.

It was impossible to refuse her charming invitation. He took hold of her hips, brought the head of his stiff *zimbriq* to the wet and slippery *kuft* he had been caressing, and pushed slowly into it.

As he had intended, the position allowed him to keep his hot body clear of Concepcion's equally hot body, except for where his belly touched her rump. He swung his loins back and forth in a steady rhythm that did not fatigue him, and very soon she was gasping to the little thrills that ran through her.

'Ah, it is so pleasant to sin!' she sighed softly. 'I shall ask Father Polycarp why this is so when I go to confession!'

Like all Santa Sabina girls, Concepcion's sexual arousal took a remarkably short time. Marcel had often thought that this was the explanation for their insatiability – it required eight or nine of their swift little climaxes to satisfy their desires. Long before he was ready, she shrieked and shook in ecstatic throes.

He made no allowances, but held her tighter yet by the hips and continued his steady thrusting – and before long Concepcion was sobbing and shaking yet again as she reached release. Twice more he made her climax, his own delayed crisis approaching by degrees. When he felt himself to be on the edge, he changed his rhythm to fast and hard strokes. Concepcion cried out shrilly and slammed her smooth-skinned bottom against him, frantic for release from her overwhelming sensations.

Marcel shuddered in ecstasy and spurted his passion into her.

When they both were calm again, he lay down on the bed feeling perfectly contented and ready for an hour's sleep to refresh himself for the evening. But Concepcion thought otherwise, and lay with her face on his belly and his dwindled *zimbriq* in her hand.

'Make me sin once more,' she begged him. 'It feels so good to be sinful!'

# 3

## Interesting Discoveries In The Dark

His Excellency the Ambassador was highly displeased to hear of Madame Jarre's indisposition, and seemed almost to hold Marcel responsible for it, and even perhaps for the discomfort of the Santa Sabina climate. If the whole truth were told, he had no great liking for Marcel and took every opportunity of thwarting his career by diverting him into meaningless and tedious tasks. From this it might easily be concluded that the Ambassador held suspicions that irregular relations perhaps existed between his charming wife and Marcel.

The affair had been brief, and was long since over, for at thirty Marcel was a little too old for Madame Ducour's taste. Nor had it ever involved any particular emotion on either side beyond a certain mild fondness, it being initiated by Madame – in what might be called a routine sort of way, just as she tried out in bed every youthful diplomat posted to Santa Sabina. Her current favourite, it was confidently rumoured, was a muscular blond twenty-one-year-old cipher clerk at the Australian Embassy.

She insisted, when Marcel had summoned his courage to ask her so delicate a question, that her husband was entirely without suspicion that anything of interest had ever occurred between herself and Marcel. If Marcel discovered a lack of respect in her husband's attitude towards him, and a tendency to give him the jobs no one else wanted, it could only be because of his own professional inadequacies, she declared, and had nothing to do with any alleged relations between Marcel and herself. Which was all very well, but as an explanation it did not go very far towards allaying Marcel's misgivings.

'Madame Jarre is your responsibility, Lamont,' the Ambassador told him. 'While she chooses to remain here in Santa Sabina you are to devote your time and efforts to assisting her. She will wish to meet local people of importance, I suppose, and to see the daily life of the ordinary people. She perhaps will desire to visit other parts of the island and inspect the fishing and farming communities – very well, you are to arrange it.'

'Understood, Your Excellency,' said Marcel, realising that he had been given a nursemaid's job, 'but for the present there is nothing I can do for Madame Jarre except to ensure that Dr La Paz visits her regularly and restores her to health.'

'Then that is what you are to do,' said the Ambassador with a shrug and a wave of his hand that indicated the interview was over. Thus relieved of duty indefinitely, Marcel took a *barossa* to the reserved beach, on the western outskirts of the city, to laze on the sand and refresh himself from time to time with a plunge into the tepid ocean.

The next day Madame Jarre seemed much improved when he made a courtesy visit to Room 416. She was out of bed and sitting in a chair by the balcony, wearing pink and white pyjamas, reading a copy of the local newspaper and drinking a glass of mango juice with ice cubes in it. Marcel found the pyjamas very *chic*.

She thanked him for looking after her when she was taken ill, and when he explained that he had been assigned to her for her stay, she thanked him again and promised to inform him when she was well enough to make a start on her ethnographic survey.

After that Marcel spent a pleasant and leisurely day about the city, much of it at a table outside the Gran'Caffe Camille, the most fashionable meeting place in the whole of Santa Sabina city – which wasn't saying much.

The only local newspaper, the *Daily Chronicles*, provided him with the useful information that *La Vierge du Rhin* was showing that evening at the cinema. Marcel had been a fan of Jean Gabin ever since, as an underage schoolboy, he had sneaked into the cinema on the Boulevard Haussman before the War to see *Pepe le Moko*. The film on offer now was an old one – but only old films ever reached Santa Sabina. Marcel had seen it in Paris a year or two before his disgrace and banishment.

The splendidly named Cinema des Grands Boulevards occupied a stretch of wasteland, round which a tall wire fence had been put up by the owners. At one end the screen stood on wooden stilts, and at the other end there was a sort of shack on high legs that served as a projection booth. The dusty earth between, beneath the open sky, held many rows of folding metal chairs. All seats cost the same – patrons bought a ticket and seated themselves wherever they wished.

Almost without exception, films screened in Santa Sabina were pirated – illegal copies made in a backstreet studio in Goa or Bombay, of miserably poor quality, sometimes with considerable sections missing, making it difficult to follow the action. The educated language of Santa Sabina being, for complex historical reasons, French, all other movies were dubbed into French by part-time Hindu-speaking translators in Calcutta, the results frequently being comic beyond imagining. It was fortunate that *La Vierge* was French made, thought Marcel, eyeing the empty rows of chairs and wondering where to sit.

A garish poster outside the Cinema des Grands Boulevards was in complete agreement with the *Daily Chronicles* that the movie would be shown at eight o'clock. In Marcel's experience that meant very little, as the cinema owner's custom was to wait for as large an audience as possible. Evidently Jean Gabin was not popular with Santa Sabina audiences, for by eight-thirty only about thirty people had filtered in and spread themselves over seats for five hundred.

As if in exasperation, the electric light bulbs strung along wires between poles down each side of the cinema extinguished themselves, and the clattering projector started up. Marcel folded his arms and made himself as comfortable as the metal chairs permitted, to enjoy the film. But this was not to be – the stocky figure and battered face of Monsieur Gabin appeared up on the screen and his well-known voice, hoarse with the smoke of a million Gauloises, made itself heard – and a young woman who had been sitting half a dozen seats away from Marcel on the same row moved in the darkness to sit beside him.

'*Bon soir, monsieur*,' she murmured.

He turned his head to look at her, thinking she was about to offer her services for fifty *tikkoos*, and he was asking himself if it would enhance the dramatic interest of the film or detract from it, to encourage her attentions. But there was something about her that suggested she was not what he had assumed. Dark as it was under the starless Santa Sabina sky, it was difficult to make out clearly her features, but she seemed to be a woman of twenty or twenty-one, with a white-toothed smile and a straight nose.

She was better dressed than the average, in a light-coloured short-sleeved frock with a belted waist. And something that was very definitely out of the ordinary – instead of the usual mop of curly dark hair she had grown her hair long, to below her shoulders, and it was tied back with a broad ribbon. There was, in fact, a certain stirring in the memory for Marcel – he knew he had seen this young woman before, but it was hard to recall where and when.

'Ah, Mademoiselle,' said he, polite as always, 'you and I are acquainted, of course. You are . . .'

'Mariana Mendez,' she said when he hesitated. 'I work at the Portuguese Consulate.'

'Exactly, I remember seeing you there at a reception a month or two back – it was the four hundredth anniversary of deposing King Pedro the Mad, or a similar Portuguese national holiday. Do you often visit the cinema?

Me, I am an enthusiast, even for the miserably poor films that are shown here.'

He had her placed now – most of the Embassies and Consulates employed suitably qualified local women as secretaries, though not in any sensitive areas, of course. They were paid miserable pittances, but thought themselves well paid – as indeed they were by island standards – and the prestige of working for rich foreigners made these secretarial positions well sought after.

His question received a very lengthy and unexpected reply – Mariana adored films, for they showed her something of the wide world outside her native land. She preferred European films to American ones, for she had concluded that the American countryside was occupied by cowboys shooting each other dead in saloons, while the cities were infested with gangsters who killed hourly with machine guns. None of that was remotely like the sophisticated and luxurious life she envisaged one day for herself.

European films – there was a different world, said she. Paris was the ideal place to live, where exquisitely dressed, beautiful and charming people dined in expensive restaurants and kissed under the trees by moonlight in the Bois de Boulogne. She had seen it all in films. Italian movies had once been fascinating, but not now, she complained, for they no longer dealt with romance and affairs between handsome young men with moustaches and women in silk dresses, but with the life of poor people, hungry and ill and without prospects. That was even worse than Santa Sabina.

'It is my dream, my ambition, my deepest desire, to live in Europe,' she confided to Marcel, her cheek almost touching his, 'and for that I would do anything – anything, Monsieur.'

She had moved so close to him that her thigh touched lightly against his, and it was impossible not to take her hands, which were almost in his lap, and kiss them. She had long fingers and well-cared-for nails, he noted, and as he lost all interest in Jean Gabin's problems up on the flickering screen, Marcel slid his arm around Mariana's shoulders and kissed the corner of her mouth briefly.

'Ah, Monsieur,' she said a little breathlessly, her eyes wide so that their whites gleamed in the dark, 'you must understand that I am not to be picked up casually in the street and *zeqqed* against a wall!'

'But of course not,' Marcel assured her, smiling a little at the unembarrassed manner in which she used the old Santa Sabina expression for what men and women did together.

'This I must insist upon,' she continued, making her point by tapping her fingers on his thigh, nearer the join of his legs than his knee. 'I was properly educated and have a Certificate of Ability to prove it, and I am employed on a regular basis in an important capacity. I can translate fluently from French into Portuguese, and back again.'

'It is evident, Mademoiselle Mariana, that you are as intelligent as you are charming,' said Marcel. His hand playing over her full breasts had discovered that her frock unbuttoned down the front from the low-cut neckline to the belt about her waist, 'but please, my name is Marcel.'

'Will you tell me all about Paris, Monsieur Marcel,' she asked softly, 'and how rich and famous people live? I would like so much to learn about their clothes and luxurious apartments and their love affairs. Is it really like I have seen in films?'

'Sometimes it is even better,' he answered, 'for the films do not show everything, for fear of making poorer people jealous – I'm sure you understand this? It will be my pleasure to relate to you in detail all you have ever wished to know about Paris – but this will take a very long time.'

Inside her open bodice his hand played with her full breasts, delighting in the feel of their smooth skin, for Mariana wore no brassière to support her bounties or to impede him. The buds stiffened immediately under his touch, and he heard her little sighs of pleasure.

'It may take as long as you wish,' she breathed. 'I hope that you will accompany me to my home after the cinema, and talk to me for hours – all night, if you please.'

Her head was on his shoulder, and though both of them stared at the screen, their attention had disengaged itself from the action there. Mariana had flipped Marcel's trousers open with a light touch and slipped her hand inside and under his shirt, to take hold of his stiff *zimbriq*. In the three years he had been on the island he had never before met a local girl who showed the slightest interest in Europe – or in anything outside Santa Sabina and constant lovemaking.

He did not let the enigma of Mariana's desire for knowledge interfere with his enjoyment of the pleasures she was bringing him. He fondled her breasts in increasing delight, his arousal mounting ever higher to her skilled handling of his throbbing *zimbriq*. For now he was content that the adventure had started – later on when they left the cinema he intended to go with her to her apartment and *zeqq* her a time or two before returning to the Grand Hotel Orient to sleep.

Her fingers in his trousers moved expertly on the hard shaft of his *zimbriq* and over the sensitive head she had unhooded. It was obvious that she was as experienced with men as every other local woman of her age, in spite of her ambitions for a life of luxury and sophistication in foreign and more civilised parts. Which was only to be expected, for although her expectations were raised, her nature was that of Santa Sabina, where *zeqqing* was as commonplace as breathing.

Drifting along in a blissful daze of sensation and undirected speculation about his new companion, Marcel was hardly aware of how aroused he was becoming until he felt the muscles of his belly clench automatically and his *zimbriq* rear up in Mariana's hand. His desire was on the very tip of spurting out – when a groan of dismay rose from the sparse cinema audience. The film had broken and the screen was blank. In truth, the films shown in Santa Sabina were always so very old and scratched and worn that it was reckoned almost a miracle if there was not at least one break during the showing.

Sometimes these breakdowns took a considerable time

to mend, especially if the film had broken several times before in the same place. The electric lights strung down the sides of the cinema came on feebly, those bulbs that were working, that is, and a chatter arose as the members of the sparse audience resigned themselves to a wait of annoying duration.

Marcel had recovered himself just in time to avoid squirting his virile juice up the back of the chair in front of him, and withdrew his hand from Mariana's breasts. He and she exchanged an understanding smile, she doing up her bodice while he did up his trousers over his frustrated *zimbriq*. Without a word spoken between them, they knew they would resume their play as soon as the film was restarted. And the outcome was guaranteed for him – and he meant it to be equally so for Mariana, for he intended to put his hand up her skirt and feel her thoroughly.

'A soft drink, Mariana?' he asked. 'Mango juice, perhaps, or coconut milk? Allow me to get you something to refresh you.'

'Perhaps a glass of iced plum juice,' she said, 'but you must let me fetch it. And what for you, Monsieur Marcel?'

'The same, and pistachio nuts for you too,' he told her.

There was no point in applying European conventions here and arguing that it was he who should be going to where soft drinks were sold, by the cinema entrance, on a rickety stall run by the one-eyed man who had the concession, and his eight-year-old son. In matters pertaining to food and drink, the custom of the island was that women served men. To enter now into a discussion with Mariana over a point of local etiquette would have been thought discourteous. He handed her a ten-*tikkoo* note, for another point of island etiquette was that all foreigners were rich and paid when they were in the company of locals.

She took the banknote which, though worth little more than one franc, was as large as a sheet of writing paper and designed to impress, with a colourful picture of President Pascal da Cunha in top hat and tails. Mariana touched his hand fondly and gave him a smile of affection, then set off up the aisle to join the queue that had undoubtedly formed at the soft drinks and nuts stall by the ticket kiosk.

While she was away, Marcel glanced around the almost empty cinema, guessing that the Jean Gabin movie would be taken off before the weekend unless it could attract more than fifty paying film fans the next night. Three rows in front of where he sat, over towards the side of the cinema, he saw in the half light someone he thought he recognised. That is to say, he thought he recognised the back of a head. In the ordinary course of events this would be improbable, for the back of one head looks much like the back of another, especially in poor lighting.

Nevertheless, Marcel was certain that there were not two men in the whole of Santa Sabina city with colourless fair hair cut very short and trained upwards like the bristles of a brush. In all candour, the style was too unflattering to be copied. The man could only be Colonel Jiri Svoboda, the Military Attaché at the Embassy of Czechoslovakia.

He was with a dark-haired woman and they were sitting close together, as if engaged in the same pastime that Marcel and Mariana had been enjoying before the film broke. But merely to begin to contemplate the possibility that the Czech diplomat's hand might be up his companion's skirt was astonishing beyond words, for Colonel Svoboda was without doubt the most humourless, dour and glacial person Marcel ever met – and that included the stone-faced Russians.

Many had in the past asked themselves why so insignificant and small a nation as Czechoslovakia, a mere province of the Soviet empire in Europe, found it necessary to maintain an Embassy to the even smaller and even more insignificant island Republic of Santa Sabina. Ostensibly, the answer was to promote the sale of Czech-made glassware, shoes, machine pistols and a variety of plastic explosives, which was absurd. The general population of Santa Sabina rarely wore shoes and had no money to buy Bohemian glass. President da Cunha equipped his police force and minute army with cheap weapons made in the bazaars of Bombay.

The truth of it, Marcel had long ago concluded, was far more sinister – it was known that the Czechs acted as cats paws for the Russians in the capitals of Europe, bribing, entrapping and blackmailing politicians. If these captive creatures were ever exposed and a scandal resulted, the Russians could disclaim all responsibility and the KGB could protest its innocence. That or something like it was the Czech mission in Santa Sabina, Marcel believed. How difficult it would be to bribe enough members of the Chamber of Deputies to swing a vote was a question not easy to answer clearly. Marcel thought it would be reasonably simple for a determined secret agent with plenty of hard cash at his disposal.

On the other hand, it had to be recognised that President da Cunha never let his Chamber of Deputies vote on any issue of the slightest importance. Even in routine trivial matters, if the Chamber forgot its duty and voted in a manner disobliging to the Presidential policy, he simply ignored it and did what he had planned to do all along. That being so, it seemed hardly worth anyone's time and money to corrupt the politicians of Santa Sabina.

Colonel Svoboda had not been in the cinema when the lights went down for the beginning of the movie. He could hardly be said to have been caught in a long queue at the ticket kiosk, for there was none. Marcel's conclusion was that the Czech had waited for the cinema to be dark before sliding in with his companion, not wanting to be seen with her. But why not, Marcel asked himself. He had caught a glimpse of her face in profile and she was, it had to be confessed, beautiful. And she was Santa Sabinan – her black hair and pale coffee complexion testified to that.

Evidently she was the wife of someone important, for ordinary husbands here paid no attention to their wives' lovers, usually being grateful that someone else had undertaken the fatiguing task of pleasuring them. But that made little sense, for there seemed no good reason why a beautiful young woman, the wife of someone important, and therefore rich by local standards, would be interested in a love affair with a middle-aged Czech having a square head and pig bristles for hair.

He was still puzzling over it when Mariana returned with two large cardboard cups of fruit juice, both leaking slightly. The projectionist succeeded in repairing the torn film in time, and the show resumed. The soft drinks were disposed of, and there had been no pistachio nuts available. Mariana cuddled herself against Marcel in the dark and soon his fingers were under her skirt and stroking her bare thighs.

'Ah!' said he softly when his roving fingers encountered not the patch of curls he expected but the thin and smooth material of knickers. It seemed that Mariana had progressed so far along the path towards her goal of becoming a sophisticated European lady that she had taken to underwear! It was this detail that convinced Marcel of the strength and importance of her drive to leave Santa Sabina and transform herself into a Parisian *poule de luxe*, with a grand apartment near the Bois de Boulogne where the suavest of lovers in expensive suits would arrive with huge bouquets of flowers and make passionate love to her for hours. Just like the movies.

It was sad, of course, to consider that Mariana's hopes were certain to be disappointed. It would take years to save enough from her salary to pay the fare to Paris. And if her strength of purpose endured and got her there, she would be compelled to live in the cheapest of rented accommodation. The men who called would be ill dressed, poorly shaven, and with breath smelling of cheap wine. On the other hand, he reminded himself, perhaps she would prefer even that to the certainty of nothing much at all happening to her in Santa Sabina.

While she retained her youth and looks, the most glamorous of moments she could expect would be when, as at present, she was able by virtue of her employment to make the acquaintance of a member of the Diplomatic Corps, who would remove her knickers to make love to her the European way – which no doubt she saw as exotic and thrilling, only because it was different from the island way. Well, thought Marcel with a touch of conceit, this evening she is lucky, for she has me. But what if it had been Colonel Jiri Svoboda – was she so anxious to liberate herself from all that Santa Sabina comprised that she would find the bristle-headed Czech acceptable?

These melancholy ruminations passed through Marcel's mind for only the short time required to slip his hand under the waist elastic of Mariana's knickers and feel down her smooth belly to between her thighs. Here again a little surprise awaited him – instead of the thick curly bush he associated with island women he touched a small triangle of neatly clipped hair. This seemed to him to be carrying her European aspirations to an unexpected level. He rewarded her by murmuring 'But how charming!' in her ear and she was so pleased that she parted her bare warm thighs in the most obliging way.

It went without saying that she had not neglected him during this little exploration of her charms. His trousers were wide open and her touch on his stiff *zimbriq* was arousing sensations of a very pleasurable type.

'Give me your handkerchief,' Mariana whispered, showing that her nature was practical as well as romantic. Marcel pulled it from his pocket and handed it to her, and she pushed it loosely inside his trousers as a precaution against what was surely to happen very soon.

Marcel sighed in rapture, feeling the moment at hand – but it was decreed otherwise by fortune that evening. Three rows down toward the screen, the bull-necked Czech and the slender lady with him rose to their feet, forming unmistakable silhouettes against the light. They had seen not even a quarter of the film because of their late arrival and present departure, a thought then somewhat hazy in Marcel's mind, his real attention being focused elsewhere, down between his legs where Mariana's hand played so very delightfully.

All the same, and against commonsense and human nature, his endless curiosity nagged and distracted him – with a faint sigh he took hold of Mariana's slender wrist and stilled her hand – and withdrew his own hand from her underwear.

'But what is it?' she murmured, disappointment in her voice.

'Between you and me, dear Mariana, there is much of intimate importance to be said and done,' said Marcel, 'and you yourself very rightly pointed out that you are no ordinary girl picked up in the street – let us go elsewhere, *chérie*, where we may in comfortable and appropriate surroundings deepen the friendship that has sprung up between us.'

'Ah, Monsieur Marcel – such delicacy and consideration,' she replied. 'I knew you were a person of unusual discernment when I first saw you.'

By then he had her on her feet and steered her by the arm out between the rows of seats in cautious pursuit of the Czech and his lady. Mariana was fumbling at the buttons of her bodice to get them done up when they passed the ticket kiosk and stood in Ferdinand Magellan Place. Marcel glanced round until he spotted his quarry among the evening strollers, heading southwards out of the square. Holding Mariana firmly, he set out to follow, his pace unhurried, in case they were noticed.

'But Monsieur Marcel, this is the wrong way!' his companion announced. 'I live in St Caterina Street, back that way.'

'Truly? But I thought it would be pleasant to have a drink together first. I am sure I have seen several bars down here.'

'But of course,' she said, charmed by his thoughtfulness and smiling affectionately at him, 'a little way along is the Dance Bar Rivoli – I am sure you know it.'

Like all public services in the city of Santa Sabina, street lighting was a hit-and-miss affair. In the main squares there stood tall and highly ornamented cast-iron lampposts, bought secondhand half a century ago from Lisbon, when a more modern and reliable system was installed there. They worked adequately – when the appropriate public employees remembered to check if the bulbs were still intact.

The Avenue of the Constitution, a most important thoroughfare, was graced with these nineteenth-century lamp-posts, and there were at least six of them outside the Presidential Palace. But elsewhere in the city, the amenity of being able to see after dark was not rated as particularly important. Ordinary streets had glassed-in lights affixed to the walls of buildings, though only at corners where roads crossed, so that street names could be read.

In the poorer districts, which accounted for four-fifths of the entire city, the only illumination after dark was provided by tiny oil lamps burning at the feet of plaster saints placed in niches in house-walls. The olive oil to keep them alight was replenished by nuns from the various convents scattered through the city, as a work of charity. If the holy sisters by chance missed a lamp or two, then a few of the Church's saints would stand unilluminated all night, and the local people would have to find their way home in darkness.

One result of this unusual system of public lighting was that lovemaking in the side streets was continuous from sunset each day to whenever the participants were satisfied. More usefully, from Marcel's viewpoint, following someone without being seen was rendered simple. Mariana on his arm chattered away happily as they strolled along, only pausing to voice a mild complaint when Marcel led her straight past the entrance to the Dance Bar Rivoli. He had seen Svoboda and his companion in the garish red lights around the doorway some seconds previously, and they had walked by.

'It is a very public place,' said he to divert Mariana, 'too many people and too much music for intimate conversation. There is a pleasant little bar further along.'

But there wasn't, and eventually the street led into Martyrs' Square, so named from the Church of the Four Crowned Martyrs that occupied one whole side of it. The Gran'Caffe Camille was in this square, but Marcel doubted profoundly whether Svoboda would take his companion there after going to such elaborate lengths to avoid being seen with her in the cinema. In this he was correct – at the edge of the comparatively well-lit Square the Czech simply disappeared, while the woman walked straight past the tables and chairs outside Camille's and crossed to the carriages standing outside the church.

'I was wrong about the little bar,' said Marcel, 'but here we are at Camille's, so this must do.'

Mariana was delighted by the choice, Camille's being known as the most fashionable bar-restaurant in the entire city. Around her at little tables sat the gilded youth of Santa Sabina city, the sons and daughters of the local well to do, and foreigners, who by definition were all rich, with their stylishly dressed wives and girlfriends.

'I think this must be a little like Paris,' Mariana said. 'Is it so, Monsieur Marcel?'

'Without doubt,' he answered, watching the woman across the Square. The Czech Colonel's beautiful companion got alone into one of the mule-drawn carriages, which set off in the direction of the Avenue of the Constitution at a shambling trot.

The *jeunesse dorée* who frequented Camille's favoured drinks that were large and highly coloured, no doubt in reaction from the workaday intoxicating drink made locally – *araq*, a fearful distillation of palm wine, that resembled pale urine and tasted much as one would imagine pale urine to taste. Imbibed in large quantities it brought on crippling hangovers, days of sickness and debility, blinding headaches, necrosis of the kidneys and liver, and rapid softening of the brain.

Svoboda reappeared on the café terrace, looking about as if to locate someone. Marcel was afraid he had been spotted during the pursuit from the cinema, and averted his face. A boy waiter hovered beside him, and without asking Mariana her preference, Marcel ordered creme de menthe frappé for both of them. Out of the corner of his eye he saw Svoboda sit down at an empty table behind him and to the left.

Mariana was enchanted by the choice of drinks, believing them to be the favourite of Parisian upper crust drinkers, ordered especially to give her a foretaste of sophisticated delights to come. She stroked the back of

Marcel's hand while she sipped at the bright violet concoction in her tall glass – it would have been unkind to tell her that the so-called creme de menthe was in reality local palm wine strongly flavoured with the coarse wild mint that grew up in the hills north of Santa Sabina city.

Her home on St Caterina Street proved to be the usual sort of apartment for those neither penniless nor well off, and up two flights of unlit stone stairs. The living room french windows stood wide open to the balconies and the street below, in vain hope of a breath of air. Madame Mendez, Mariana's mother, forty and with a shapeless figure under a brightly pink cotton frock, sat on a bamboo chair by one window, half in the room and half out on the balcony. Marcel assumed she was indulging the hobby of watching who went past in the street, and with whom.

She made a great fuss of Marcel when he was introduced by her daughter and learned that he was French and a diplomat. She saw his potential value to Mariana instantly, and to herself at one remove, and she took every care to play the gracious hostess to him. He was made to sit in the most comfortable chair while she bustled out to the kitchen to make coffee and open a bottle of wine. Marcel knew beyond all possibility of doubt that the wine would be locally grown and vile. Whether it was the climate or the soil, the slopes of Santa Sabina had never yet produced a decent bottle of wine, and never would. But courtesy demanded that he should drink whatever he was offered and praise it.

Meanwhile, while Madame occupied herself with these domestic duties, Mariana showed Marcel her magazines. She had been given them by the Portuguese at the Consulate where she worked and also by other foreigners she had met. They were in the main women's and fashion magazines – French, German, English and American – with glossy illustrations of impossibly charming models in expensive clothes. There were pictures of social and cultural events at Vienna, Paris, Milan, and colour photographs of the interiors of the homes of vicomtes, millionaires and film stars.

'Are any of these like your apartment in Paris?' she

enquired in all seriousness, and Marcel explained that he thought it not worth while to keep a home in Paris during his foreign service, but that his Mama lived a little outside, at Neuilly.

'In a château, naturally,' said the irrepressible Mariana. He was spared the necessity of answering by the return of Madame Mendez with her tray of refreshments. She poured him a glass of white wine and he was able to glimpse the gaudily printed label – *St-Pommery du Lac Beau Rivage*. Like much else on the island, it was a grandiloquently meaningless name for a very inferior product.

To encourage her daughter's prospects, Madame Mendez retired to bed after one small glass of the ill-tasting wine. Mariana took Marcel by the hand and led him across the sitting room to a long bamboo settee with thin grey cushions. He expected that she would sit beside him and drape herself about his neck, but first there was the question of impressing him. To do that, she stood in front of him, her chin up, knees together, feet turned slightly outwards, in a pose copied from a fashion model in her magazines.

When she had his full attention, she took off her dress, each movement of arms and body carefully thought out to be graceful. The point of it, he saw at last, was to show him that she wore knickers – a garment unknown to all but the rich of the island. To Marcel's knowledge there was only one small shop in the city that sold imported female underwear, and the prices there were formidable. Mariana could have spent three months' salary there for two tiny silk garments – unless of course she had been on terms of close friendship with a foreigner, like himself.

'Very pretty, Mariana,' he said, knowing she was waiting for him to praise her. 'In those delightful little knickers you are even more charming than ever.'

'When I am alone and looking at my magazines I always think of myself as *Marie*, not Mariana,' she answered softly. 'It is more *chic*. When I get to Paris I shall change my name to Marie forever.'

She sat across his lap, her arm round his neck, and he

played with her full bare breasts to his heart's content. When at last he slipped his hand down the front of her tiny French knickers to feel between her legs, she was already on the very brink of a climax. He could guess what tremendous effort of will it cost her to continue playing her role of European sophisticate, when her whole nature surely urged her to revert to the immemorial traditions of Santa Sabina – to push her man down flat on his back and straddle him for rapid satisfaction.

Her bare back arched, her thighs splayed outwards, and with a gasp of relief she went into a frantic sexual climax, Marcel's fingers teasing it out for as long as he could.

'Ah, Marie, we shall become very good friends, you and I,' he murmured in her ear. 'Let us go to your bedroom and make love to each other all night.'

# 4

## A Day Of Scholarship And Culture

When Nanette Jarre felt well enough to begin her ethnographical work she requested Marcel to show her the national library, for it was useful to begin by consulting local works of record, she said. Marcel explained that only one library, national or otherwise, existed in Santa Sabina city, and none at all elsewhere in the island. This was the Augusto da Cunha Memorial Library, named in honour of a nineteenth-century president and member of the da Cunha dynasty, and indeed founded with his own collection of books after his demise.

Further, Marcel explained, the public were allowed into the heavily ornate building which housed the Library, but never to handle the books, which were regarded as a national treasure of incalculable worth.

'What then do they do in this remarkable Memorial Library if they are prohibited from reading?' asked Madame Jarre. She was looking composed and pretty that morning, in a silk blouse and white linen skirt. Evidently she was slowly becoming accustomed to the unrelenting heat of the island.

'They go to admire the portrait paintings of old Augusto and other members of the notable da Cunha family,' said Marcel with a tiny shrug. 'His fourth wife was an outstandingly beautiful woman. They can look at his parade uniform and ceremonial sword in their glass cases, and admire a copy of the Constitution of Santa Sabina which is on display.'

'Nonsense!' said Nanette. 'Why do they really go there – if they do?'

'For the most human of all reasons,' Marcel confessed with a broad grin. 'The da Cunha Memorial Library is a meeting point for young men and women who wish to make new friends, as is the National Museum, the Martyr's Church and the fruit market, but the library and museum are a cut above the others and attract a better type of seeker, if you understand me.'

'You mean these places are haunts of prostitution?' Nanette asked, frowning slightly at Marcel's indirectness of speech.

'No, no, no – there are other and clearly designated places for that,' he told her. 'When I said new *friends*, what I meant was new sexual partners. These people are absolutely obsessive in their demands, and no shame attaches to the constant pursuit of new experience. Or to be more precise, new partners for the same old experience. As you would expect, recognised places have over the years come into being for casual meetings.'

'And the national library is one of them? Already I can see that my survey will uncover some interesting ethnic practices.'

During their stroll through the city to the Memorial Library Marcel took the opportunity of acquainting Nanette with a part of the history of the ornate building in which it was housed. It was built by the Portuguese when Santa Sabina was theirs, as a monastery for the Little Brothers of Compassion, a religious order a Bishop intended to instal and foster, so that someone at least would pray for his soul. But the Order did not prosper at all, the youths of Santa Sabina being sexual athletes from an early age and disinclined to be recruited into celibacy.

'But there are nuns here,' said Nanette. 'I've seen them in the square from my hotel window. So the cloistered ideal is not entirely disregarded.'

'There are three or four convents in the city,' Marcel

agreed with a smile. 'They are girls' schools and provide an education of sorts to the daughters of those who can afford to pay their fees. As to the holy sisters themselves, while I personally do not disparage their chastity, it ought not to be forgotten that they are all pure Santa Sabinans by birth, nature, upbringing, and temperament. That being so . . .'

It was unnecessary to complete his sentence, he thought, but Nanette stared at him oddly.

'Are you sure you are not judging these people by standards of your own?' she enquired. 'Unchaste nuns – this is the stuff of eighteenth-century anticlerical pornography and therefore suspect. Are you perhaps prejudiced against the local population because of the discomfort of the climate?'

Marcel came to a standstill in surprise, and stood facing her on the cracked pavement outside the Memorial Library.

'Believe me, Madame,' he said earnestly, 'my feelings toward the people of Santa Sabina are benign and respectful. I have a great many friends here, I am pleased to say. But you will find it necessary in your work to understand the Santa Sabinans and their culture to accept that continuous sexual activity is the key to all that goes on here.'

'I find that impossible to believe,' said Nanette. 'It seems to me that you are projecting your own obsessions on to others, an unhealthy and unprofitable state of affairs.'

With that she swept into the library. Marcel shrugged at the thought that she would soon learn the true state of affairs and followed her inside. By virtue of the undeserved status locally accorded to foreign diplomats, he was easily able to persuade the Director of the library to allow Madame Jarre access to his priceless books.

Naturally, they were not on open shelves to invite visitors to take and handle them – they were behind dusty glass, locked safely from prying fingers. The Director, a melancholy man of perhaps fifty, dressed in a dark suit and a stiff celluloid collar most inappropriate to the climate, but lending him a dignity of sorts, unlocked bookcase doors and showed the distinguished visiting ethnographer the volumes pertaining to the history of Santa Sabina and its people.

They were old, some of them very old, and mostly bound in red leather with fading gilt tooling. There was nothing written or printed after 1901. The very earliest volumes went right back to the Portuguese period of the island's complicated history and were written in either Church Latin or sixteenth-century Portuguese. Assisted by the deferential Director, Nanette took a dozen or more of the most promising books to a long table equipped with a reading lamp and seated herself for what might become a long stay.

Meanwhile, Marcel had been browsing further along the shelves made accessible by the sad-looking Director, and had found more interesting publications. He selected a few to take across to Nanette's table, and perched on the edge of it while he showed her his find.

'Monsieur Augusto da Cunha was interested in ancient Roman history,' he observed with a smile. 'His bookplate with family coat of arms is in this valuable copy of Suetonius' masterpiece – *The Twelve Caesars*.'

'In which language?' Nanette asked, taking the book.

'Translated into French,' said Marcel, watching her face while she opened the book, 'dated 1785 and illustrated to depict the personal preferences of each of the emperors.'

Nanette had paused at the beginning of the chapter dealing with the Emperor Tiberius. The first page of it was occupied by an engraving which showed Tiberius naked on a type of ancient Roman chaise longue. A naked girl sat over his face, her thighs parted on either side of his head, and a second girl, who was equally naked, knelt between his legs and applied her mouth to his stiff *zimbriq*.

'It seems that Monsieur da Cunha's interest in erotica was no less enthusiastic than your own,' Nanette commented impassively as she turned the pages. She stopped at the chapter on the mad Emperor Caligula, and studied the engraving that introduced Suetonius' account of the imperial tastes. The picture showed a naked girl bending over, and Caligula standing behind her, his *zimbriq* thrust into her from the rear. And behind him stood a young man, also naked, hanging on to his Emperor tightly while he made vigorous use of the imperial back door.

'A versatile man, this Caligula,' said Marcel.

Nanette said nothing. She closed the book and put it down.

'But there is more,' said Marcel cheerfully, handing her more leatherbound volumes embossed with the da Cunha crest. 'I have found this fascinating nineteenth-century edition of the Marquis de Sade's *Justine*, complete with eighteen illustrations. One of them is particularly amusing – it shows the incident in the story where poor Justine is stripped and violated by four lecherous monks.'

'Enough!' said Nanette quickly. 'You may choose to waste your time on these outmoded male fantasies, but I have serious work to do, Monsieur Lamont. Perhaps you will be so good as to leave me in peace to continue.'

'As you wish, Madame. My intention in drawing your attention to these books was merely to demonstrate the truth I mentioned earlier today – that the key to understanding Santa Sabina and its culture is to realise that sexual activity between changing partners underlies everything that goes on here. We Europeans do not at first believe this, but there is something in the air or the water – who knows what – that acts as an aphrodisiac on those who live here. As you will discover, Madame Jarre.'

'What nonsense!' she exclaimed. 'I really believe this is an attempt on your part to establish a sexual relation with me! I can appreciate that an unmarried man posted far from Paris and living in the restricted society of the diplomatic world must be prey to certain frustrations. I have no wish to be impolite, for you were very kind to me when I was unwell, and I must rely on you for the progress of my work here. But it is impossible for me to solve your personal problems.'

Marcel felt that he had been dealt with. He smiled at Nanette – his extra-charming smile – and took his leave with a reminder that he would call for her at seven that evening to escort her to the concert, as requested by His Excellency. He was reasonably certain that a few hours unattended in a place known throughout the city as a meeting point for those seeking new adventure was as good a way as any of immersing Madame Jarre in the amusing sexual anarchy of Santa Sabina.

In this he was proved correct, as he learned when he knocked at the door of Room 416 in the Grand Hotel Orient a few minutes to seven that evening. Nanette let him in, and asked him to pour drinks for them both. She had ordered a bottle of champagne to be sent up from the hotel bar, and it stood in an ice bucket on the side table, with two tall glasses. Nanette had been putting on her earrings when he knocked – one gold and pearl hoop hung from her earlobe, and she went back to the mirror to affix the other while he popped the cork from the bottle.

Marcel smiled at the label half peeled off from its immersion in cold water. It said *Dom Cliquot-Bollinger Finest Champagne*, and below that in smaller letters was the falsehood *Produce of Chateau Yquem, Rheims, France*. It was, of course, locally made palm wine, watered down and sugared to hide its characteristic taste, and impregnated with bubbles from a cylinder of carbon dioxide. He shrugged and poured two glasses – *Dom Cliquot* had the merit of being extremely cheap, as well it might!

Nanette completed her attention to her appearance and took a glass from him. For the concert she had put on a short evening dress in white, cut off the shoulders, nipped in at the waist, and with a skirt that flounced out at knee level. It made her look younger than her years, thought Marcel, studying her with appreciation. Her legs were very good, but her bare shoulders were a trifle thin, perhaps. Her light brown hair frothed round her head in curls, setting off her attractive face perfectly.

They drank to each other, and Marcel noted that she

pulled a wry little face when she tasted the vintage. But her manner to him was friendly and open, as if there had been no disagreement between them at the Memorial Library earlier that day. It was not long before he became aware of the reason for this.

'Monsieur Lamont, I feel I owe you an apology of sorts,' she said.

'Please,' said he, charming as always, 'we shall be in each other's company very often while you are here and I hope that we may become friends. My name is Marcel.'

'And mine is Nanette, as you know,' she replied, ready enough to fall in with his suggestion. 'To continue, I must admit that I disbelieved most of what you said to me this morning – it was all too male ego oriented, it seemed to me. It still is, but at least I have come to see that you were telling the truth.'

'There is a certain irony in accusing a diplomat of speaking the truth, Nanette. Nevertheless, outside working hours I make it a rule never to lie to the people I like. What brought about your change of heart?'

'After you left the library I got on with my work – skimming through books and making notes of useful items to come back to later on. Gradually I became aware that a procession of various good-looking young men was passing through the room where I sat – and their interest was not in the books or paintings. It was very surely in me.'

Marcel nodded, his smile sympathetic.

'Perhaps because they saw me as a foreigner,' Nanette went on, 'none of them addressed me in words, but only with shy smiles. It was distracting, but I tried to ignore what was going on and continue with my work. Then one of the young men – he could not have been more than seventeen or eighteen, came up to my table and leaned on the far side, staring down at me. I was about to ask him to go away, when he made an obscene gesture.'

'Ah yes,' said Marcel, 'I can guess. He formed the thumb and forefinger of one hand into a ring and poked the forefinger of his other hand through it – is that not so?'

'You have seen this done, evidently.'

Marcel shrugged and told her it was the traditional approach of the islanders to each other, men to women and women to men, to enquire if the other was interested.

'It is not regarded as obscene here,' he explained, 'but as a useful introduction with a perfectly clear meaning, without any waste of time. If the person thus approached is not interested, a slight shake of the head is sufficient, and the adventurer will move on without hard feelings, to try elsewhere.'

'In a public library though!' Nanette exclaimed in reproof. It seemed to Marcel that she had a scholar's exaggerated sense of the importance of collections of old books. Erudition and learning were all very well in their way, but living was about men and women, not dusty old volumes.

'As I explained,' he said, 'the library and the museum have a reputation for attracting the better type of prowler. If it is of any interest to your survey, I can escort you to the fruit market, where the ordinary type of person goes in search of fun and frolics. You will be able to observe the mating rituals in safety and convenience – you will not be approached while I am with you. Had I remained in the library this morning, you would have been left alone.'

'Then what it comes to is this,' said Nanette, displeased, 'a woman on her own is fair game here for men to pester with their obscene suggestions?'

'Yes,' Marcel agreed, 'and a young man alone is fair game for Santa Sabina women of all ages to approach with suggestions of an immediate *zeqq*.'

'Immediate what?'

'Ah, excuse me – I forgot you have not been here long enough to become familiar with the few words of the old Santa Sabina language that are necessary for day-to-day survival. The verb *to zeqq* means to make love, though its precise significance is much more basic and Rabelaisian than that. But you should not therefore think it is an obscene word – it is used without any embarrassment by all, priests, nuns, and local gentry. There has been some debate among the learned on the origins of the Santa Sabina language, of which you must be aware.'

'I have read the published papers and hope to make some study of the question while I am here,' said Nanette, nodding wisely.

Marcel refilled their glasses with the bogus champagne.

'Some say it was the aboriginal tongue of the people who were here before the Arabs came in the eighth or ninth century – the date is obscure,' he told her, 'but others claim that the so-called Santa Sabina language is no more than a mongrel dialect making use of words taken from the various languages of the island's conquerors – the Arabs, the Genoese, the Portuguese.'

'And what is your own view?' Nanette asked. 'For I see you take an interest in the people and customs here.'

'I do not know enough to have a properly informed opinion,' said he, 'but when did that ever stop a man from having his own idea about anything? If the *patois* theory were true, then one would expect to find as many French-based words in it as Arabic or Italian words, for Santa Sabina was a colony of France for a hundred years almost.'

'And are there any?'

'None I have ever been able to distinguish. But of course, in the towns the language of everyone is French. Out in the rural areas only the village priests understand French, and all the people speak the Santa Sabina language, which is impossible for us to learn, there being no grammar books or dictionaries.'

'I shall certainly want to visit some of these areas,' said Nanette thoughtfully. 'Will it be difficult to arrange?'

'Not in the least. When you are ready, tell me and we will go by bus to the north and then on muleback or foot to visit any number of villages you choose. They are all alike, of course.'

The musical concert to which Marcel had been requested by the Ambassador to escort Nanette Jarre was to celebrate the seventy-fifth birthday of President da

Cunha's mother, and was therefore an occasion of public importance. Several nations had taken the opportunity to ingratiate themselves with the president in their own way – the British had sent a Royal Navy frigate which anchored a mile off shore and fired a nineteen-gun salute for the old lady – an act of noisy and unnecessary barbarism, in Marcel's view. The Americans had presented her with an enormously long Cadillac limousine complete with built-in cocktail cabinet, but she had been housebound for the past dozen years, and it was improbable that she would have much use for the vehicle, even if it could be safely driven on roads outside the city.

His Excellency the French Ambassador, on behalf of his nation and government, had the honour to present to Madame da Cunha an exquisite Sèvres porcelain dining service for thirty-six people. Marcel approved the choice, though it was with a rueful smile that he imagined the uninteresting and restricted local cuisine served on plates of such quality. The Russians had, presumably on the advice of someone with more sensitivity than was normally to be found in the Kremlin, despatched to the island a string quartet to play a birthday concert for the President's mother.

It seemed the KGB had learned by some devious route that as a girl she had been fond of the music of Alexander Glazunov, and on her honeymoon trip had met him in Paris, where he settled in the 1920s after retiring from the Leningrad Conservatory.

In truth, the Russians had pulled off a diplomatic *coup* with their choice of birthday gift, and had won a great victory over the other powers. Even more galling was that President da Cunha had decided to make use of the concert as a political event by issuing invitations to all ambassadors to be present with their ladies. Not that he leaned towards the Russians – he was too crafty to become involved with anyone at all – but by seeming to favour them he was conveying the message that others would have to do better to catch up with the USSR, which meant thinking of more things to give him.

The birthday concert was held in the Theatre des Beaux

Arts, a large baroque edifice built in the seventeenth century by the Jesuits, who had established themselves on the island with the intention of ruling it by spiritual and religious terror. But a certain megalomania seized upon the holy fathers, alarming the Portuguese Archbishop when he observed that the Jesuits' modest chapel was larger and more splendid than the Sistine Chapel in Rome. Very naturally, he took steps to protect his own position by having the Order cleared out of the island, even though he had no jurisdiction over them.

The building then became the property of Holy Church, in the eyes of the Archbishop, but the Portuguese Viceroy thought that too convenient and annexed it in the king's name. All that this meant was that the grandiose former Jesuit chapel was used for secular purposes. With modifications over the years, it became the venue for dramatic performances, auctions of furniture and other goods, Masonic Lodge meetings, musical recitals, banquets given by politicians for supporters, cockfighting tournaments, and other typical local entertainments.

His Excellency the French Ambassador, Jean-Jacques Ducour had naturally been allocated one of the best boxes for the concert. He and his wife, in full formal evening rig with sashes, medals, honours and decorations, received the friends and guests they had invited to join them. The Ambassador appeared much taken by Madame Jarre, and lingered over her hand after he had kissed it while he detained her in conversation. He acknowledged Marcel's presence with a curt nod, and in return received a polite bow. Madame Ducour was rather more welcoming to Marcel, and smiled graciously at him when he kissed her hand. She also engaged the attractive ethnographer in conversation, but one must presume it was on different topics from those raised by her husband.

Glancing round with an expert eye, Marcel noted that the wily president had filled the Theatre des Beaux Arts with everyone of political importance to him. The two tiers of boxes housed diplomats and their entourage, government ministers with their wives and hangers-on. The eighty-four members of the Chamber of Deputies sat in the front stalls with their ladies, and behind them were the rows of senior civil servants, high-ranking army officers, and others beholden to President da Cunha for their position.

The Czech contingent occupied a side box on the second tier, their priority not being high. Colonel Jiri Svoboda, hard faced and stiff haired, was deep in conversation with his Ambassador, Marcel noted, and from the manner in which the two men leaned their heads towards each other, their discussion must be of an essentially confidential nature. Military attachés were not in the usual way of things considered of any great importance in a country so poor and isolated as Santa Sabina, and it appeared to Marcel that the Colonel's true function was perhaps other than stated.

Nor was it difficult for him to pick out the woman who had met Colonel Svoboda in the Cinema des Grands Boulevards. She was in a box with half a dozen other well-dressed Santa Sabinans, only two along from the French Ambassador's box. In a pale tangerine evening frock that displayed her slender shoulders and much of her full bosom, she was exquisitely beautiful and exceptionally desirable. Marcel recognised at once the man in a dinner jacket sitting beside her. He was Enriquez da Motta, the Minister of Industrial Developments.

The title was impressive, but the post was without function, there being no development in industry or trade in the Republic – da Motta had the appointment for the salary and perquisites that accompanied it, because he was a cousin of President da Cunha. But then, every government minister without exception was related to the President's family. To be appointed to a job without responsibility showed that da Cunha thought his cousin an idiot, good at nothing, for whom provision had to be made.

Nevertheless, to be quite certain he had correctly identified the lady, Marcel pointed her out to Madame St-Beuve, friendly wife of the Embassy Second Secretary, and enquired who she might be. Genevieve St-Beuve was the type of woman who knew everyone worth knowing, their provenance, background, pedigree, merits and faults, connections, liaisons past and present – in short, she was a living breathing reference book. She was also, Marcel had personal reason to know, an agreeable companion in bed, if perhaps a little more formal than the occasion required.

Madame St-Beuve confirmed that the lady was indeed wife of Monsieur da Motta, and that her name was Graziosa. They had two children, she added, both girls. Before her marriage her name had been Braganza, one of the celebrated Hundred Families who between them owned everything there was worth owning in Santa Sabina. Then dropping her voice to a secretive murmur, Madame St-Beuve informed Marcel that it was reliably said that Madame da Motta had engaged in an imprudent friendship with a certain dashing young man at the Italian embassy, and that this ended only when her husband complained and the offending diplomat was packed off back to Rome.

That was interesting if true, thought Marcel. A fervent young Italian, and now a dour middle-aged Czech. It didn't make sense in those terms. There must be more to this than met the eye and it would be useful to find out more. At this moment all those present in the Theatre des Beaux Arts rose to their feet and bowed towards the Presidential Box as Pascal da Cunha made his appearance, his wife on one arm and his mother on the other. He was arrayed in pristine tails and white tie, his entire chest gleaming and glittering with the absurd number of decorations conferred upon him by foreign governments to secure his favour.

Three trumpeters in the scarlet parade uniform of the Army's Presidential Bodyguard Brigade blared out the brisk if somewhat uninspiring Santa Sabina National Anthem, after which everyone sat down again, cleared their throats, rustled their programmes and in general prepared themselves for the music. All members of the Russian string quartet had surnames indicating a Jewish descent, Marcel noted – it was a comic irony that the Kremlin had sent abroad to assist their diplomatic plans members of a minority they continued to persecute.

The compositions of Alexander Glazunov were not, it had to be admitted, of any particular interest to Marcel. But individual taste was of no importance whatsoever on an evening when music was merely a political weapon. He sat as comfortably as the seat he was allocated allowed, folded his hands and let his thoughts range over the two questions that occupied his attention – what was the true reason why Graziosa da Motta had met Svoboda, and second, what was the best way to get Nanette Jarre into bed?

The interval, when it came, was an extended one, to give all present plenty of time to move around and talk to each other, besides unhurriedly enjoying the champagne and cold snacks served in the boxes. After a while, Marcel took a stroll along the corridor running behind the boxes, and went out into the foyer and then the street beyond, in search of a cooler ambience. But there was no cooler place to be found, and he headed back into the theatre to quench his thirst. At least the champagne offered here was French, though of a very inferior vintage, as one well expected in Santa Sabina.

In the foyer he encountered his ambassador's wife, ending her chat with Portuguese friends. She commandeered Marcel to escort her back to the box, and he gave her his arm, wondering why she had been moving round alone. The answer, he decided, was that she had been looking for her current young friend – the blond-haired cipher clerk.

'Did you find him in this crowd, your Australian friend?' he enquired politely.

'Ah, do not speak to me of Australians!' Jacqueline Ducour exclaimed. 'They are uncivilised savages!'

'I am sorry to hear of it,' said Marcel, keeping a smile from his face. 'He has disappointed you, this one?'

'On the reserved beach he seemed a young god,' she said, with the tiniest catch in her throat at the splendid memory, 'blond as Apollo, with huge muscles – oh, those mighty thighs of his! The first time I touched him I thought my heart would break for joy! I wanted him to be mine – to do what I pleased with!'

'Of course,' said Marcel, who knew very well what it was to belong to Jacqueline, however briefly, for her to make use of, 'but what was lacking in this sun-golden young athlete?'

'Athlete indeed!' said Jacqueline bitterly, 'his prowess was only in swimming and weightlifting and similar ridiculous male pastimes. In matters of love all these muscles are without use. In this respect he is not strong – he is feeble!'

'My sincere regrets, dear Jacqueline,' said Marcel. 'Could he not manage it even once as you prefer?'

'Do not remind me of his incompetence,' she said, 'the memory is too distressing.'

They had reached the curving access corridor behind the boxes when the electric lights flickered twice and went out. Without being told they knew that the entire city was in darkness, and they were not in the least surprised. The antiquated generating station which supplied power to the capital failed two or three times a week. Normally it required at least twenty minutes or half an hour to get the worn-out machinery operating again, but the inhabitants of Santa Sabina city had their own alternative arrangements. Institutions of importance kept bottled-gas lamps ready at hand for these inconvenient breaks in supply, others brought out old-fashioned oil lamps.

The Theatre des Beaux Arts relied on neither of these methods of illumination. In accord with its dignity and status, it used candles, set in elaborate, though cracked and dusty, crystal candelabras set on the walls. Naturally, it would require some time for employees to make their way right through the building to light up whatever candles remained in the fittings. Meantime total darkness prevailed.

'Stand still,' Marcel advised Jacqueline, 'it would be most painful to bump into a door or other obstruction.'

There were other people in the corridor, of course, and

they too had decided to remain safe where they were until they could see again. A hum of chatter, interspersed with laughs, sounded through the darkness, and under cover of this Jacqueline moved close to Marcel, till he felt the softness of her bosom against his arm and her lips grazing his cheek in a fleeting kiss.

'Tell me, Marcel,' she whispered, 'why is it that I come to you when I am desolated by the clumsiness and futility of other men? Do you know the reason?'

'How can I say?' he murmured back.

Her hand touched his chest gently and moved slowly down until she could slip it into the waistband of his trousers and feel down further yet until she had his limp part clasped in her hot palm. He felt the tip of her wet tongue touch the corner of his mouth and slide between his lips – and his *zimbriq* grew quickly stiff and long. If it had been any other woman but Jacqueline he would by then be caressing her breasts and belly through her thin evening frock. But her way was different, as he had every reason to know, and he kept his hands down by his sides and let her direct the course of action.

The simple truth of it was that Jacqueline Ducour, behind the facade of haughty good manners thought appropriate for the wife of an ambassador, was a predator of handsome young men. But her way was not that of the she-wolf, dragging them down to devour their flesh whole, but the silent rapacity of the vampire bat, that settles gently on a sleeping victim and takes pleasure of his body without his knowledge – until too late he wakes up to find his strength draining from him.

Her hand was sliding delicately up and down Marcel's upright *zimbriq*, and the tip of her tongue vibrated cleverly for a moment inside his mouth, arousing him furiously.

'Your Australian friend,' he murmured, 'was he indeed clumsy and futile – or was that your disappointment speaking?'

'Imagine it,' said Jacqueline, 'we were in a hotel room and I was almost delirious with the anticipation of stripping naked his sun-tanned and muscular body! Off came his underwear – and my heart sank like a stone in a well! The *zimbriq* revealed was no larger than my little finger, I swear it, even when it stood hard! All the rest of this absurd man was huge, except for the part that mattered the most!'

'How truly appalling to you, *chérie*,' said Marcel, knowing that his own had swollen to a most satisfactory size under the teasing manipulation of Madame Ducour's fingers. 'An impossible situation for you, a total debacle.'

'What was one to do?' Jacqueline asked. 'Bitter regret did not prevent me from seeing if anything could be done. But alas, this fradulent Apollo at once tried to roll me on my back and penetrate me! And even in that he was useless, for a premature release of his tribute merely wet my underwear and provided no satisfaction for either of us!'

The passage remained dark, the surrounding conversation rose high enough to cover all that Marcel and Jacqueline might then say to each other.

'You may touch me now,' she whispered, her mouth at his ear.

Moving with delicate ease, he reached down and brought a hand up under her frock, until he could lay his palm lightly on her bare belly. She sighed into his mouth and moved her feet apart a little to separate her thighs. Under his hand her warm belly was like satin to the touch, and at her urging he slid his hand down inside her loose silk knickers.

'You are the only one who is right for me, Marcel,' she told him in a whisper. 'I could love you, but you do not love me and my heart breaks each time that I have anything to do with you.'

Madame Ducour's declaration was some distance from the truth, it must be admitted, and perhaps she did not fully acknowledge to herself what the truth was. To take a less romantic view of the relations between them, she felt a proprietorial affection towards Marcel because it amused him sometimes to let her have her way with him.

'But I adore you, *chérie*,' he said, 'you know that.'

The tip of his middle finger glided along the sensitive lips of her *kuft*, then pressed inside and parted them.

'Marcel!' Jacqueline exclaimed in sudden admonition. 'Do not presume!'

Her long thin fingers with their pointed and scarlet-painted nails caressed his twitching *zimbriq* with a light but very sure touch.

'Tell me that you love me, *chéri*,' she murmured, 'tell me, or you will break my heart.'

The sensations that rippled through Marcel's entire body were so divinely devastating that it seemed to him his moment of crisis had arrived. But Jacqueline recognised very well the onset of the critical instants – her hand in his trousers moved as swiftly as a striking snake, she had his zipper down, his jerking *zimbriq* exposed, and was tugging him towards her, using it as a handle.

With fingers that trembled with passion, he pulled aside the short leg of her knickers, and she guided him straight to the goal of his desire.

'Kiss me, Marcel,' she murmured in the dark, her hot mouth on his, and she had raised him to such a pitch of intense emotion that he thought he was about to discharge his passion into her hand. But at the same time he knew she would never permit that – Jacqueline was expert in ensuring her own pleasure.

'Gently, *chéri*,' she whispered to him while pressing the end of his *zimbriq* into the waiting split between her thighs, 'show me that you love me.'

But she was teasing him deliberately with her words – and not entirely without emotional cruelty – for he was so aroused that the mere act of sliding into her brought on his climax at once. He gasped and jerked as his passion spurted into her. And this was precisely what she wanted – not for her the thrill of being mastered and used by a man; her delight was found in extracting his virile essence before he could penetrate deep and rub his wet flesh on her wet flesh.

At the instant she felt Marcel's spurting release between the lips of her *kuft*, she uttered a sigh of rapture and held on to his shoulders throughout her gentle ecstasy. It was to be brief – a glimmer of light showed far down the corridor as employees of the theatre moved towards them, lighting candles along the way. Marcel tucked away his exploited part and quickly zipped up his trousers. Jacqueline snatched the silk handkerchief from his breast pocket and wiped between her legs.

'I can always rely upon you, dear Marcel,' she said, pushing the wet handkerchief back into his pocket. 'Tomorrow afternoon,' she said, calm and fully in possession of herself, 'I shall come to your room in that dreadful hotel you choose to live in. Expect me at three o'clock.'

'Alas, I must excuse myself, Jacqueline,' he answered, taking her arm again to lead her to the Ambassador's box now that it was possible to see the way. 'Madame Jarre has asked me to show her around the city tomorrow, and His Excellency's orders were to accommodate her wishes in everything.'

'Not in *everything*,' and Madame Ducour's tone was cold and displeased suddenly. 'And that is something else I had in mind to speak to you about – the way you were staring at that woman earlier this evening made it obvious that you want to get her into bed. She has already told me of how you stripped her naked the day she arrived – how could you!'

'Believe me, there was no intention on my part . . .' Marcel was excusing himself when Madame cut him off short.

'You are to leave her alone,' she said in her haughtiest tone of voice, 'understand me? Stay away from her, or it will be the worse for you. I shall be at your hotel tomorrow at three – do not disappoint me.'

# 5

## An Alarming Ultimatum Is Delivered

There was no arrangement for Marcel to take Nanette Jarre to the fruit market the next morning. It was an excuse on the spur of the moment to avoid having to meet Madame Ducour. But alas, the flimsy evasion had been dismissed out of hand – no one ever yet had succeeded in denying the Ambassador's wife whatever she had set her heart upon.

That being so, Marcel idled the morning away. At breakfast he had seen Nanette and enquired about her plans for the day, and was told that she proposed to return to the Augusto da Cunha Library for a further inspection of books on the history of the island and its people. She would, she promised, not be alarmed when handsome young Santa Sabina men approached her and made obscene gestures – she would act on Marcel's advice and get rid of them with a smile and a shake of her head.

After she left the hotel, Marcel remained on the terrace with a pitcher of iced papaw juice and wrote long-overdue letters to his mother in France and to friends elsewhere. Now that he was relieved of other official duties in order to chaperone Nanette, there was no reason to go to the embassy. He formed a hope that her stay would be a prolonged one, and decided to ask about her plans, so that he could devise ways of increasing the scope and length of her researches.

The morning passed pleasantly, and at one o'clock he ordered lunch. The cuisine of the Grand Hotel Orient left much to be desired – but that was equally true of every restaurant, hotel and snack bar in Santa Sabina. He settled for the table d'hote, priced on the menu at the equivalent in *tikkoos* of twelve francs. It was a typical island meal of grilled swordfish served cold with shredded palm kernel mixed in a type of salad with a red-leafed vegetable called *frolo*, for which there was no French name. Nor was there ever likely to be.

After that he finished his carafe of white wine with a modest helping of soft cheese – it was made with goat's milk and had ground cashew nuts in it – and went up to his room. He had an hour to shower and change and rest before Madame Ducour was due at three.

The tepid water of the shower refreshed him slightly, though the heat was intense. He splashed himself under the arms, over his chest and belly, and between his legs, with almost the last of his *eau de toilette*. For a visit from Jacqueline Ducour – a secret visit – he considered that informality was appropriate in clothes, and put on a white sports shirt with short sleeves, pale blue trousers and woven straw sandals made locally. He sat in a rattan chair by the open window to wait – it might be just a little cooler if he moved his chair out onto the balcony, but that was to invite trouble. Doing so would make him visible to everyone who passed through San Feliz Square – if anyone who knew him also saw Madame Ducour entering the hotel, an obvious deduction would be made.

Marcel's curious on-off affair with his Ambassador's wife had begun three years before, very soon after he had been posted to the island republic. It was not he who took the initiative – he would never have dared to make advances to Madame Ducour after the unfortunate circumstance of the politician's charming wife in Paris and his exile to Santa Sabina. The human imagination shuddered and recoiled from a contemplation of where those who offended on Santa Sabina were posted – what lower depths could exist to receive those who were foolhardy enough to run a risk of even further demotion?

And of course, as he discovered within ten days of being on the island, almost every Santa Sabina girl could be had for the asking. The question of the Ambassador's wife did not enter his thoughts, svelte and stylish though she was, and by a long way the best dressed and best cared-for European woman in this tropical backwater. She was no young girl, of course – she was close to her fiftieth birthday – but she had kept her good looks and her figure marvellously well.

All that was of no interest to Marcel, busy exploring his new surroundings and coming to the astonished realisation that the island women were remarkably obliging. But that was only a male viewpoint, as if women were merely there for his own pleasure. Madame Ducour saw matters in reverse – young men were there for her pleasure, and she very quickly took advantage of Marcel.

It happened so very casually that he did not believe that it was happening at all. He was in his hotel room at about five in the afternoon when he heard a tap at the door. To his surprise there stood Madame Ducour, looking regally cool in a white silk blouse and skirt and a broad-brimmed straw hat with a scarlet ribbon round it, like a gondolier.

She was inside the room in an instant and had the door closed and her back to it. She said she had come to inspect the hotel where he had chosen to live, it being of importance that those attached to the Embassy paid proper attention to protocol and the maintaining of the status and dignity of their position. It sounded very improbable to Marcel that His Excellency's wife would concern herself with such a matter, but he smiled his charming smile and invited her to inspect his quarters.

She looked about the room, her brown eyes lingering for a few seconds on the broad bed and its old-fashioned brass head, then at the writing table and bamboo armchairs set near the window to the balcony. She crossed the room on high-heeled open-toed white glacé shoes to peep into the bathroom, where there was no bath but only a shower and a drain set in the tiled floor. She opened a door of the wardrobe and looked in at Marcel's clothes neatly hanging inside.

She made no remarks or comments on what she saw or what she thought of it. Nor was any necessary, for without understanding how it came about, Marcel found himself lying with her on the bed and kissing her delicately, her tall slim beauty seeming to invite that type of kiss rather than full-mouthed passion. Her eyes were open and she was staring at him while he kissed her – and more than that, it was her hand between his thighs, not his between hers, and she had unzipped his trousers before he knew it and was holding his fast-growing part.

'Madame,' he said softly, 'you are very welcome, even though you have taken me by surprise.'

'My name is Jacqueline,' she said, 'and you may stop being surprised and stroke my breasts.'

Marcel opened her fine silk blouse and undid her brassière to free her breasts for his hands to feel. He thought them perhaps a little slack, which was not to be wondered at, but still very provocative. They were of a smaller size, the right size to be held in a man's hand, and their buds were well developed and a handsome russet colour.

'You may kiss them,' Jacqueline murmured, and Marcel was slightly amused by her assumption of dominance, for as yet he knew nothing of her personality. But she was the Ambassador's wife, and he had no intention of offending her.

He kissed her half-parted lips again, then lowered his head and kissed the prominent tips of her breasts and glided the end of his tongue over them. The fragrance of the expensive perfume from Paris that she had sprayed in her hair and on her neck and breasts filled his nostrils and made his mind whirl in sensuous delight. He gazed up into her face in open admiration, and was ravished by the expression of voluptuousness in her large brown eyes. At that moment Marcel was unable to believe his luck. He was making love to an elegant Parisian lady, a tremendous treat for him – and a wholly unexpected one

– after three weeks of making love to a se[...]
siastic but unsophisticated young Santa[...]

Jacqueline's fingers were long and t[...]
and she understood how to use them to [...]
men into doing what she wanted. Her f[...]
patterns up the stiff shaft of his *zimbri*[...]
sensitive head, making him shiver with [...]ous sensation. He kissed her breasts in adoration, hardly knowing that she had his belt unbuckled and his trousers round his knees, his shirt up and his undershorts gaping wide. Her fingers wheedled about his throbbing part, raising him to a high degree of excitement – and so far he had done nothing but kiss her breasts.

To regain a proper male initiative, Marcel put a hand under the hem of Jacqueline's silk skirt and slid it upwards gently inside her bare thighs. But she stopped him at once, grasping his wrist with her free hand, the other still busily arousing him.

'Not until I tell you,' she said, her wet tongue licking at the corners of his mouth and then over his eyelids, hurling him into a frenzy of erotic sensation. He let her continue, to see what it was she intended, and a moment came when she let him raise her skirt and remove her loose-legged white silk knickers – and by then he was so aroused that the sight of her neatly trimmed little patch of nut-brown hair almost caused him to deposit his passionate tribute on the inside of her bare thigh.

She did not let him touch her brown-curled and thin-lipped *kuft* and when at last she permitted him to enter her, Marcel was within a heart-beat of the climactic moment. Even as he slipped his jumping *zimbriq* into her soft wetness, the crisis overtook him and he spurted his passion before he was more than three or four centimetres inside. This he had assumed to be a disaster, but not so – to his amazement Jacqueline was shaking beneath him in the throes of a genteel climax of her own.

And as he found out, that was the way she wanted it, the only way she wanted it. She had about her some mysterious influence of the South American vampire bat, choosing strong and handsome young men for her

...d lulling them expertly while she battened very ... on their virile powers. She took just what she ...ted from them and gave very little in return.

That was three years ago, and while Marcel waited for her he knew she had not changed, but he was curious why she had turned to him last evening at the Theatre des Beaux Arts. Jacqueline was not a woman who acted on impulse, all that she did was for a reason and carefully calculated. She had not seduced him in the darkness for her pleasure – at least, that was not the main reason. Nor was she visiting his hotel room today only for the sake of a sexual climax or two, though doubtless that would be her pretence.

He heard the tap at the door and let her in quickly before anyone passed in the corridor and saw her. She wore a frock of moss green shantung silk, loosely belted about her commendably slim waist, and a green straw hat. Marcel took her hands in his, kissed them both in exaggerated homage, then took a step toward her and lightly kissed her cheeks.

'*Chéri*,' Jacqueline murmured, 'it is always so pleasant to be with you. Have you anything cold to drink?'

'Champagne?' he asked doubtfully, knowing she would turn up her elegant nose at the local imitation. 'No? Peach juice?'

'Too sweet to be drinkable. Have you no orange juice?'

He had, and busied himself pouring a glass for her. When he turned round to face her again, she had taken off her beautiful Paris frock and hung it in the wardrobe. She had also removed her shoes and was sitting on the bed, the pillows behind her back to support her in a half-sitting position. Her hands were behind her back undoing her little white lace brassière. She was bare-legged, for not even the grandest lady wore stockings in the heat of Santa Sabina except on the most formal evening functions.

'Your orange juice,' said Marcel.

'Later. Come here, Marcel, I need you.'

She had never said that to him before, or to anyone else. She was extremely arousing to look at, her long slender body naked but for loose-fitting knickers in fine apricot silk, her round little belly button just visible above the waistband, and her toenails painted the same bright shiny scarlet as her fingers. It was no hardship at all to lie beside her on the bed and rain tiny kisses on her well-shaped breasts.

'I can only stay a moment,' she murmured, stroking Marcel's face gently. But she always said that, even on occasions when she had stayed three or four hours with him. It meant nothing.

Her hand was inside Marcel's trousers, her fingers dancing lightly over his fast-stiffening *zimbriq*, teasing it to full stretch. Her other hand was on the nape of his neck, holding his face against her soft little breasts.

'Jacqueline, you are adorable,' he sighed, knowing well what was expected of him. Madame Ducour was no ordinary woman of a certain age who parted her legs for young men to pleasure her. She had the experience of thirty years of sexual adventure and she had gained an ability to mesmerise her partners into a sort of erotic delirium, from which they woke only when she drained them of their virile strength. In her Marcel recognised a most rare talent, and he respected her for it.

Her smooth flat belly above her knickers was highly inviting – Marcel had an urge to lick it, but he knew Jacqueline would object to any advances he made. He looked up from her breasts to her face, seeing a delicate thin smile on her lips.

'You were staring at my belly,' she said. 'I could feel your thought. You wanted to kiss it and put your tongue in my belly button – do not deny it, Marcel.'

'The thought is a delightful one,' he admitted, 'but in fact I was thinking of kissing your charming *gublas*.'

'That is a most inelegant word, *gublas*,' Jacqueline said with a tiny sniff of disapproval. 'What an extraordinary language is Santa Sabinan! *Gublas* – it makes my breasts sound like great puffed out footballs of flesh, fit only for the peasant women of this miserable island.'

'Ah, no, no,' Marcel assured her, 'your breasts are *chic* and elegant, *chérie*, you may believe me. I find them delicious.'

She was a little flattered by his praise and permitted him a tiny reward for pleasing her vanity.

'You may kiss my belly if you wish,' she said graciously.

Marcel moved with care and tact so as not to make her regret the licence she had granted him. He bent his back and placed a kiss on her warm belly as glancing as a butterfly's wing on the petal of a flower. When that seemed to be acceptable, he did it again – and then repeated it many times, moving slowly to cover the smooth flesh of Jacqueline's belly with kisses. He saw that her brown eyes were closed and her mouth slightly open, and her fingers had ceased to move on his *zimbriq*.

With his nose he eased the waistband of her silk knickers a centimetre or two down, reaching with extended tongue to touch her lower, and lower still, as the waistband slipped a little under his gentle pressure. But the tip of his exploring tongue had covered no more than half the journey between belly button and curls before Jacqueline withdrew her permission.

'Enough,' she murmured, and clasped a hand under his chin to bring his face back up to hers. He kissed her mouth, and on his stiff and throbbing *zimbriq* her fingers recommenced their play. But something had been achieved, for it was quite soon after that she gripped his hard part tightly and asked him to remove her knickers.

She turned on her back for this, but still propped up against the pillows, half sitting, so that it was not possible to lie on top of her. Marcel slipped the flimsy silk garment down her long legs, which instantly parted wide, displaying her neatly clipped little patch of nut-brown curls and the long thin lips of her *kuft*. Marcel bowed his head at once and pressed a warm kiss on them, as if in affectionate greeting to a dear friend. Jacqueline ran a hand over his hair and round his ear, stopping him from using his tongue to rob her of control.

She was ready for him – ready in her own terms, that is, and she allowed him to flatten the pillows under her head while she moved down the bed until she could lie flat on her back.

'Come to me, Marcel, *chéri*,' she murmured, her glowing brown eyes staring at him with mesmeric intensity. By then her deft manipulation had excited him to very nearly the limit of desire – unless she moved with the greatest care now she would spoil all that she had done.

He was still wearing his shirt and trousers down somewhere round his ankles, but there was no time to undress. He rolled over to place his belly on Jacqueline's and his fingers reached for her *kuft*, to part the lips for a rapid penetration. But she stopped him – her hand was there first, prevening his touching her and opening herself to receive him. He slid forward to put the engorged head of his *zimbriq* between those long thin lips and he was shaking with excitement, hardly more than an instant removed from the sexual crisis.

Jacqueline's hand still held him tightly, so that it was not possible to slide into her, and then she kissed his face with little pecking kisses. Her fingers slid skilfully up and down his shaking part, throwing him into a delirium of sensation. As the first spasm of discharge gathered in his belly, she knew it and let go, her hands grasping his hips to pull him slowly into her. There was not the least opportunity of a quick and savage thrust into her depths, for she still was in control, her hands guiding and setting the pace.

'Ah Jacqueline!' he sighed while she let his *zimbriq* slide slowly into her, centimetre by centimetre, spurting its desire as it entered. This was the moment to which all her skill and experience were directed, and even in her supreme triumph she retained control. Her lustrous eyes were staring unfocussed, her mouth hung slackly open, her belly was palpitating in and out – her own critical moments were upon her!

But not until Marcel had completed paying his homage to her did she relax and let nature take its course. When she knew she had drained his virility, her arms went limp, he sank limply on her belly, the movement pushing his exploited *zimbriq* right in to the limit. Only then did she cry out and shudder under him in a genteel little climax.

They lay side by side, only their fingertips touching, while their overheated bodies cooled a little – as far as that could be achieved in the sultry climate of Santa Sabina. Jacqueline was first to recover her energies and speak.

'I truly adore you, Marcel,' she said, 'you understand me so perfectly and do not try to interfere in lovemaking. If only I could trust you to remain content with what I give you, I would take you as my permanent lover. But you are unreliable.'

'I regret you find me so,' he answered, amused by her total presumption that the world ought to revolve about her pleasure, 'but I have a high regard for you, Jacqueline, and although we do not often make love together, there exists an understanding between us which revives whenever we kiss.'

'I have something to tell you, *chéri*,' said Jacqueline, not troubling herself to comment on his statement of faith, 'it is this – my husband believes I am having an *affaire* with you.'

'I knew it!' Marcel exclaimed, sitting upright in a suddenly startled movement. 'That is why he treats me as he does – but I asked you this a long time ago, not once but several times, and you denied that he suspected anything.'

'I was mistaken,' she replied coolly.

'And so is His Excellency – we are *not* having an *affaire*. We have never had an *affaire*, you and I.'

'Then what shall we call it, *chéri*? I admit that months have passed when we have not seen each other, except for the usual round of diplomatic parties and perhaps on the reserved beach. At these times you have occupied yourself with short and brutal exploitations of local women, in the idiotic way that men do.'

'And you, my darling, have occupied yourself in seducing any handsome young men who arrive on the island to take up posts at any of the embassies. Your Australian Adonis with the tiny part was only the most recent in a long parade of simple-minded men you have used for your pleasure.'

Marcel spoke with more heat and less consideration than usual because the news that the Ambassador suspected him had entirely upset his equilibrium.

'Oh Marcel, don't be unkind to me,' said Jacqueline, and she turned on her side to face him and stroked his face gently. 'I need you, *chéri*.'

There was that word again! Why on earth should she *need* him, except as a plaything when she had nobody else in tow?

'The truth is,' she continued, 'that although perhaps we may say that we are not having an *affaire*, others may not see it as we do. For example, I have consulted my diaries for the three years since you arrived in Santa Sabina, and in that time you have made love to me forty-three times.'

'Good God, such accuracy!' said Marcel. 'But I did not know you kept a diary. If you record everything in it, then it must be an exceedingly compromising document. I dare not think what His Excellency would do if it fell into his hands!'

'Of that there is no fear,' Jacqueline assured him. 'None at all.'

'Then what has put this suspicion in his mind, tell me that? On the occasions you and I have met secretly we have been very discreet.'

'It is I who have allowed this slight suspicion to form in his mind,' she astonished him by saying, 'not by chance, but for a reason.'

Marcel stared at her, round-eyed and open-mouthed, his power of articulate speech in suspension.

'Listen to me,' she said in a businesslike tone, 'I am sick and tired of this wretched island and everything it represents. For me the years of youth and vigour will soon be past – I have no wish to stay here and become old and grey eating the awful food and with only a handful of friends to amuse my days.'

'I understand that,' said Marcel, beginning to see something of the emotions that were driving her. 'We share this desire, you and I, to return to Paris to live, not remain as exiles in this curious place. But I still do not follow your reasoning in alarming His Excellency.'

'There is no need to keep calling him that in the privacy of your bed,' said Jacqueline, tapping Marcel's chest impatiently. 'As his wife of twenty-four years I am unable to think of any particular way in which Jean-Jacques is excellent.'

'Nevertheless . . .' said Marcel hesitantly.

'I have pleaded and argued with him to retire early from the diplomatic service so that we can go back to France this year. But he exhibits a stubborn determination to stay as Ambassador here until the normal age of retirement. As you are well aware, the only chance of being transferred away from Santa Sabina to another appointment is to enjoy the friendship of a powerful Minister in Paris.'

'If one had that,' said Marcel sadly, 'one would not be sent here in the first place.'

'Exactly. So you see my problem?'

'Clearly. But I do not see your solution.'

'I intend to let Jean-Jacques discover incontrovertible proof that you and I are lovers. He will not wish to put his career, as he foolishly calls it, at further risk by insisting on a divorce. I know too much about him for that, and as the saying goes, a scorned woman is an implacable enemy.'

'Then what will he do?'

'He will agree to a separation, with proper provision for me. It not only a question of his salary – he has investments in France. As soon as a lawyer has drawn up an adequate document for signature, I can be on a ship on my way to an airport and a flight home.'

'I admire your arrangements,' said Marcel, who did no such thing, 'but what of me? How can I continue to work here at the Embassy if His Excellency hates and despises me for *zeqqing* his wife? It will be impossible.'

'I prefer you not to use those dreadful Santa Sabina words,' Jacqueline said. 'I do not *zeqq* and I do not permit any man to *zeqq* me! What happened between you and me a little while ago was a delicate expression of exquisite desire, surely you must understand that much!'

'But of course,' Marcel soothed her, 'delicate and beautiful, just as you are yourself, Jacqueline. But to answer my question – what of my position after you have left for France? Have you thought of that at all, *chérie*?'

'Naturally – I have given it all possible consideration. What will happen is quite simple – Jean-Jacques will write a report in which you will feature as a Don Juan, a Casanova, a wrecker of marriages, a despicable and untrustworthy person who for his own selfish motives has seduced the wife of France's Ambassador and sullied the sanctity of marriage. He will recommend, indeed he will demand, your immediate recall. As a result you will be ordered back to Paris, and be free of this miserable island. I am ready to receive your thanks for planning this.'

'My thanks,' said Marcel, his mouth turning down, 'oh yes, my thanks are certainly due! My God – don't you know what will happen to me in Paris? I shall be sacked. I was posted here in the first place because an important person discovered me in bed with his beautiful wife one afternoon. A second time and I am finished.'

'Ah!' said Jacqueline, 'I did not know that. But no matter – you are young and intelligent and you will find employment with no great difficulty.'

'That I doubt profoundly – I am trained for nothing except the diplomatic service. It is impossible to imagine myself in the employment of some large commercial organisation. No, you must abandon this plan of yours, Jacqueline, and explain away whatever suspicions you have implanted in your husband's mind. I refuse completely to be revealed as your lover!'

'But you *are* my lover,' she retorted, 'you cannot deny that you have been for three years.'

'I shall deny everything! I shall say that you made advances to me most improperly and I refused you, out of proper respect for His Excellency. They will think you accuse me for revenge.'

'Don't be stupid, *chéri*, my husband will not believe that. It is his settled opinion that you are an immoral person. To hear that you have made love to me forty-five times will confirm his opinion absolutely.'

'Your arithmetic is incorrect,' said Marcel. 'It was only forty-three before and to that we have added one.'

'It will be forty-five in a moment,' Jacqueline replied calmly. 'Now that I have you alone I mean to take every advantage of you.'

'I refuse!' said he. 'I will not be your toy if you intend to ruin my career, such as it is, and cause me to be turned out on the streets penniless and without prospects.'

'You begin to be tiresome,' Jacqueline told him, 'be silent now and lie still.'

'Never! Go to your Australian Adonis and persuade him to let you try again! Perhaps if you take great care he will last out long enough to give you what you want.'

'Marcel,' she said in a warning tone, 'you go too far! Give me one good reason why I should not rescue myself from years in this living hell by revealing the truth about you and me to my husband.'

'Because – oh God, I give up!' he said in exasperation.

'Ah *chéri*, I cannot bear to hear you speak in that tone of voice,' she said, wheedling, 'it will break my heart. I adore you – with you I would run away from this miserable island even if we had to starve together in an attic room. I want you to be happy, whatever it may cost me in deprivation and unfulfilled dreams and ambitions.'

During this preposterously untrue statement, her hand rested on the inside of Marcel's thigh, stroking gently upwards.

'There is something about you, Jacqueline, that I can never resist,' he told her, 'even when I know you are lying.'

'Do not treat me so unkindly,' said she, her hand very close to the join of his thighs, where his *zimbriq* lay limp and small after its recent exercise.

'Unkind – me!' he murmured, rolling his eyes upwards.

'You adore me really,' she said. 'I know that, *chéri*. It is why I always come back to you, no matter how badly you behave.'

To hear himself accused of behaving badly towards a woman who only made use of him when she had no one else available almost took the breath from Marcel's body. Before he could collect his wits to make a suitable reply, Jacqueline raised herself from the bed and deposited her long elegant naked body on top of him with her legs outside his.

'And if I say no to your number forty-five?' he asked.

'Give me your tongue, Marcel,' she said and took it into her mouth and touched the tip of her own to it. Marcel could feel his *zimbriq* stirring along his belly, and Jacqueline too felt the tiny movement against her own flesh.

'Put your tongue out further,' she told him, raising her head to look down into his face beneath her, 'and open your eyes – look at me when I am making love to you!'

Marcel thrust his tongue out as far as it would go, so far it was almost painful, and Jacqueline's mouth descended over it and engulfed it completely. He felt her sucking at it strongly and the sensation aroused him furiously. He placed his hands on the lean hot cheeks of her bottom, but she refused the embrace at once. She gripped his tongue between her teeth to prevent it escaping her, and pulled his hands away from her. She pressed his arms down on the bed at his sides with a hard jerk that was a wordless order to keep them there.

His *zimbriq* had become long and stiff. Jacqueline sucked hard at his tongue, and at the same time started to slide her body a little backwards and forwards on him. The tiny movement rubbed the russet buds of her breasts on his chest, the pleasure that gave her being doubled by the consideration that she was using him, while he remained passive. And at the same time she knew she was arousing him by the sliding of her belly over the head of his swollen part. Marcel kept his eyes open, as bidden, and Jacqueline's shining brown eyes were open.

Jacqueline was in her most rapaciously delightful vampire-bat mode, Marcel knew. Her eyes stared into his at short range, and if it had been possible to draw out his soul through his eyes as she was drawing out his virile essence with her belly, that is most certainly what she would have done. But metaphysics are not a subject for study by a chic Parisian lady, and Jacqueline had learned to be content with draining young men of their seed and at the same time planting in their heart a seed of her own – a tiny seed which would grow in time into a hot yearning to be dominated emotionally by her.

Soon she felt Marcel pressing his belly upwards against hers eagerly, and she too was trembling and aroused, but still very much in control. This time when his hands crept from where she had pushed them down on the bed and slid lightly over her hips to caress her bottom, she made no objection. As for Marcel, he was dizzy with sensation, straining his tongue upwards into her open mouth, his eyes wide and fixed on hers.

With each beat of his heart his *zimbriq* grew stronger and more insistent against the smooth skin of Jacqueline's belly. A few moments more and the crisis would be reached – she felt its inexorable advance and used her skill and experience to time it precisely. When Marcel's mouth gaped wide to moan in climactic release, she raised one hip and slipped her hand between their bellies. In an instant she had hold of his shaking *zimbriq* and guided the velvety head to the moist split waiting for it.

Her timing was accurate – Marcel had penetrated no more than two centimetres into her warm wetness when his *zimbriq* gave a great leap and gushed out its warm desire, spurt after spurt of virility drained from him for her delectation. At the feel of it in her, she gave a delicate little cry, like the tearing of silk, and collapsed onto Marcel's shaking body in an ecstasy of triumph.

When they were able to converse rationally, Marcel asked if she still intended to destroy his career and disgrace him.

'But you know I adore you far too much to ever hurt you,' she replied softly. 'You must help me to get away from this place, or I shall die and be buried here if I have to stay much longer – I implore you to assist me.'

'In every way I can,' he assured her, touching his lips to her belly in the lightest of kisses. The sheen of perspiration was on her skin, and Marcel brought a soft linen handkerchief from a drawer and wiped gently between her breasts, down her belly and between her parted legs.

'Everyone says you are very clever,' she murmured, 'even my husband says so, though he dislikes you. Very well then – make use of your cleverness on my behalf. Devise a way to get me to France with an adequate settlement from Jean-Jacques.'

'That may take some time,' he said with a shrug.

'But not too long,' said she, her beautiful brown eyes on his face. 'I cannot endure more than another month in Santa Sabina. If you are incapable of thinking of a practical scheme by then, I shall with reluctance be compelled to give my husband proof that you are my lover.'

# 6

## Some Secrets Are Not Secrets At All

The visit to the fruit market took place on the next day after Jacqueline had informed Marcel of her impossible demands. There was little point in succumbing to anxiety, for he was hopeful that some scheme would occur to him in time to prevent her from going to His Excellency with the news that she was being *zeqqed* by a member of his embassy staff.

And it was completely false, in Marcel's opinion, for he did not consider that he had ever *zeqqed* Jacqueline Ducour. Nor for that matter had she ever *zeqqed* him, properly speaking. He had on a number of occasions permitted her to use him in her games. It was true that these games involved his *zimbriq* and Madame's *kuft*, if one wished to be wholly candid about their relations, and that the outcome was a shared sexual climax – no, that was not correct, Madame Ducour did not share anything, she brought about her own sexual release by teasing him to one by hand.

All things considered, it was totally misleading to imagine that what he and she did together – or rather what she did to him – constituted what was normally meant by *zeqqing*, to employ the word in its day-to-day meaning. But on consideration it was doubtful if the Ambassador would understand these distinctions.

Nevertheless, life went on, and something would surely turn up before the threatened confrontation with His Excellency became necessary. And life did go on next day in the form of taking Nanette Jarre to see the famous fruit market – at her request. It seemed that during her day in the library examining the archives of Santa Sabina she had been approached by so very many young men making lewd gestures to signify their interest that she had reached an acceptance of Marcel's assessment of island motivation.

On this day she was cool and elegant in a sleeveless summer frock of dusty pink silk. The walnut-brown curls round her head were glossy and light, her face had lost the pallor of illness and her manner was vivacious. Altogether she was as attractive a companion for a morning stroll as could be found anywhere on Santa Sabina island, and Marcel was delighted to accompany her. About her neck there hung on a long cord an expensive-looking camera, which he assumed to be for taking a few snaps of local sights – insofar as there were any worth photographing.

The fruit market was held daily in one of the public squares in the poorer part of Santa Sabina city, no more than fifteen minutes stroll from the Hotel Grand Orient. It had an official designation – Dom Olispo Place – but no one called it anything but the fruit market, and whoever Dom Olispo had been, he had centuries ago been forgotten. In the middle of the square stood an old and cracked marble fountain and basin, long since out of order and dried up, though perhaps it had once been the source of drinking water for those who lived in the tall and crumbling old tenements round the four sides.

The space between fountain and buildings was filled up with ramshackle wooden stalls, some with torn and faded awnings over them, some without. Here was on show in huge profusion all the fruits of Santa Sabina – peaches, figs, oranges, melons large and small, coconuts, papaws, mangoes, tangerines, guava, breadfruit, pomegranates – and many of strange appearance for which there were no names other than the local ones.

In addition to the abundance of ripe and luscious fruit this was also where the other sweet-juiced product of the island was on display – the coffee-skinned and black-haired young women of Santa Sabina, rolling their unrestrained bosoms and big round bottoms under their skimpy cotton frocks. Some of them stood behind the stalls to sell, many more walked about with straw shopping bags, chattering and picking out the bargains. Marcel led Nanette slowly through the good-natured crowd, letting her drink in the peculiar atmosphere of the fruit market.

'My observations of the past few days are certainly confirmed as valid here,' she said after a while, 'underwear appears to be unknown.'

'Only rich ladies influenced by European magazines and movies trouble themselves with undergarments,' Marcel said with a nod. 'The women you see here about you – whether twelve years old or thirty-five – are wearing nothing whatsoever underneath their brightly coloured frocks.'

'But the poorer people also see the imported movies,' Nanette objected. 'Why have they not taken to wearing knickers at least – is it simply a question of poverty?'

'Not entirely, though it is true that the average person is extremely poor by our standards here. A more practical reason in my opinion is the climate – wearing nothing under the frock helps a little to keep them cool. It serves the further purpose of making the men hot – the effect of seeing all these charming bodies hardly covered is very provocative.'

'My experience in the library was that the men here need no provocation,' was Nanette's comment. 'They stared openly at my breasts and made circular movements on their own chests. They leaned over the writing table and made that obscene gesture of their fingers. They rubbed themselves between the legs while they smiled at me. There was one youth – he was no more than seventeen or eighteen – who got his penis out and waved it at me.'

'But none of this disturbed your concentration?'

'To be truthful, knowing on your advice they could be shooed away without difficulty, I found their antics amusing.'

Marcel shrugged and smiled at her words and continued with his explanation of why underwear did not appeal to the majority of Santa Sabina women.

'The most telling reason of all,' said he, 'is also the most practical of all. Quick and casual lovemaking goes on all the time, and by pulling her dress over her head, a woman can be instantly naked. And if the act proposed is too casual even for that, then she has only to raise her dress to her hips and stand with her legs apart – *et voila!*'

'So you say,' said Nanette, not without certain scepticism. 'But I have yet to see any evidence of this.'

'We will promenade slowly around the square,' Marcel replied, 'and we will keep close to the buildings. You will have every proof of my assertion before we have completed the circuit.'

They made their way between stalls and gossiping women to the edge of the square, turned and strolled along the south side. A ground floor window stood open with the shutters only partly closed, giving an oblique view over a high sill into a sitting room. It was ill furnished, the wooden floor bare, only a pair of rickety bamboo chairs and a round-topped table to be seen.

Lengthways against the white-painted wall opposite the window – no longer a clean white but a neglected and faded yellow-grey – stood a wooden bed with a thin mattress. One leg had broken and that corner of the bed was supported on a pair of cracked brown building bricks. But the focus of attention was not the decor or lack of it, but on the two people in the room. A youth of nineteen or twenty lay on his back on the bed, wearing a multicoloured shirt and plain blue trousers.

Over him in the traditional Santa Sabina position for making love squatted a woman five or six years older than he. She was naked and sat with her knees up to her shoulders and a look of concentration on her moon-round face. Her companion's trousers were wide open and she was bouncing up and down briskly on his embedded *zimbriq*.

Marcel and Nanette stood side by side, hardly breathing, very still, watching the action in the room.

'But they may be married,' Nanette said in a whisper, 'there is no evidence this is a casual encounter, as you call it.'

'He is some years younger than the woman,' Marcel said in explanation. 'That would be most unusual – local custom is that marriage partners should be of equal age, preferably within two or three months. The ideal marriage partner is one born on the same day as yourself.'

'Why?'

'I've not the least idea. It is a local superstition. There are so-called Presenters who make their living by checking on birthdays in church registers, no other records being kept of births, and charging a fee for bringing together young men and women with identical birthdates.'

'Perhaps the idea has a certain charm,' said Nanette. 'When is your birthday, Marcel?'

'The first of April,' he admitted, 'the year is not important.'

'There are some months between us,' she said, 'mine is on the eighteenth of August.'

'I shall remember that,' he said, 'and if you are still here then, we shall celebrate it together in style. But to continue what I was telling you about these two who are *zeqqing* – it is certain they are strangers to each other. She chose him among the stalls and brought him in to her room.'

He was surprised to hear a click beside his ear, and glanced at Nanette. The expensive-looking camera that had hung round her neck during their walk from San Feliz Square was now up to her eye, and she was pressing the shutter release as quickly as the film could move itself on.

'Is the light good enough inside there?' he asked, eyebrows rising at Nanette's sang-froid.

'With this film and shutter speed I can almost take pictures in the dark,' she answered. 'Oh, look!'

Down on the bed the young man squirmed and arched

his back in what most obviously were the final moments. The woman was riding him hard and fast, her plump coffee-coloured breasts rolling up and down to the movement of her body. Then her head went back and her mouth gaped in an ecstatic cry as she reached her goal. *Click click click* went Nanette's camera.

'Perhaps she is a street woman and he has paid her for this,' she suggested to Marcel, still busily taking pictures.

'Impossible,' he replied. 'No one of his age would dream of paying a woman to *zeqq*. Some of them demand presents from older women before they will perform.'

While he was speaking, Marcel took the ethnographer's arm and led her away from the window and further round the square. She was not even blushing faintly, he noted, and he asked if she found the sight interesting from a scientific point of view.

'To *zeqq*,' she said, repeating the word, 'that strikes me as a most appropriate verb to describe what we observed. But to answer your question, sexual customs and mating rituals are of immense interest to a scientist making a study of a particular culture. The positions adopted give an insight into the normal social relationships of the culture and the influence of its history. Though it would be necessary to observe many couples in the act of *zeqqing* to determine what is the normal usage.'

'Not at all,' said Marcel, 'what you saw is the normal way of it here – the man under and the woman over. If you will glance into the alley we are passing, you will see something else.'

It was the usual narrow alley, hardly more than a metre and a half wide, that led into a courtyard behind the tenements. Half way along it were two doors facing each other across the stone cobbles. Both doors were set back in the wall a little way. In the doorway on the right stood a young couple, pressed closely together in the tiny space available.

In reversal of what one used to the ways of casual lovemaking in Paris would have expected, it was the boy who stood with his back against the door. The girl held her bright orange frock up at the front as high as her waist, and standing with her feet well apart, was *zeqqing* her companion rapidly.

'But they are so young!' said Nanette. 'No more than sixteen I am certain, the pair of them!'

'The children here are incredibly advanced in sexual games,' Marcel informed her. 'If these two are sixteen, they have been indulging in the delights of *zeqqing* for three or four years at least, and have tried out hundreds of partners.'

'I do not think so,' said Nanette in open disbelief, 'for if that were true every female in this city would be pregnant, but we have seen no more than one or two big bellies all morning.'

'The Church has taught them that it is sinful to conceive out of wedlock,' Marcel explained, 'and the girls prevent this by chewing *qagga* leaves. This is a wild plant that grows here. The dried leaves can be bought at any pharmacist.'

*Click click click* went Nanette's camera, recording the scene for her learned studies. Tiny as it was, the sound reached the girl's ears and she turned her head to look over her shoulder, not missing a beat of her vigorous action. She saw the foreign couple in their fine clothes watching her at her pleasure, and grinned at them broadly, her white teeth shining in her dusky face. To be discovered in the act did not embarrass her, but it did Nanette, who turned away red-faced and walked quickly on.

Marcel caught up with her in a few strides and touched her arm lightly.

'There is no harm done,' he said, 'and no need to feel guilty about seeing Santa Sabinans at their amusements. It does not discommode them in the slightest. You will see many such scenes as you travel about the city and the country – it is impossible to avoid the sight for long.'

'But to do it so openly!' Nanette exclaimed.

'Why not? Santa Sabinans feel no shame about the act of love and they waste no time seeking privacy. They do it as naturally as breathing. They *zeqq* each other so frequently that for them it is normal to slip into a doorway or behind a tree for a few minutes. Afterwards they kiss and go their separate ways.'

Nanette had recovered her scientist's objectivity.

'The female partner was again in control of the action,' she commented. 'Is that usual, in your experience of the island?'

'Absolutely,' said Marcel helpfully, 'the normal position is the one you observed first, the man down flat on his back for the woman to ride. In fact, the Santa Sabina name for it is the *mule ride* – which to my mind always has suggested that the men here are held in no great esteem by the women. But perhaps I am wrong with that. The standing-up position against a wall or a tree is known as the *belly to belly*.'

'You speak with the confidence of one who knows,' Nanette said thoughtfully. 'Am I to assume that you have conducted some experiments of a personal nature with indigenous females?'

It seemed an extraordinarily impersonal way of asking if he had *zeqqed* any of the local girls, and it made Marcel smile.

'You would be entirely correct in that assumption,' he said.

'And you confirm the local reversal of the traditional roles in the sexual act?' she asked.

'You may take it as fact that to persuade a Santa Sabina girl to lie on her back to be *zeqqed* is very nearly impossible,' he informed her.

'I find that strange indeed,' said Nanette, 'and impossible to reconcile with the historical fact of the island's colonisation for centuries by Arabs, Italians, Portuguese and French – nations very well known for the overdeveloped egotism of their males, who ruthlessly suppress all signs of female aspiration.'

Marcel stared at his companion in amazement to hear himself and his compatriots viciously slandered in this way. *Male ego* – what in heaven's name could she mean? The words were without meaning, the accusation was monstrous! However, his diplomatic experience came to his aid, and he returned a mild answer.

'Things are not always as they seem,' he began, and then with relief drew Nanette's attention to a couple almost concealed by a stack of empty wicker baskets by a house wall. They had been used to bring in the fruit from the growers, and put out of the way until the market closed. The stack was almost two metres tall, and between it and the wall was a narrow space that made Marcel think of the pretty girl he had *zeqqed* between the bales on the dockside while waiting for the steamship *St Fiacre* with Nanette on board to tie up. What was the girl's name? She wore a red skirt – Carmelita, that was it.

By standing not far from one end of the stack of big wicker baskets and pretending to be looking at the market stalls, it was possible to see out of the corner of one's eye the pleasant activity being conducted in semi-privacy. Two youthful Santa Sabinans were standing close to each other between baskets and wall and Marcel's attention had been caught by a quick movement of the girl's hand as she flipped up her thin frock to reveal a bush of dark and curly hair where her thighs joined.

After a pause for inspection, the youth put his hand over her dark-haired *kuft* and felt it for a while. The girl moved closer to undo his trousers and put both hands inside, returning the compliment with evident enthusiasm.

'Take care!' Marcel whispered to Nanette, on seeing her lift her camera to her eye. 'It would be a pity to disturb them. Let us walk on and see what other sights there are.'

'Wait one moment,' she whispered back, adjusting her camera settings.

In truth, Marcel was curious to see how the lovers intended to manage affairs in the confined space. His guess was that one of them, girl or boy, would stand against the wall, while the other pressed up tight in a *belly to belly*. That certainly was how he would arrange it himself, if he were behind the baskets with the girl. He was surprised to see her push her companion down until he sat on the stone flags, his back to the wall and his knees up, then position herself right above the upthrust *zimbriq* sticking out of his trousers.

*Click click click click* went Nanette's camera, but happily the subjects of her candid photography were far too engrossed in each other to catch the little sound. Her hand was between her spread thighs, opening herself as she descended on to the ready spike of flesh that awaited her. In another second it was inside her and she was jerking herself rapidly up and down.

Marcel was patient while Nanette took another dozen or more pictures, then led her gently away. By the time they completed their circuit of Fruit Market Square they had observed, and she had photographed, no less than ten couples who were *zeqqing* in corners, doorways, alleys, farm carts and other useful little spots. Nanette had shot many rolls of film of all this activity and was putting her scientific training to work at making sense of what she had seen that morning.

'It is obvious to me that the social customs of Santa Sabina are devised entirely for the benefit of the male,' she said, staring at Marcel as if he were personally responsible for this deplorable condition.

'Ah no, that is only one's first impression,' he said, making for the Gran'Caffe Camille for a cooling drink, to be followed by a leisurely lunch. 'It was my own impression when I arrived here from France. But the true situation reveals itself.'

'And what is the true situation?' Nanette asked sceptically, letting him see that no non-scientist could possibly understand the complications of a foreign culture.

'It is now obvious to you that *zeqqing* is continuous,' Marcel said, 'and entirely without restraint. But the people here have no sense of the continuity of time – they seem not to believe that there will be a tomorrow after today. Or even an afternoon after this morning – or another hour after the present hour. As a result, they are impatient in all things, including *zeqqing*. They snatch at pleasure, and in doing so they lose it.'

'But how can you say that?' Nanette asked. 'Those we have observed this morning achieved satisfactory sexual climaxes in an unusually short time. Is it that you have objections of some egotistic type to being mounted by a woman?'

105

'By no means,' he defended himself, 'the idea is charming in my opinion. But alas, in the instant that a Santa Sabina woman impales herself on a *zimbriq* she is transformed into a machine for *zeqqing* and ceases to be a desirable human being. She hurls herself up and down so furiously that she and her companion are finished in a matter of seconds – you noticed that yourself.'

'I took that to be an ethnic characteristic,' said Nanette.

'However it is explained, it is the cause of disappointment in Europeans who indulge themselves in casual encounters with Santa Sabinans,' Marcel assured her. 'No sooner are they at her home than she jerks down his zipper and seizes his *zimbriq* with a heavy hand. There is scarcely time to get her frock over her head before she has him down on his back on her bed and is over him and has him inside her. Then it is only a question of how fast she can slide her *kuft* up and down on him – usually no more than twenty times before all is over.'

Nanette stared at him strangely and suggested it might well be possible that the problem lay not with the women of Santa Sabina – perhaps it was he who was the victim of an all-too-frequent male sexual disability, that of premature emission?

'Certainly not!' he exclaimed in indignation. 'I would have you know, Madame Jarre, that as a lover I am held in esteem by several ladies here – European ladies, I mean.'

'And that includes Madame Ducour, wife of our Ambassador?' Nanette asked with a sardonic smile.

'How absurd!' said Marcel, his heart sinking. 'What do you mean by that?'

'Only this – I saw her going into your room in the hotel only yesterday. It was about three in the afternoon. Ambassador's wives do not visit men in hotel rooms except for one purpose. I trust you were able to satisfy Madame Ducour's expectations and that when she departed she still held you in esteem.'

'Dear Nanette,' said Marcel, controlling his emotions with an effort, 'you ought not to jump to hasty conclusions at what you saw. You may be sure there was a perfectly good and proper reason for Madame Ducour's brief visit yesterday.'

'Very brief,' said Nanette. 'I was on the terrace outside the hotel having a drink before dinner when I saw her leave – about half past six, that was. Over three hours! You must be indeed a remarkable lover, to detain her that long.'

At last it dawned on Marcel that for all her straight-faced lack of expression, Nanette was making fun of him, and had been doing so for some time. He gave her a broad grin to show that he understood at last.

'Isn't it terribly dangerous for someone in your position to be *zeqqing* the Ambassador's charming wife?' Nanette asked as if in all innocence. 'Wouldn't he be annoyed if he found out?'

'It would be disaster,' he answered lightly, 'but since life is a catastrophe anyway, what is one more misfortune?'

They reached the terrace of the Gran'Caffe Camille and sat at one of the little round tables under the striped awning. Marcel noticed that at the far end of the terrace sat the beautiful Graziosa da Motta, talking animatedly. But she was not with the bristle-haired Czech – her companion was another woman, finely dressed but twenty years older, her mother perhaps. The glasses on the table before them contained a drink of bright green colour, which he knew was a Santa Sabina imitation of absinthe.

A very young waiter in open white shirt and long white apron greeted Marcel and asked what he might bring.

'The drinks here are a little strange,' Marcel told Nanette. 'They try hard to reproduce the aperitifs we have in Europe so there is not the expense of importing them. The ingredients are grown on the island and are a sort of approximation of what you expect to taste. You are already familiar with the champagne, so-called, and in general it is not to be recommended. But it is more palatable than most of the other drinks.'

The waiter nodded happily and went off to fetch a bottle of what the picturesque label described as *Veuve*

*Bollinger Brut* – three lies in as many words! Graziosa da Motta glanced along the terrace and Marcel caught her eye and inclined his head to her. She smiled vaguely and turned back to her companion.

'She is very beautiful,' said Nanette, 'who is she? Another lady who holds you in high esteem as a lover, in spite of your problem?'

Marcel ignored the joke and explained that she was the wife of the Minister of Industrial Developments, and that he knew her by sight, from the endless round of diplomatic receptions. Then it occurred to him that he had not at the time understood fully the implication of what Nanette said earlier about seeing Jacqueline entering his room in the Grand Hotel Orient. Here was something which might perhaps be explored further – and to his advantage, he hoped.

'My room and yours are on different floors of the hotel,' he said with a smile. 'May I ask where were you going when you saw Madame Ducour enter my room?'

Nanette looked at him and shrugged.

'But of course,' he said, 'you were coming to see me – isn't that so, Nanette?'

'To be perfectly frank, yes. There was some small detail I wished to ask of you – the exact opening hours of the Memorial Library. But it was of no importance.'

Naturally, it was nothing of the sort, her cancelled visit to Marcel's hotel room. He understood very well that she was under the mysterious spell that Santa Sabina cast over every person on the island, Europeans as well as those born there. A compulsion to *zeqq* affected all alike, by day and by night. Santa Sabinans succumbed to it as children and started to *zeqq* each other by the time they were twelve or thirteen and regarded their compulsion as a simple fact of life. Foreigners whose calling brought them to the island were already adults, but they were affected equally and found the compulsion strange and, for some, disquieting.

In Marcel's informed opinion, Nanette had been on her way to his hotel room the previous day for the excellent reason that an overwhelming urge for *zeqqing* had manifested itself. A pity that Madame Ducour was due at the same time. Marcel intended to have lunch served on the terrace, but knowing now that Nanette was in a receptive frame of mind, he changed plan.

He explained that the Gran'Caffe Camille provided facilities that had been familiar in Paris half a century ago, but which had gone the way of the horse-drawn carriage and the gaslight – namely, the private room for diners wishing to entertain their *petite amie* in comfort and seclusion. Nanette said she found it enchanting, this romantic relic of the past, and asked whether it was possible to be shown one of these rooms.

Marcel made the arrangements, and ten minutes later, as soon as the bottle of *Veuve Bollinger* was empty, he led her into the Caffe and upstairs, where the half-dozen private rooms were. In open-eyed astonishment she stared about the small old-fashioned dining room for two. The furniture was of mahogany, inlaid with marquetry flowers, the seats were upholstered in red plush, and on the walls were long crystal mirrors.

'But how bizarre,' said Nanette, 'to find the comic decadence of the *belle époque* lingering on in this remote tropic island. To an ethnographer Santa Sabina is a living museum, where the Portuguese have left their names, the Arabs their dark eyes and scimitar noses, the African slaves their dusky complexion, the Italians their amiability, the French their civilising manners.'

Marcel shrugged and said she ought not to forget the heritage of the original island dwellers, whoever they might have been, and their excessively relaxed attitude towards sexuality. But Nanette dismissed the idea with the condescensions of a trained scientist towards a layman.

'We shall find,' said she, 'that these attitudes you find so interesting can be explained without recourse to theories about an original Santa Sabina racial group – they are the outcome of generations of slavery and colonisation.'

They sat side by side on a long banquette, comfortable and well cushioned, as was to be expected in a private room. Marcel explained the intricacies of the menu while they drank another glass of champagne.

'Not even we French in the hundred years we ruled here could teach fine cooking to the inhabitants,' he said ruefully. 'The cuisine is typical of the place and there is no more to be said about it. Cattle do not thrive here, neither beef nor sheep, so what is represented as beefsteak or other meat dish is in fact mule flesh. The animals you see about the city, in the shafts of the carriages and carts – when they are too old to work they are sold to the butchers. Or there is goat, cooked in a variety of ways, none of them very interesting.'

'Santa Sabina is no place for a gourmet,' said Nanette. 'What do you advise, Marcel?'

'The fish – it is always freshly caught and good, though some of it is unfamiliar to the European palate.'

She agreed to let him order for her, and after consulting the menu with care and asking questions of the waiter, he ordered a simple meal for two of cucumber and sour melon soup, followed by sea slug stuffed with peanuts and caraway seeds, and braised in white vermouth. The waiter assigned to them flitted silently in and out, serving the food and filling their glasses. When at last they ended the meal with thick slices of a yellowish goat's milk cheese speckled with cumin seed, he set out coffee and a bottle of so-called cognac on the table and left them alone.

While they ate Marcel asked what Nanette intended doing with the many photographs she had taken that morning of Santa Sabina couples at their amusements. She surprised him by saying that some would be included in her report when she submitted it. The thought gave rise in his mind to curious questions about UNESCO and its activities. On the other hand, he had already noted her dry sense of humour, and perhaps she was teasing him.

Unfamiliar though the food was, and suspect though the drinks were, the effect of both combined in the right proportion was to put Nanette in a good humour.

'Now that I know the secret of your rendezvous with Madame Ducour,' she said, her eyes sparkling in a mischievous manner, 'it is only fair that you should know a secret concerning her husband, the Ambassador.'

At once Marcel stared at her in great interest.

'At the Theatre des Beaux Arts,' she said with a smile, 'at that absurd concert for the President's grandmother or whoever it was, when the lights failed – you recall?'

'But of course,' said Marcel, remembering vividly the moments when Jacqueline had pleasured him in the dark corridor. But no, that was not correct – what Jacqueline had done was to pleasure herself, making use of him for the purpose.

'The Ambassador was asking me about my work and I had moved to sit next to him in the box while we talked – when *paf*! out went all the lights. His Excellency told me not to be alarmed, and explained that the failure of the electricity is a regular occurrence in Santa Sabina city. I wore my short white off-the-shoulder dress that evening, if you remember – the one with the flounced skirt – and suddenly I felt the Ambassador's hand down the front of it while he was talking to me so casually.'

'Well, well!' said Marcel with a smile. 'What did you do?'

Nanette shrugged.

'I was very surprised, as you can well imagine,' she said. 'I hardly knew what to do when this hand began to fondle my bare breasts. Should I be outraged, should I scream, smack his face – but he is a very distinguished man, Monsieur Ducour, and so I did nothing at all.'

Marcel sighed and said he wished it had been himself with her in the box when the lights went out.

'I'm sure you do,' she answered, 'but I expect you were with a woman somewhere else in the theatre, taking advantage of the darkness and general immobility.'

'Not at all,' he lied sturdily, 'I was out in the foyer with the Portuguese Consul when the lights went out, and we strolled out into the square to smoke a cigarette until we could see our way back.'

'That's as maybe,' said Nanette, who appeared to have formed a distinct view of Marcel's character. 'Anyway, during the time His Excellency was telling me how long it normally took them to restore the lighting, I felt his hand on my thigh – high up and inside my skirt.'

There could be detected a note of amusement in her

voice that caused Marcel to listen intently while he refilled her glass with pale golden cognac.

'No doubt you found it pleasant enough to permit him to enjoy his beastly molestation,' he said with a smile, 'and why not?'

That was not the response Nanette expected and she accused him of cynicism.

'By no means, dear Nanette. I have told you of the effect on everyone of this island – a continuing sexual arousal that will not be denied. What happened between you and the Ambassador was only natural.'

'Nothing much did happen,' she told him, 'he had a good feel of me, and then the theatre staff came round lighting candles, and that was the end of it.'

What a pity, Marcel was thinking, what a pity His Excellency had not been given the time or opportunity to do more. Anything that could be used against him by Jacqueline was of importance, yet on reflection Marcel realised that even if the Ambassador had *zeqqed* Nanette, it would be insufficient as evidence. More than that was required, for the Ambassador certainly knew about his wife's repeated infidelities and would never trade off one marital misdemeanour of his own against her interminable list! But it was encouraging to hear that His Excellency was tempted, and perhaps something to his discredit could be arranged.

By now Marcel was cupping a round little breast in his hand through the dusty pink silk of Nanette's frock, and she made no objection. He told her she was beautiful and adorable, that it was his most ardent wish that they would become the closest and dearest of friends.

'Why not?' she replied, and kissed him on the cheek. 'As you say, it is only natural here to do what the Santa Sabinans do.'

Marcel returned the kiss, on her lips, and her mouth clung to his. Their kiss became passionate, until at last he pressed her down gently to lie at full length on the cushioned banquette. As his hand caressed her thigh up under her frock she asked him if that was what usually happened in a private room.

'What else are private rooms for?' he asked, his *zimbriq* at full stretch and twitching in his trousers. 'The waiter will not return now until I ring for the bill.'

He wanted to see her naked and kiss every part of her, but he was afraid she would not go along with that in a restaurant. It would perhaps be better to take her back to the hotel and make love there, but it was important to him to establish between them an intimate relationship here and now. He lay beside her on the red plush cushions, his fingers finding their way into her tiny knickers to play over the curls of her *kuft*.

Immediately he discovered something important about her – her nature was to be active in everything. Even while he pressed a gentle fingertip into her moist split, he felt her hands reach for his belt-buckle and undo it. A moment later his trousers were wide open and her hand inside to grasp and manipulate his stiff *zimbriq*. Her hand was cool, his belly was hot, and the contrast aroused him intensely.

'You must take my knickers off,' she murmured, 'if you hope to achieve anything worthwhile.'

It was the work of a moment to slide them down her legs and over her bare feet, for she had kicked her flat shoes off when she lay down on the banquette. She opened her legs, and Marcel leaned down to kiss her bare thighs. But she was too aroused to delay matters further, and urged him with her hands to put his belly on hers and lie on her. He shed his jacket and tie faster than ever before in his life, and mounted her. Her hands were down between her legs, to guide him straight into her wet *kuft*.

He kissed her mouth, her face, he licked her closed eyelids, he turned her head between his hands and thrust his tongue into her ear – and all the time he was *zeqqing* her frantically – and she was responding with a rhythmic jerking of her belly to meet his stabs.

'Nanette, Nanette,' he moaned in a delirium of sensation, and she sighed, 'yes, yes, faster, *chéri*! until his hot desire came surging up from the depths of his being and into her clinging *kuft*. As she felt the first throb inside her,

Nanette uttered a faint wail of climactic delight, and jerked underneath him fast and furiously.

When they were able to speak rationally again, she opened her dark brown eyes and smiled up into Marcel's face.

'That was very nice,' she said. 'Pay the bill, *chéri*, and we will go back to the hotel and do it again with our clothes off – yes?'

'Oh yes,' said Marcel.

# 7

## *A Reputation For Generosity Can Be Bought Cheaply*

While Nanette Jarre continued her research into the history of Santa Sabina and its people at the Augusto da Cunha Memorial Library, Marcel had even more time than usual on his hands. He was not expected at the embassy, being assigned to Madame Jarre for the whole of her stay, but he had not the least intention of sitting in the library watching her examine the old books.

Before nine o'clock he was waiting in the street outside the Portuguese Consulate, watching for Mariana Mendez to arrive for work. She was late – it was nine-fifteen before she came round the corner, but it was of no importance, for there was so very little to do at any foreign legation that working hours tended to be irregular. A look of surprise crossed her pretty face as she caught sight of Marcel, then she hurried up to him looking pleased.

While they exchanged greetings, her eye lighted on the wicker hamper on the ground beside Marcel and she asked if he meant to go away somewhere.

'On a picnic,' he told her, 'with you, for it is much too hot to work in an office today. Tomorrow you can tell them you were not feeling well, and no one will mind.'

She agreed at once, delighted by his plan to pass a whole day with her. They strolled at leisure through the uncrowded city streets to Vasco da Gama Square, where the buses started from and came back to, bought tickets and climbed aboard one waiting empty and idle at the stop for Vilanova. From long experience of the local public transport Marcel knew the timetable to be mythological – the bus would depart, not when due, but when the driver decided.

Only two main roads ran out of Santa Sabina city. One of them followed the coast southwest, past the Reserved Beach and along the low shore through groves of coconut trees, frangipani and bougainvillaea. This road went as far as Selvas, a fishing port on the far west side of the island, several hours' journey away. The other road followed the northwest coast, which rose up high and rocky just a few kilometres outside Santa Sabina city. It ended at Vilanova, a large town in the foothills of the Sierra Dorada mountains in the far north of the island.

Not that Marcel had any intention of going that far – almost a whole day journey by bus. With Mariana cuddled close against him, her hand resting lightly on his thigh, he watched for the whitewashed kilometre stones marking off the distance from the city, and at the eleventh stone rang for the bus to halt.

Mariana was puzzled by all this. She had thought he meant to take her to the reserved beach, and the idea of being accepted by the foreign community for whom it was reserved pleased her – but at the same time the thought of having no swimsuit dismayed her with the prospect of appearing fully dressed among European ladies in stylish beachwear. But Marcel told her he wanted that day to take her to a secret beach he knew, a place where no one would see them, where no swimsuits were needed, and they could be alone all day.

At the point where they left the bus the road ran along the cliff face, about halfway up. The rocks rose steeply up on the left towards the top, and fell equally steeply to the right to the sea below. But not very far from the eleventh kilometre stone was the beginning of a track slanting downwards, nearly parallel with the road, and it was along this that he conducted Mariana. The rough track descended sharply, hidden from above by straggly thorn bushes, clung to the outside of a rocky spur above a sheer drop, then descended at last into a little cove.

It was, as Marcel had said, a secret place, known to only a few. He had been shown it two years before by Sherri Hazlitt – the daughter of the American Ambassador at that time – a clean-scrubbed straw-haired brainless and pretty California girl with whom he had enjoyed a brief but extremely complicated *affaire*. She had long since returned to the United States, leaving Marcel with the knowledge of the secret beach as her gift to him.

In fact, it was very small – no more than a narrow strip of sand between large rocks, where little waves ran in and expired without a murmur. Mariana stood looking about her in something approaching dismay – this deserted cove was hardly the type of sophisticated venue she longed for – it compared badly with the magazine pictures she had seen of the beaches at Cannes and at Nice, where elegant young ladies sunbathed luxuriously, amidst the admiration of handsome young men.

'What is in the hamper, Monsieur Marcel?' she asked.

'Marvellous things for you, Marie,' he replied, careful to use the French name that pleased her, 'and you shall see! But first, a little dip in the sea to cool us after the bus ride.'

It was not much after ten in the morning and the temperature stood at 30°C under a completely overcast sky. Marcel stripped naked and ran out into the sea until it was deep enough for him to dive and swim. As always, the water was warm, but it helped to reduce the temperature of his sweating body. When he turned, he saw Mariana standing in the shallows and waiting. She had taken off all her clothes, but she was reluctant to get wet – the islanders never sat in the sun if they could find shade, and the only ones who went into the sea were fishermen falling in by accident.

Marcel swam strongly back until he felt the bottom under his thrashing feet, then stood up and waded up to where the little waves broke over Mariana's ankles. She was very desirable, her skin a charming *café-au-lait* tint, her brown-black hair hanging down her back in a riot of curls, her breasts round and full, the bush below her smooth belly trimmed to a small triangle. In fact, he thought, she could almost be taken for a European with a heavy sun tan, which was her aspiration, though an unlikely one ever to be fulfilled, alas.

His *zimbriq* began to rise while he walked towards her. He put his arms round her and pressed her body to him, so wetting her breasts and belly, and cooling them a little.

'Ah, that's what you brought me here for, not for a picnic,' she said lightly, her hand sliding between them to take hold of his upthrusting part. 'You think that's all Santa Sabina girls are good for, don't you?'

'Why no,' said Marcel, stroking the satin skin of her bottom with both hands. 'I think you are adorable, Marie, but if you don't want to make love, then I shall respect your wishes.'

Whatever her aspirations, she was Santa Sabinan at heart and had never in her life refused a stiff *zimbriq*. She smiled and turned away from the empty sea to lead him up the beach by his outstanding part, as if it were a handle. Up under the cliff he spread his shirt out on the sand for her to lie on, knowing she would be pleased by this little attention.

She lay with her knees upwards and outwards, displaying the pretty *café-au-lait* petals between her thighs, under the little delta of black curls. Marcel sat beside her to fondle her breasts and kiss them.

'What very beautiful *gublas* you have, Marie,' he murmured.

'No, I don't like you to use that word,' she said, staring up into his eyes. 'It makes me sound like an ordinary girl who is picked up in the street by anyone. You know I am different.'

She sounded so much like Jacqueline Ducour that Marcel could only with difficulty prevent himself from smiling. The protest was the same, though the two women were a world apart.

'But of course, *ma chérie*,' he said at once, 'you are a young lady of refinement and distinction, and I respect you greatly. I have the honour to tell you, Marie, you have very beautiful breasts.'

Hearing a Frenchman use her French name and the French word for her bountiful assets brought a smile of satisfaction to her pretty face and friendly squeeze of his throbbing *zimbriq*. To show her that he truly respected her, Marcel slid his hand down her smooth belly to caress the fleshy lips of her *kuft*.

'Tell me the truth, Monsieur Marcel – do you go with ordinary girls from the streets sometimes?' she asked.

'But that would be highly inappropriate,' he said evasively. 'As a foreigner and a member of the diplomatic corps one must exercise a certain prudence.'

'How can *zeqqing* be imprudent, when everybody does it all the time?' said Mariana. 'But it is true that for you it would be inappropriate to *zeqq* the ordinary girls who offer themselves in the cafés and squares. You are too important and magnificent a person to waste your time with common girls without underwear or the elegance to lie on their back for you.'

Marcel's fingers were playing gently within her slippery *kuft* and he was impressed by the degree of self-control she exerted to lie still with her legs apart when her every Santa Sabina instinct surely was urging her to roll him over on his back and impale herself on his upright part. Evidently Mariana Mendez was determined to transform herself into a European no matter what the cost. Ambition so very zealous ought to be rewarded, though there were limits to what Marcel could do for her.

'How charming of you to think of me as important,' he murmured with a little smile of affection. 'In the circumstances I must agree that to go with ordinary girls would be inappropriate. My good fortune was better than I had any right to expect when you and I met in the Cinema des Grands Boulevards.'

She was sighing gently now as she struggled to keep herself in check under his manipulation, and her bare thighs trembled in a manner most provocative. But aroused though she was almost to the point of climax, she did not abandon her questioning.

'You *zeqq* the foreign ladies here,' she said with an effort, 'the wives of the diplomats – yes? Tell me!'

'But of course,' said Marcel, thinking of Jacqueline and her curious little ways of lovemaking. 'Why do you ask, *chérie?*'

'It interests me,' she said faintly, her eyes rolling upwards to show the whites as she teetered on the brink of ecstasy and still fought to control her shaking body. 'Is it different?'

'*Ma chère Marie*, you have made love with European men before me,' said Marcel, enormously aroused by her battle to stave off her sexual crisis while she probed for answers. 'You know if it is different or the same.'

Before she could pursue her enquiries any further, her moment arrived. Her back arched up from the wrinkled shirt she lay on and with a shriek of delighted release she shook and shuddered her way through a long sexual orgasm.

Inflamed beyond the point of reason by her bodily response to his stimulation Marcel lay quickly on her palpitating belly and pushed in between the parted lips of her *kuft*, swiftly sliding his *zimbriq* into her warm and slippery depths. Mariana, feeling herself penetrated at last, hugged him to her with loud gasps and cries, heaving her belly up and down under him in frantic desire to extend and enhance her sexual climax. Marcel plunged and moaned in rapture, his fingers sinking deep into the flesh of her soft round breasts.

'*Je t'adore*, Marie,' he sighed as his frantic desire spurted into her.

'*Mon amour!*' she moaned, her feet hooked over his bottom to drive him deeper yet with rhythmic kicks of her heels.

When they were again tranquil he kissed her lightly and sat up to open the wicker hamper and show her what was inside. Food and wine, of course, prepared and packed by the kitchens of the Grand Hotel Orient – cold cuts of swordfish with mango sauce, roast legs of chicken wrapped in reddish *frolo* leaves, boiled rabbit stuffed with pounded cashew nuts – a veritable feast. The labels on the wine bottles declared with more recourse to imagination than truth *Chablis St-Denis Grand Clos* but the wine had become too warm to drink. Marcel set the bottles in the sea between rocks, to cool them down a little.

Of greater interest to Mariana than the delicacies were the magazines Marcel had obtained from Madame St-Beuve, who seemed to subscribe by post to every well-esteemed publication. There were two copies of *Vogue*, almost a year old, a *Harper's Bazaar* of the same vintage, back numbers of *Paris-Match*, of *Elle* and *Chic*. Marcel himself had donated a copy of *La Vie Parisienne*, only a month out of date. Marie fell on the publications with cries of glee, flipping through the pictures enthusiastically. She flung her arms round Marcel's neck and hugged him to her big bare *gublas*.

'But there is more,' he said, grinning in genuine pleasure at her unrestrained enthusiasm.

From where he had concealed it at the bottom of the hamper, underneath the wrapped food and plates to eat it from, he drew out a small flat package wrapped in tissue-paper and handed it to her. Mariana opened it to reveal a pair of elegant knickers in magenta silk, trimmed with black lace. He had bought them from a shop on Independence Place, opposite the Presidential Palace – the only shop in the entire Republic of Santa Sabina that imported underwear and other *chic* items for the wives of diplomats and ladies of the Hundred Families.

Mariana stared awestruck at the present, then rose trembling to her feet and put the knickers on, staring down round-eyed at the flimsy silk clinging about her loins. A moment later she fell to her knees to throw her arms around Marcel, also on his knees by the hamper, and shower fervent kisses on his face and mouth, until he was overwhelmed by her gratitude. From now on he could do no wrong in her eyes, and whatever he asked would be done at once.

When at last she calmed down a little she was going to remove her pretty knickers and put them away where no harm could come to them from sand or sea, but Marcel persuaded her to keep them on. He wanted to admire her a little in them, he said, and he promised to take every care nothing untoward happened to them. Mariana arranged her bare back against a tall smooth rock, and with Marcel's shirt spread under her bottom to protect her new treasure from the silver-white sand.

'If I may ask you something, Marie,' Marcel began casually, 'I try as part of my profession to understand how your country is organised and governed, but we foreigners often get things wrong, I'm sure. My question is simple – what would happen if the President died unexpectedly?'

'But an election, of course,' said Mariana, surprised by so obvious a question. 'There is an election every five years by law. If President da Cunha died between elections there would be a special one. The Vice-President would be head of state for the few weeks necessary to organise affairs.'

'Yes, I understand that,' said Marcel, who in fact understood the processes of government of the island thoroughly. 'There would be four or six weeks when Vice-President Joaquim Cuando was in charge. But at past elections, there has never been more than one candidate, a da Cunha. No one has ever stood against the da Cunha candidate in the hundred years or more that Santa Sabina has been an independent republic.'

Mariana nodded, her attention still on the charm and elegance of her magenta knickers. She was running a fingertip lightly over the silk to feel its smooth texture. Politics seemed to be an irrelevance to a young woman as happy as she was just then.

'Everyone respects the da Cunha family,' she said, 'they are the largest landowners, the richest and best educated of the Hundred Families. No one would ever dare be so disrespectful as to oppose them in an election.'

'So I believe,' Marcel agreed, certain that if anyone stood in opposition he would disappear overnight, 'but my question is this, Marie – if President Pascal da Cunha were to become ill and die unexpectedly, who would be elected next President?'

'His son,' she replied without thinking. 'Ah, no – that would not be possible. His son is only twelve years old. Madame da Cunha kept having daughters for the first ten years of their marriage – there would be a problem, Monsieur Marcel.'

'A problem which those interested in politics must have given consideration to,' he said, 'which includes all of the Hundred Families. As I understand your constitution, if no candidate is forthcoming, the Chamber of Deputies has the power to nominate one. He then stands for election and becomes President.'

'They teach us that at school,' said Mariana, 'but I forgot. The problem has never arisen before.'

It was Marcel's chance observation of Colonel Jiri Svoboda of the Czech Embassy meeting in secret with the beautiful wife of the Minister for Industrial Developments that had reminded him of a certain reputation the Czech Secret Service had acquired. It was known that they had bribed or blackmailed members of the French Senate, the Federal German Bundestag, the British House of Commons and the Dutch States-General. There remained not the slightest doubt in Marcel's mind that they could get control of the Santa Sabina Chamber of Deputies if they tried hard enough.

To what purpose? That was obvious – a change of government and the installation of a more sympathetic regime, headed by a president ready to sign agreements to set up foreign naval and air bases on the island and to allow exploitation of whatever oil and minerals reserves were to be found in the mountains and off the coast, and so on, and so on. And all this on behalf of and paid for by the Czech's masters – the KGB and the Kremlin.

For a diplomat it was something to think about carefully, but not to trouble a charming young lady with – especially one who sat with her back to a rock and her knees up, and wearing only silk knickers. Marcel was lying on his side – he put his hand between her parted thighs to stroke the smooth light brown skin up towards the spot where magenta silk covered her clipped dark curls. The lace-trimmed legs of the knickers were loose enough for him to pass his hand inside and lay his palm on her belly.

'You asked if I had been with other foreigners before you,' she said, her black eyes shining as she looked fondly down at him. 'Why did you ask?'

'I didn't precisely ask,' said Marcel. 'I naturally assumed a charming and refined young lady like you had been pursued and courted by many discerning men. It would be very strange if it were not so.'

'There have been three,' Mariana said, smiling affectionately at him again, 'but never anyone like you, Monsieur Marcel. You are unique – I adore you with all my heart.'

'And I adore you,' he said, stroking her smooth belly gently. 'Who were these others, Marie – will you tell me?'

'If you wish. The first of them was Senhor Tomas Pinto, who was the Vice-Consul when I first went to work at the Portuguese Consulate, the year before last. He was very kind to me, but he was an older man and wore himself out *zeqqing* me. After some months he could only do it if I sat on top of him, in the Santa Sabina way. That did not please me.'

Marcel nodded in sympathy, seeing quite clearly that a friend who could only *zeqq* in the manner Mariana was trying to escape would be of little interest. Pinto had downgraded himself from exciting foreigner to middle-aged local without knowing it.

'Senhor Tomas went back to Lisbon for early retirement,' said the girl, 'then a friend of his at the Brazilian Embassy became my friend – Senhor José Barbosa . . .'

'Ah, I am acquainted with him,' said Marcel.

He had also met Barbosa's wife at diplomatic functions and thought her a most beautiful and exotic woman of the vivacious and dark-haired Latin American type. She wore low-cut frocks at cocktail parties, to show off most of her superb bosom – and it was Marcel's opinion that she would be a tigress in bed.

'He treated me very well, Senhor José, and told me about the high society in Rio de Janeiro,' Mariana went on. 'He taught me how to dance rumba and samba and tango – he liked very much to dance naked with me, after my mother had gone to bed and we had the living room to ourselves. But there was a problem – he came to see me so often that his wife found out and objected.'

'Ladies of her temperament are famous for their jealousy and fits of rage,' Marcel said, shaking his head sadly.

'There was a confrontation when she came to the apartment one evening and saw us together. She screamed and cursed and kicked poor José between the legs and tried to pull out my hair but I ran away naked, down the stairs and up the street, and hid in a yard until she dragged him away.'

'And you have not seen him since, I suppose?'

'Oh yes, sometimes he escapes from the Senhora for an hour or two and comes to *zeqq* me, but not very often, for she watches him closely now, and it is always very sad.'

'When did you see him last?' asked Marcel, curious as ever to hear more of the anarchic sexual pleasures of Santa Sabina. Inside Mariana's knickers his hand moved slowly and gracefully over the satin skin of her belly.

She looked at him thoughtfully before answering, uncertain to what extent he too suffered from the emotions of jealousy that afflicted foreigners so painfully.

'It was the evening you and I met in the cinema,' she said at last. 'Senhor José asked me to meet him there for an hour – not that we could *zeqq*, but I could stroke him in the dark and give him pleasure that way. But he did not arrive by the time the film started – and there you were, to carry me off to the Gran'Caffe Camille!'

'And your other friend, the third one? Who is he?'

'He is very nice, but also very strange, I think. He works at the Swedish Embassy and his name is Sven Johansson. He is their priest, but he likes *zeqqing* very much. He explained to me that the Swedish religion does not order its priests to be celibate, like the Catholic Church, but I cannot tell if this is true or not. What do you think, Monsieur Marcel?'

'I have met this man at the Swedish Embassy, at a

celebration of their King's birthday,' Marcel said with a grin. 'He is the embassy chaplain. The Swedes are a species of Protestant, and their pastors are permitted to marry and have children, if they wish. I think it is a sin for them to *zeqq* other women – but what do I know of these heretical practices?'

Truth to tell, it was not only at the Swedish Embassy that Marcel had encountered the Reverend Johansson. He had seen him more than once at Madame da Silva's establishment on the Avenue of the Constitution. At Maison da Silva were to be found the prettiest, cleverest and most willing girls in all Santa Sabina city, and at a very reasonable price. To be charitable, perhaps the Swede was there to call the girls to repentance, but Marcel thought it unlikely, having seen him go upstairs with various girls and descend twenty minutes later with a foolish smile of satisfaction on his face.

'Is it different with a priest, Marie?' he asked. 'Tell me.'

'There is nothing to tell, Monsieur Marcel. He comes to my home, always with a present, and takes his clothes off and lies on the bed and asks me to feel his *zimbriq* until it stands up stiff. Then he asks me to place myself on hands and knees and he *zeqqs* me from behind. I think this must be the Swedish way, because when I suggest lying on my back for him, he refuses.'

'It's not a particularly Swedish way, as far as I know,' said Marcel. 'I think it must be his way to *zeqq* without looking you in the eye, which might perhaps make him feel guilty. He is not a suitable friend for you, Marie.'

'Now you have become my friend I shall send him away. I do not want anyone else but you.'

She took his head between her hands and pulled him closer to her until his face was between her breasts. The spicy smell of her flesh was very exciting and the breast to which he pressed his lips was soft and enticing. His eyes closed in delight when he felt her hand clasping his *zimbriq*.

'It is stiff again,' she said, 'I think you want to *zeqq* me.'

She spoke no more than the truth – in her hands it had grown to full size and strong again. She glanced down, then back to his face with an enquiring expression.

'Is it the French way, what you do to me before you *zeqq* me – or are you like Monsieur Sven, that you have some secret reason of your own?'

'I don't understand what you mean,' said Marcel, his fingers tracing the soft lips of her *kuft* inside her knickers. 'What is it you find unusual? I lie on your beautiful belly and push up inside you – *et voila!*'

'No, before that,' she replied, 'you caress my *kuft* until you make me *zboca*, and only then do you put it in me properly. You did this the first time we made love, on the settee at home in my apartment, and you did it again today here on the beach. Why do you do this to me, Monsieur Marcel, is it a French custom?'

'I don't think so,' he said, smiling at her, his fingertips pressing softly into her slippery warmth to find and stroke her little nub. 'It is something I like to do – to watch your face while you *zboca*. It is a caprice of mine, to enjoy the look of ecstasy in the critical moments – there is no mystery, I assure you, *chérie*. If it displeases you, I shall not do it again.'

'No, no!' she exclaimed at once, very anxious not to disturb him in any way. 'I like it when you do it to me, I like it very much when you show me that you are master and can do whatever you like with me. I asked only because I have never before had a friend who did this before *zeqqing* me.'

And to prove that she was telling the truth, she splayed her legs wide on the shirt she was sitting on, to let him play with her wet *kuft* to his heart's content. But now that his personal little caprice had been made the subject of rational discussion to be defended, Marcel had lost interest in continuing with it for the present. He knelt between Mariana's knees and lifted up her legs to pull her knickers off and smack her bottom just a little. She giggled and ran her hands over his belly and soon his stiff part was in her again, forcing open the long fleshy split of her *kuft*.

Well-mounted on her belly, with her legs around his waist to pull him in close, he swung his loins backwards and forwards in a steady, strong tempo that made Mariana sigh and gasp to the thrills that ran through her. She swung her hips upwards boldly to redouble the strength of Marcel's thrusts, and he held her rump clasped in his hands and let Nature take its course, for it was unkind to restrict her exuberance, however overzealous.

She was trying to retain some control of herself, he knew – it was not a simple question for Mariana of *zeqq-zeqq* – getting a male part inside her and bouncing up and down fast to bring on the climax quickly, and then do it again and again, until her partner was unable to continue. That was the way of it with the ordinary girls of Santa Sabina, as she called them, the common girls who let themselves be picked up in cafés and bars – even in cinemas!

But it was not her imagined European way, not what happened after the tender love scenes she had seen in imported movies, where beautiful women wore *haute couture* frocks by Chanel and Dior – where hands were kissed by handsome young men wearing white tie and tails, who took them to expensive night clubs to drink champagne and dance to a ten-piece band, who held them in their arms while slipping diamond necklaces round their throat. Romantic embraces on a terrace under the stars were surely the prelude to something more refined, more elegant, than simply squatting over a man for *zeqq-zeqq*.

Yet for all that, Mariana was greedy for sensation and when she felt her critical moment approaching, she heaved her belly faster and wriggled her loins under him. Marcel gave a long cry as he fountained his passion into her *kuft* and she writhed and panted in ecstasy.

'You are magnificent, Monsieur Marcel,' she told him when her throes subsided, 'but you have made me very hungry. Can we eat now?'

Marcel laughed and climbed off her well-fleshed body and went to get the bottles of imitation Chablis from the washing waves that he hoped had cooled them a little. Mariana put her magenta knickers on again and set out plates and food from the hamper. They ate and drank and chatted and rested. She asked him what family name she should take when she went to live in Paris – it seemed to her that Mendez did not sound French. Marcel gave the question some thought and offered Manet, Marne and Menton for consideration.

When they had finished eating and two bottles were empty they dozed for half an hour. Eventually Marcel persuaded her to come a little way out into the sea with him – without her precious knickers, of course. She held on to his hand firmly and waded out till the sea was up to her waist.

He coaxed her out a little further, by caressing her bottom and running his hand between her thighs, until the sea lapped at her big soft breasts. He bowed his head to lick their salty buds, making her giggle and take hold of his *zimbriq*, which was soft and small, a condition she was able to transform. Marcel would have liked to *zeqq* her standing up in the sea, the swell lifting them up and dropping them down. But inborn Santa Sabina aversion to the sea ruled that out, and he put an arm round her waist and led her back to shore.

At about four in the afternoon Mariana said that she ought to make her way home, for her mother would be expecting her back from the Portuguese Embassy. They packed away the remains of the meal and climbed the steep track up to the Vilanova road to wait for a bus back to Santa Sabina city. It was a long wait until one appeared, but they were in no hurry and the time passed easily.

Madame Mendez was surprised but pleased to learn her daughter had been out with Marcel all day instead of at work. Evidently she had greater hopes of him than of the foreigners Mariana had made friends with before. She made him very welcome and showed exquisite tact by announcing she had been just about to retire to her room for a late siesta when she heard them at the door. So saying, she disappeared.

'We must wash off the sea salt,' said Mariana, taking Marcel by the hand to lead him into the bathroom – though there was no bath in it, only a shower. She undid her belt and pulled her short frock over her head, slipped off her flat-heeled white shoes and posed for him proudly in her magenta silk knickers before she removed them.

Marcel kissed her breasts and squeezed her bottom through the thin silk before stripping off his own clothes. With arms about each other's waist, they stepped together under the shower and let the tepid water cool their sweating flesh to the extent it could. Mariana took the soap and washed all over Marcel's body, starting with his hair, letting the cascade rinse out the salt from his swim. By the time she reached his *zimbriq* the touch of her hands on him had caused it to stand stiffly up again.

She giggled and handled it with affection, then continued on down his legs to his feet and toes. Then it was her turn to be washed – Marcel had her lean against the white-tiled wall with her arms above her head while he soaped under her arms and down her body. When the lukewarm water washed away the lather from her breasts, their dark buds were standing prominently. He put his head down and sucked them in turn.

'Do you think my breasts are too big, Monsieur Marcel?' she asked. 'I have noticed that the foreign women here mostly have small breasts. Except for Madame Barbosa, who came here to find her husband and scream at him. And a few others I have seen.'

'Your breasts are a delight, Marie,' Marcel assured her, 'not too big by any means, but charmingly right, for my taste.'

It was the most natural thing in the world to stroke them and play with them while he told her his view. Then his hand moved downwards and circled on her smooth belly until her feet slid apart for him to feel between her thighs.

'Do you also find my *kuft* charming?' she asked softly, her eyelids half closed over her dark brown eyes. 'I think that you do, because you want to feel it all the time.'

In truth, Marcel's fingers were caressing the warm folds of flesh between her legs. Left to his own devices he would have continued his gentle titillation until she reached her climax and afterwards *zeqqed* her standing against the wet tiled wall. But Mariana had something else in mind. She tugged him towards her by his stiff handle and pressed it between their bellies to hold it still.

From above the shower head cascaded water down on them, over her soft breasts and down between their bellies, giving them an almost-cool sensation.

'May I ask you something?' she said, her cheek against his and her mouth close to his ear.

'Anything you like, Marie,' he answered, continuing the slow rocking against her that produced tiny thrills of pleasure from the rub of his upright *zimbriq* on the wet skin of her belly.

'I have read somewhere that in foreign countries men and women do not always make love with *zimbriq* and *kuft*, as we do,' said she, 'but sometimes a man will *zeqq* a woman's mouth.'

'Yes,' Marcel agreed, his curiosity aroused, 'but you did not read about that in any of your magazines. They do not write of this in *Vogue*, I think, nor in *Paris-Match*. Not even in *La Vie Parisenne*. Who told you of it?'

'Monsieur Sven showed me some photographs he brought with him from Sweden,' she confessed at once, wriggling her belly slowly against Marcel's imprisoned part.

'*Oh la la!*' he exclaimed in amazement. 'The more you tell me of this man, the less I understand why he is a priest! But the pictures – were they of him?'

'It is impossible to say,' said Mariana, shrugging slightly, 'they were of a girl with yellow hair taking a stiff *zimbriq* in her mouth. The photograph was taken close, and all that was to be seen of the man was from his waist down to his knees. But it was not Monsieur Sven, I think, because I never saw his *zimbriq* stand so long and hard as the one in the picture.'

'Why did he show you this – because he wanted you to do it to him, was that it?'

'Oh no, he never *zeqqed* me in any way except on my hands and knees. It was because I asked him why he always wanted to do it from behind and never lying on top of me like other foreigners that he said Europeans had many different positions for making love. This I found very interesting, because I want to know all I can about your customs before I go to live in Europe. Do you have other ways besides lying on top of a woman to *zeqq* her?'

Marcel's gently sliding against her belly had begun to arouse her, he noted. Her breasts were pressing rhythmically on his chest as she breathed faster, and her fingernails were digging sharply into his bottom. Or perhaps it was not his movement but the thought of unknown and exotic ways of making love, ways untried in Santa Sabina, where a man rolled onto his back was soon despatched by his partner.

'This formidable Swede was telling the truth,' Marcel said, 'we also use our mouths to make love.'

'Let me try it,' she said at once, and was down on her knees in the shower basin before he had time to agree. Now it was he with his back to the wet tiles, and Mariana's hands easing his legs apart. She cradled his dangling *castazz* in the palm of her hand and held his upright *zimbriq* in the other, bending forward to suck the swollen head into her mouth.

Marcel uttered a sigh of pleasure at the sensations that soon flicked through him. He rested his hands on Mariana's shoulders and felt her satin-smooth skin under his palms while he stared down intently at what she was doing to him. Her attentions had brought his *zimbriq* up to full stretch – fifteen centimetres of hard throbbing flesh – and her tongue lapped over the purple head she had unhooded.

'*Ah, Marie, chérie!*' he sighed, eagerly admiring the way in which his stiff part quivered between her clasping fingers and tried to thrust itself up higher still. Her shining brown eyes glanced up to meet his, and he murmured '*Je t'adore*, Marie . . .' His whole body was trembling and his legs were shaky under him, and still the sensations grew more exquisite as Mariana sucked half of his *zimbriq* into her hot and greedy mouth.

Her ambition to be European in every way made her a very fast learner – it seemed to Marcel no more than a few seconds since she had slipped down to her knees and started, yet already the unmistakable sensation that he was about to *zboca* was surging through his belly! He shuddered in spasms of ecstasy and cried out to feel his hot passion spurting up into Mariana's mouth.

# 8

## At Times The Poor Have Their Uses

After a few days Nanette announced that she had for the present completed her researches in the Memorial Library, having gained a good working knowledge of the accounts of the island and its people written by local scholars. When Marcel enquired what she would prefer to study next – the provincial towns, the peasants and their village life, the fishing communities – she surprised him by saying she wished to investigate the urban poor in Santa Sabina city.

'But why?' he asked.

'To see to what extent the traditional ways have been debased by urban living,' said she. 'As I understand it, it is only the inhabitants of Santa Sabina city who come into contact in any way at all with foreigners. The results will be interesting.'

'It is true that the diplomatic community rarely venture out of the city,' Marcel agreed, 'the reason being that there is no reason – the countryside here has nothing to offer, no scenery of note, no architectural sights, no hunting, no festivals – in brief, nothing but villages and fields, right up to the Sierra Dorada mountains, which are bare, featureless and uninteresting even to rock-climbers. The life of the country people is bound to the usual agricultural cycle, planting, reaping and planting again. Everything of interest, such as it is, exists only here in the city.'

'Well then,' said Nanette, 'you understand why I want to look at the poorest type of people here. I have seen the well to do, and their style is a distant imitation of our European ways.'

'Very distant,' Marcel said, shaking his head sadly over the Santa Sabina cuisine and wines.

'Which is the poorest part of the city?' she asked, 'and why is there no street map available?'

'It has never been worth anyone's while to produce one,' said he. 'The local people know their way around their city, and the foreign community is too small for sales of a street-guide ever to be profitable. The average diplomat needs to know how to get from his embassy to his house, and the way to a few acceptable restaurants. To that diplomats' wives add a knowledge of where the reserved beach is. And that's it!'

'Describe the city to me,' Nanette said.

Marcel embarked on a lengthy exposition of the names of the main thoroughfares and how they linked the principal squares, in which were to be found every establishment, official or not, which might be of interest to her. The poorest quarter was the northern part of the city, he explained, San Simeon as it was called, a warren of narrow streets and alleys.

Nothing would satisfy Nanette but to be taken there the next day. So it came about that at ten in the morning he and she sat at a café on the inappropriately named Boulevard Royal, beyond which lay the San Simeon quarter. It was a nondescript sort of boulevard, the Royal, running straight as a ruler for perhaps a kilometre and a half between anonymous buildings, scruffy palm trees planted along either side of the carriageway.

The café was so tiny that it had only two tables outside on the pavement – scuffed and dented and of metal, from which the white paint had long since worn away. A sign so faded as to be almost indecipherable announced it as the Café-Bar Napoleon, and the proprietor himself came out to ask what they wanted. He was a fat man wearing a string vest and baggy khaki shorts, his paunch hanging over his belt like a collapsing balcony. Marcel ordered two glasses of iced mint tea, for the heat of the day was already oppressive enough to make them perspire, even when they were sitting down.

The iced tea was served in squat glasses that were so thick that they were opaque, but to sip it was mildly refreshing. Marcel was hoping still to persuade Nanette to abandon her intention of exploring the slum quarter, but she ignored his suggestion and started to ask questions about his experiences with Santa Sabina women. He answered frankly, seeing no reason to conceal anything from her if it was of use to her research into the habits and customs of the people. After much intimate detail, she eventually enquired how many of them he had *zeqqed*.

Marcel shrugged to signify 'Who can say?'

'It is not my way to keep count,' he said. 'What would be the purpose?'

Nanette said there was something she wished to tell him – and he smiled a little when she informed him that in the interests of science she had investigated Santa Sabina sexual behaviour with the aid of a young man she met in the Memorial Library.

'I congratulate you on your professional attitude,' he said. 'Where did this investigation take place, if I may ask?'

'He approached me while I was reading and said he found me so beautiful that his heart would break if I refused him. This was more interesting than having obscene gestures made at me, and I decided to accompany him to see how these things are done among the better type of person here.'

'What sort of youth was he?' asked Marcel.

'Good looking, seventeen or eighteen years old, I estimate. His name was Jorge, he said. I expected him to take me to his apartment, and he told me it was usual on these occasions to go to the woman's home. Naturally, I didn't want the complication of taking him to the Grand Hotel Orient, and rather than lose his opportunity he showed me a small hotel in a side street where a room could be rented for a pittance.'

'Your research was very thorough,' said Marcel. 'What sort of sexual behaviour did the subject exhibit?'

'Not at all what I expected,' Nanette informed him without a glimmer of a smile, 'but extremely interesting. After the usual preliminary kisses and caresses, instead of Jorge undressing *me* he stripped himself naked and stood with his hands on his hips for me to admire *him*, though not in a conceited way – more an offer of himself to a superior. I found that strange.'

'But interesting – scientifically speaking?'

'Of course. I went along with the curious behaviour pattern he was exhibiting – I caressed his body until he became very highly aroused. A firm stroking of his belly seemed to give the best preliminary results.'

Marcel pictured the scene in his mind – a pale coffee-skinned youth standing naked and trembling in a run-down hotel bedroom while the distinguished French ethnographer Madame Jarre felt his belly and bottom! In the interests of scientific research, of course.

'Preliminary?' he enquired. 'In what sense?'

'As a prelude to handling his *zimbriq*,' she replied, 'which needless to say was fully distended and remarkably stiff.'

How could it be otherwise, Marcel asked himself.

'Unthinkingly, I let him become excessively aroused,' Nanette continued. 'I think they may be over-sensitised sexually, young Santa Sabina males, for in a very short time he ejaculated into my hand. That was not what I wanted, and I concluded that the experiment was a failure.'

'No, no – they are very resilient,' said Marcel with a smile, 'male and female.'

'So Jorge assured me when he saw my disappointment. While he sat on the bed to recover his strength I took off my clothes to observe what effect a naked female body had on him.'

'With stimulating results, I am sure,' Marcel commented.

'Oh, very much so. He hurled himself off the bed and lay full length on the floor to lick my feet, and so on up my legs, very slowly. It was an extraordinary sensation, the feel of his hot breath and the tip of his tongue on my skin.'

'Surely he touched you with more than the tip of his tongue,' said Marcel. 'His hands, for example?'

'Not once! He kept his hands behind his back so firmly that I assumed Santa Sabina males regard this as the correct thing to do during the early stages of sexual connection. Naturally, the touch of his tongue caused me to become aroused, and as it seemed he might be in some way inhibited by a non-local partner I took the initiative at the appropriate time. I lay on my back on the bed and held out my arms to signify he should assume the upper position – but instead of mounting me, he began a lengthy explanation of what he insisted was the proper way to make love – namely, with *him* on his back and me above.'

'As I told you, when we visited the fruit market.'

'I thought you might be embellishing the truth a little. But confronted with a young man who seemed to understand no other position, I had to accept that this was the local way.'

'And you continued your research to a conclusion?'

'But of course. Jorge's male organ had become usefully stiff again and so I straddled him on my knees and took ten or twelve photographs of him in the traditional Santa Sabina male mating posture. It delighted him that I found his body pleasing enough to take pictures of.'

'And then you *zeqqed* him,' said Marcel.

'As you say. Twice, in fact. They are very resilient, you are right about that.'

'What conclusions did you draw from the investigation – or is it necessary to repeat it with a few more youths to establish the facts?'

'It is impossible to base a theory on only one example. Jorge may not have been typical of Santa Sabina males – his behaviour patterns may be deviant. I shall repeat the investigation many times with different subjects before I can be sure of my facts, and only then will it be possible to formulate a theory.'

'You have come to a very suitable country for research of the type that interests you,' Marcel was amused to inform her. 'No Santa Sabina young man will refuse his fullest collaboration to a beautiful French ethnographer. Population statistics here are completely unreliable, being based on guesswork, not counting, but there must be some thousands of handsome youths here in the city alone. And when you have investigated enough of the urban dwellers to be satisfied, there are many thousands more out in the countryside. Your researches could last a lifetime!'

'I cannot stay longer than a month on this first visit,' said Nanette, 'my preliminary report on the ethnographic potential here must gain me the support and finance needed for a second and much longer stay later in the year – a stay of six or seven months, with an assistant or two for the statistical work and a fund to employ local secretarial and other employees.'

'But I cannot believe that UNESCO will finance research into sexual behaviour on this obscure tropical island!'

'I shall not present my application for funds in those terms, you may be sure,' she answered, smiling at last. 'Ethnography offers a large and complex field of study, Marcel. And now, if you have finished the iced tea, may we begin our exploration of the San Simeon district?'

Marcel shrugged and they set off. Not far along the Boulevard Royal from the café a narrow street between tall buildings led northwards. A barely legible sign announced to anyone who cared that this was the rue Recamier, and before they had proceeded a hundred metres it became very obvious that this was where the poor lived. The rue Recamier led between decrepit old tenement buildings, where the paving stones were broken and dirty, where lines of tatty washing were strung across the street, where few windows had any glass in them, and whatever paint had once been on doors had peeled off generations ago.

'As you may observe,' said Marcel, 'there is nothing here but dereliction and squalor.'

'Not so,' Nanette retorted, 'there are people.'

And so there were, people young and old, men and women, many children, but with nothing to do, it seemed, and nowhere to go. Where alleys only a little more than a metre wide led from the rue Recamier into unimaginable areas of dilapidation, small groups of two or three young men could be seen leaning against crumbling walls and chatting over shared cigarettes. At open ground-floor windows were women with elbows on the sill, gazing out to see who passed by and call a greeting.

Further along away from the boulevard Marcel and Nanette came to a succession of tiny one-room shops. At some a wooden box or two displayed cheap vegetables, at others dried fish dangled in strips from hooks. Some were offering well-used and rickety furniture, some were selling poor-quality clothing brought from the back-street sweatshops of Calcutta. There was not a shoe shop to be seen, Marcel pointed out, thinking it was useful to an ethnographer to know that the very poor of Santa Sabina wore no shoes, either in the city or in the country.

Nanette had brought her camera and shot pictures of anything and anyone she found of interest along the way. No one minded – they smiled at her, men and women alike, when they realised they were the object of her interest. Especially a girl on a balcony close to where the rue Recamier ended at a stone fountain with running water, and was transformed into the rue Bernardette to the left and the rue Grandpère Emil to the right.

It was the balcony of an apartment a floor up from the street and the young woman was leaning over the iron rail, arms folded on it and her heavy breasts lying along her arms. She was about twenty, Marcel guessed, and pretty in what he thought of as the customary Santa Sabina way. Her raven-black hair was arranged in a fringe over her forehead, and she wore a bright yellow frock that only just reached her knees.

She waved and smiled when Nanette aimed her camera up at her, and when Marcel smiled back, she pouted in a kissing gesture at him. In another moment she pulled her frock up to her hips and exhibited her bare brown thighs and the curly black bush where they joined. *Click click click* went Nanette's camera, while she asked Marcel why the girl wanted to be photographed like that.

'It is not for your camera that she shows her *kuft*,' he said, 'she does it as an invitation to me to go up to her apartment and *zeqq* her.'

This view of her intimate charms through the ironwork of the balcony was making Marcel's *zimbriq* stir in his trousers, as if anticipating pleasures to come and desiring to be ready in good time. Then a young man appeared on the balcony beside the girl, yawning and stretching his arms as if waking up. He wore only a pair of wrinkled white duck trousers, his bare chest smooth and hairless, as was usual with Santa Sabina men. Like his girl he too was about twenty years old.

*Click click* went the camera, and Marcel kissed his hand up in gallant farewell to the girl above, but she smiled and slid her feet apart on the balcony and touched her exposed *kuft* with the fingertips of one hand, while beckoning to him with the other. A thought entered Marcel's mind, and with an enquiring look on his face he pointed briefly to Nanette, shooting pictures with her expensive camera to her eye, and then at the man up on the balcony. The query was instantly understood and by way of reply the young man grinned and passed a hand over the front of his trousers, where his *zimbriq* might be thought to be concealed.

'We are invited up to their apartment,' Marcel told Nanette, gently pulling down her arm so that the camera moved away from her face. 'A unique opportunity presents itself to engage in an interesting cross-cultural experience.'

Nanette was looking up at the young man stroking the front of his trousers, a thoughtful expression on her face.

'So I see,' she said. 'There exists here the possibility of a comparison of the social and sexual responses of two racially unmatched couples. The prospect is a fascinating one and not to be missed.'

'You know what you will have to do?' Marcel asked, smiling at her matter-of-fact description of what he himself thought of as *mixed doubles*.

'One cannot know in advance,' she rebuked him, 'but I assume as a working hypothesis that when we go up to the apartment the male subject will open his trousers and lie on his back for me to spike myself on him. The interesting question then will be how quickly he responds to my sliding movement on him – whether his sexual orgasm precedes or follows my own.'

'That is only the first interesting question,' said Marcel. 'Then comes the second. How often can he achieve the climax – more times than you, or fewer?'

It was improbable that the couple on the balcony could hear the soft-voiced conversation down below, but even without words they both seemed to have grasped the substance of it. The young man grinned cheerfully down at Nanette and flicked open his trousers to let his stiff *zimbriq* jut out, pale brown in colour as if sun-tanned. The girl continued to slide her fingers over her bared *kuft*, her mouth open and her tongue vibrating in the direction of Marcel.

He and Nanette turned to each other and grinned in a manner that could only be characterised as conspiratorial. Their minds were made up. They looked up at the couple on the balcony once more and waved to show they were pleased to accept the offer – at which the young man began to slide his hand up and down his stiff length very slowly, a dreamy look in his eyes as he gazed down at Nanette's upturned face.

Arm in arm, Marcel and she went to the crumbling street door and entered. Marcel led the way up an unswept and gloomy flight of stairs, and on the first landing found a splintering door of once brown but now greyish wood. It stood half open, as if in permanent invitation to whoever passed this way. Marcel did not trouble himself to knock – he pushed the door open and went in, Nanette following close on behind.

As one might well expect in the sordid quarter of San Simeon, the apartment was of the smallest and most basic. It consisted of one room in which were contained all that was required for sleeping, washing, cooking and eating. There was an unpainted wooden table with two rickety-looking chairs, a low bed without either headboard or footboard, a small spirit-burning cooker standing on a shelf, and a cheap bamboo washstand with a basin and a metal canister for water.

The bed was broad, and sagged badly in the middle as a result of years of hard use, but the thin woven blanket thrown over it looked reasonably clean. Marcel took in the surroundings at a single glance, and then the young couple came smiling from the balcony to welcome them. The girl's name was Immaculata and the boy's was Cosmo.

'What marvellous names they have!' said Nanette, smiling.

Marcel introduced her and himself only by their first names.

'But how interesting,' said Nanette, glancing about. 'I must have a picture or two for my record. Would you describe this as a typical San Simeon dwelling, Marcel?'

He shrugged and did not answer, for Immaculata had the total lack of patience of all the islanders – she had no time to fool about with photography when *zeqqing* was in prospect. Her yellow frock was over her head in a flash and thrown aside, her arms around Marcel's neck and her naked belly and *gublas* pressed to him. He reached round to fondle the cheeks of her bottom while he exchanged kisses with her.

Cosmo at the same time made his own somewhat more restrained approach to Nanette. He moved close to her on his big bare feet and pressed his throbbing *zimbriq* into her hand. Marcel heard a nervous giggle from her direction, but was by then enchanted by the feel of Immaculata's smooth skin and lost interest in what Nanette might be doing, or having done to her. And Immaculata was concerned to discover what particular advantage Marcel had to offer, and not interested in seeing what her boyfriend did. She undid Marcel's trousers and pulled out his *zimbriq*, nodding in pleasure to find it was of substantial length and thickness, and satisfactorily stiff.

But before she became more intimately acquainted with it, she remembered something, and turned to speak to Nanette.

'I have seen at the movies that foreign ladies always wear a little garment underneath their clothes to cover their *kuft*,' she said. 'Blonde-haired Mademoiselle Brigitte Bardot and the American lady Mademoiselle Marilyn Monroe I have seen, and many others. Let me see yours, Mademoiselle Nanette.'

Without waiting for agreement, she released Marcel and pushed aside Cosmo, went down on her knees and undid the waistband of Nanette's grey skirt. Down it slipped to her ankles, revealing her tiny white knickers, through which the shadow of dark curls could be seen. Immaculata ran her fingers over the smooth silk, her tongue sticking out between her lips in concentration.

'Very pretty,' she announced, 'prettier than in the movies. But why, Mademoiselle Nanette? Perhaps in a colder climate it is necessary to keep your *kuft* warm, but here in Santa Sabina you will be too hot.'

'It's not entirely a matter of practicality,' Nanette replied with a smile at being addressed as Mademoiselle. 'Two hundred years ago Frenchwomen went as bare-bottomed as you. But social customs change and nowadays we all wear knickers of some sort.'

'All?' Immaculata asked, her fingers still feeling the soft material that covered Nanette's fleshy split. 'Even poor women in your country wear these?'

Nanette nodded and said to Marcel she found it strange that a people colonised and nominally Christianised by the Portuguese, Italians and French had never been taught European concepts of modesty. He shrugged and reminded her the islanders had become an independent republic in the era of the Emperor Napoleon when knickers had only just been invented.

'But give it a little more time,' he said ruefully. 'Already our fashion magazines and movies have taught ruling class Santa Sabina women to wear them. Soon they will become universal, and part of the strange charm of this island will disappear.'

Immaculata was not listening to this sociological chitchat – she pulled Nanette's knickers down her legs and off, to see if a Frenchwoman differed in any way from herself where her thighs joined. When her questing fingers assured her there was nothing to choose between Nanette and herself, she grinned and brought her investigation to an end. Marcel had been fascinated by this display of unsophisticated curiosity, his stiffness twitching a little while he stared at Nanette's neat thatch of curls.

Immaculata stood up and laughed at the rapt look on his face, then spread herself on her back on the bed, legs wide apart and her bare feet dangling down on the floor. Marcel transferred his stare to the black-bushed *kuft* she was offering him, noting the fullness and the prominence of the fleshy mound between her plump thighs.

Without doubt, Santa Sabina girls were bodily well made for the act of love they indulged in constantly. In his three years on the island he had never seen a young woman who was skinny, or who had undersized breasts. And as to the size and shape of their *kufts*, he had always found them to have well-grown and fleshy lips pouting through the thatch of black hair, as if to kiss and then swallow every *zimbriq* that approached.

He stripped naked quickly and sat beside her on the bed, his fingers caressing the delight she was exposing fully to him by parting her legs so widely. He opened the lips to stroke inside over her fair-sized bud.

'You like the feel of my *kuft*?' she asked with a grin. 'But you needn't think I'm going to let you *zeqq* me the foreign way – I won't let you lie on top and squash me. If that's what you want, do it to Mademoiselle Nanette – she must be used to it.'

Marcel grinned back at her and got completely on to the sag-backed bed, lying on his back. At once Immaculata was above him on her knees and had his upthrusting part in her hand to guide it between her straddled thighs. Her other hand prised herself open, and with a long fast movement she sank down, driving his *zimbriq* deep into her. There was not even an instant's pause before she was bucking her body up and down on him, making him feel her full weight sitting on his belly at each downstroke, and threatening to rip his treasured part from his body at each upstroke, so fiercely was the grip of her *kuft*.

'That's the way to do it!' she exclaimed, and her big soft breasts flopped up and down to her lively movements, 'not that ridiculous foreign way you *zeqq* Mademoiselle Nanette! She will learn our ways, and in future she will *zeqq* you, understand?'

Marcel rolled his head sideways on the bed, to where Nanette had Cosmo on his back and knelt between his outspread thighs to stroke his belly. She had taken off the rest of her clothes and her pale skin shone with perspiration from the heat of the room. But there was little time for Marcel to take note of what Nanette intended to do to her passive partner, for Immaculata's bouncing up and down was having its effect.

The strength of her assault was causing him to shake and jerk with excitement – and to pant loudly as tremors of pleasure surged through him. In the incoherence of his thinking as mind gave way to sensation – it seemed an incredibly short time since Immaculata had impaled herself on him – he felt his crisis arriving. 'Too soon!' he gasped as she sat down hard on him and made his sticky passion gush up into her quaking belly.

Immaculata cried out in triumph to feel his surge inside her, and jerked her body on him in ecstatic spasms so fierce that he thought he would be pummelled to death beneath her. But he knew from his past experience that the sexual crisis of Santa Sabina women was brief and intense, and within seconds Immaculata was calm again and grinning at him as she climbed off his belly.

He glanced sideways to observe Nanette's scientific progress in her ethnographic study of Cosmo's sexual responses. She had advanced to a position of dominance in the proceedings, being seated firmly on Cosmo's belly, and evidently with his *zimbriq* embedded inside her. But unlike Immaculata's performance of the Ride of the Valkyries, Nanette was rocking herself gently back and forth, a contented smile on her pretty face.

Poor Cosmo was not used to this treatment – he expected to be ridden hard and fast, to be used almost with contempt – and he squirmed between Nanette's thighs and jerked his loins upwards in an attempt to make her use him properly – that is to say, as roughly as a Santa Sabina woman would. The look on his face brought a smile to Marcel's lips – Cosmo's eyes were glaring, his brow was wrinkled and his teeth were grinding together. In short, his whole face was contorted in an expression that seemed to be compounded of incomprehension and frustration.

'That's not how we do it,' said Immaculata, who was stretched out beside Marcel to watch the foreign lady's progress. 'I must show her the right way.'

She leaned over Marcel as if to tap Nanette on the arm to get her attention and explain how a man ought to be *zeqqed*, but he took her wrist and stopped her.

'She knows perfectly well how to go about it,' he said with a smile. 'It is her choice to *zeqq* him slowly the first time.'

Immaculata grunted doubtfully, but made no further attempt to intervene. She lay across Marcel's chest, elbows planted on the bed and her chin supported on her hands, while her dark brown eyes watched Nanette's every up and down movement. Marcel put a hand on her upturned bottom to stroke the plump cheeks fondly, his other hand playing lightly with her dangling breasts.

Nanette continued her gentle lullaby rocking on Cosmo until she had aroused herself too highly to maintain her self-control any longer. Her closed eyes blinked open, she breathed in so deeply that her little round breasts rose in a most provocative manner – and without warning she was transformed into a dynamic *zeqqing* machine running at maximum power. She rammed herself up and down on Cosmo with a brutality that made him cry out in alarm – or perhaps it was relief that he was at last being used hard for a woman's pleasure.

'Ah, yes – at last!' exclaimed Immaculata, and wriggling her bottom under Marcel's caressing hand. 'Now she will have him!'

And have him she did, in only a few strokes! Cosmo's mouth gaped wide open in a long throaty rasp and his loins bucked up between Nanette's gripping legs as her sliding *kuft* drained him of his virility to prolong her own ecstasy.

Though Immaculata had scorned the prelude, she was impressed by the finale. When Nanette dismounted from Cosmo and lay down between him and Marcel to rest a little, the Santa Sabina girl scrambled over Marcel to lie beside her, heedless that her heel struck him between the legs and made him wince. Marcel moved towards the edge of the bed to give the two women space between himself and Cosmo, who was with eyes closed and chest panting up and down.

After the performance she had witnessed, Immaculata displayed a childlike curiosity in Nanette's sexual equipment. She felt her breasts, evidently comparing them to her own – to Nanette's disadvantage, evidently, for Immaculata's were much bigger and had more prominent buds. Her attention was then turned towards Nanette's expanse of smooth white belly and its central dimple, and then at last to her neat little tuft of dark brown curls.

'What a thin little bush,' said Immaculata, 'there's hardly enough to cover your *kuft* properly. Is it a French fashion to keep it cut short?'

Marcel heard Nanette say that her curls were untrimmed and as nature intended, and he raised himself on an elbow to look over Immaculata's pale brown shoulder. He was in time to see her run her hand over Nanette, from her belly button to down between her parted thighs, her fingertips trailing slowly along the moist pink lips of Nanette's *kuft*.

'Nothing wrong with this bit, Mademoiselle Nanette,' she said with a chuckle. 'I began to think you'd never had a mule ride before, when you started, but you put Cosmo through his paces! Look at him, the lazy creature – half asleep already!'

Marcel heard Nanette's tiny gasp when Immaculata pressed her fingers into the lips between her thighs.

'I'm sure that wasn't Cosmo's first ride today,' said Nanette with a giggle, her legs twitching along the bed as her Santa Sabina friend explored inside her with joined fingers.

'Men are the mules,' Immaculata explained to her, 'and women ride them – you remember that. We don't have your foreign ways here. I took a ride on Cosmo first thing this morning when I woke up, and he went back to sleep afterwards while I got up to make myself coffee. He can't be tired after one little ride.'

Her curiosity satisfied that foreigners were made to the same pattern as indigenous Santa Sabinans, she removed her hand from Nanette's *kuft*. To Marcel's surprise he heard Nanette start to question Immaculata – evidently scientific interests were not to be neglected. She asked at what age Immaculata had begun to *zeqq* males, what was her estimate of how many men she had since then done it to, for how long had Cosmo been her boyfriend, how many times a day did she *zeqq* him, had she always lent him to other women, how many other men did she pleasure herself with besides Cosmo – and on and on and on, endless questions to make a man's head spin!

Immaculata seemed flattered to be asked about her love life, and answered the questions in detail. 'Eleven, twelve times a day' he heard her say, 'three or maybe four men I know who live nearby I visit most days and *zeqq*. Sometimes my uncle visits me to be *zeqqed*, but not more than three or four times a week, he being more than forty years old now.'

Poor old uncle, thought Marcel, past it at forty and worn out by the incessant demands of his womenfolk. But still, he retained enough interest to visit his young niece for a workout now and then. It was unlikely he could afford to buy *datra*, the herbal extract used as an aphrodisiac by aging Santa Sabinans, and so his thrice-weekly *zeqqing* was a considerable achievement.

No, Immaculata continued in reply to the next question, she had no babies yet, but she was thinking of marrying Cosmo and would then stop eating the *qagga* leaves. Yes, on the nights he came home too drunk to be of any use to her she *zeqqed* herself with her fingers until she fell asleep. Why was she thinking of marrying Cosmo? Because his birthday was just four days before her own in September, with only a year between.

Left to himself, Marcel surrendered to the heat of the day and fell into a light sleep. When he woke up again he saw Nanette and Immaculata sitting up and talking to each other as if they were old friends.

'Your boyfriend's ready for it again,' said Immaculata with a grin, noticing that he had woken with a stiff *zimbriq*.

She reached out to take hold of his proud possession and slid her hand up and down it a few times.

'Ah, he likes that!' she said, feeling his hard length throb in her clasp. 'Ride him, Mademoiselle Nanette, while I rouse up my lazy Cosmo and straddle him. We'll gallop side by side, you and I – if I can hold myself back to your slow pace.'

'No need,' said Nanette, 'I've a better idea. You take Marcel and I'll get up on Cosmo – we'll race them against each other.'

The thought amused Immaculata enormously, and she threw a leg over Marcel.

'Wait!' said Nanette, 'we have to start level. You're not to put his *zimbriq* in you till I've got Cosmo's standing up stiff. Otherwise you have an unfair start on me.'

'I don't need a start,' said Immaculata, laughing at her. 'I shall beat you easily, you will see – I shall make Monsieur Marcel's *saksak* come squirting out of him before you have Cosmo even a little excited.'

She sat over Marcel grinning, his *zimbriq* in her hand ready to insert when the race started. Marcel stared up at her plump brown-skinned breasts – though she was hardly yet twenty her *gublas* dangled somewhat slackly from constant handling, but they were still arousing to look at and to touch. He put both his hands on them and gave them a squeeze.

'My mule is itching to gallop,' she said to Nanette. 'Hurry up, before he bolts with me.'

Marcel twisted his neck to stare at Nanette and see what she was doing. She had arranged Cosmo on his back with his legs out straight and his feet slightly apart, and was sitting over his loins. She was rubbing his *café-au-lait zimbriq* between her fingers to stiffen it, and as soon as it raised its head she steered it to her ready split and sank down to force it in.

'Ready!' she told Immaculata, who at once raised herself on her knees high enough to position Marcel's twitching *zimbriq* to her liking. She sat down on him, driving it in so hard it made him gasp.

'Ready,' she announced.

'Go!' said Nanette.

At once Immaculata slammed herself up and down on Marcel with an enthusiasm that could almost be described as demonic in its intensity. Her soft brown breasts bounced up and down furiously to her movements, and her hot *kuft* slid up and down the length of Marcel's embedded part with a brute force that made him fear he would be ruined for life by this merciless barbarity. It was not for the first time that he asked himself what effect it had on the psyche of the average Santa Sabina male to undergo many times a day the experience of a frantically aroused woman over him, pounding him into whatever he lay on.

'Ah, ah!' he heard Nanette squeal, and he looked sideways to see her riding an astonished Cosmo faster and harder than even Immaculata. So much so, that she had brought on her own crisis – her slender back was arched in climactic spasms and her hands were clasping and squeezing her own breasts. An instant later Cosmo jerked up between her legs, his open eyes showing only the whites, and he gasped out 'Yes, yes, yes, yes, yes!' as he felt his passion spurting from him.

Entirely undeterred by losing a race in which she had started favourite, Immaculata rode Marcel in a frenzy, her breathing ragged and noisy through her gaping mouth. He stared down along his own body to where his engorged *zimbriq* plunged into the wet fleshy lips lost in the bush of black hair between Immaculata's thighs. He felt the quick surge in his loins, and moaned while he shuddered and shook in climactic release.

It seemed to him that her slippery *kuft* clenched his spurting part like a strong hand, and in the same moment she began to cry out – a high-pitched screeching much like the sound of the brightly coloured parakeets that lived in wild nut trees outside the city. '*Aiee!*' she screeched, her head thrown back and her pale brown belly rippling with sensation.

Afterwards there was laughter and congratulations between the two women, and Cosmo put his trousers on and went out to a bar nearby and came back with bottles of the local beer for all. As Marcel well knew, this was a truly atrocious brew, to be drunk only in an emergency, but happily the bottles had been kept in a bucket of cracked ice and the drink was at least refreshing.

Refreshment of any kind was welcome, for he was sure that when the women had got their breath back they would want to change mules and race him and Cosmo against each other again.

# 9

## Unauthorised Disclosures

For the people of Santa Sabina there was never any difficulty in finding a place to *zeqq* a friend – the poor did it standing up in a doorway or alley, the better off invited their friends home with them, even if the family was in, and did it there in somewhat more comfort. The ruling classes, whose marriages were usually arranged for them on dynastic lines, took more care not to let their spouses know what they were doing – they made much use of small hotels where rooms were available by the hour.

The diplomatic community took pains to conceal liaisons, for the very good reason that broken marriages might well result if husbands and wives became aware of each other's amusements. The moral code by which they were bound was more restrictive than that of Santa Sabina, and lovers called on their girlfriends at home in the afternoon, when husbands were at work – or visiting girlfriends of their own. Ladies too nervous of the servants to risk having lovers call at their homes had their rendezvous in a hotel room.

Marcel had never had the least compunction about inviting his girlfriends, married or not, to the Grand Hotel Orient, and the hotel proprietor, Monsieur Costa, never minded in the least. Jacqueline Ducour had no qualms about visiting his room there, nor did many another diplomat's wife with whom he was on terms of intimate friendship. Except for Madame St-Beuve.

Genevieve St-Beuve was married to the second most important person at the French Embassy, but she was so excessively proud of her ancient family that she conducted herself as if she were superior to the Ambassador's wife. She regarded her husband's family, the well-connected St-Beuves, as beneath her socially, since she could name her ancestors all the way back to the time of King Louis XI. However, neither his connections nor her own faultless pedigree had saved Monsieur St-Beuve from being posted to Santa Sabina.

Marcel had pondered more than once on what sort of offence a man as intelligent as Honore St-Beuve could have committed. He seemed not overinterested in women, even when they were to be had for the asking in Santa Sabina, nor did he seem to have the least interest in boys, or in gambling or in drinking, or other of the usual vices that got people into difficulties. It was a mystery that would only be solved if St-Beuve or his wife chose to reveal it. The unspoken rule in Santa Sabina was identical with that of the Foreign Legion – no questions asked!

Madame St-Beuve was a most elegant and attractive woman – and one who was extremely protective of her reputation. There were no rumours about her, no names linked to hers, no one had ever been able to state with the least conviction that she indulged herself in love affairs. Yet in the nature of things, everyone knew that she must do so. It was simply that she covered her tracks so well not even her best friends could prove anything.

Marcel knew for certain that she amused herself with lovers, for he was one of them, and had been for the past year. But to be Madame St-Beuve's lover was at best a part-time occupation – her security arrangements made it impossible to meet more than two or three times a month. Other women were necessary to fill in the long gaps between.

Besides which, there was the question of her unusual approach to love. One could say it was exclusively for the taste of real connoisseurs, and not for the average man who asked for no more than to lie on his girlfriend's belly and thump away to their mutual gratification. All things considered, two or three times in a month of Madame St-Beuve's capricious style of lovemaking was sufficient for Marcel. And for most others, he suspected, for he was sure she had others to oblige her.

On the other hand, a rendezvous with her was interesting for yet another reason – the ingenuity she employed to find places to meet was as good as any espionage arrangement between secret agents. 'A small white house not far past the 21-kilometre stone on the Selvas road', would be her directions, or perhaps 'room 3B of the Hotel Eiffel Tower' or once 'the apartment over a grocer's shop on the corner of the rue Robespierre'.

Marcel was amused and charmed by the extraordinary nature of the locations, as much as by Genevieve's misplaced caution in discovering them. Was it a touch of paranoia in her, or was she simply devising entertainments for herself, to relieve the long tedium of exile in Santa Sabina? He could never entirely make up his mind, and when he put a question to her, she only smiled as engimatically as Mona Lisa and made no reply.

It was with no surprise that he learned by telephone that she would be pleased to see him at three that afternoon – at number 171 avenue King Alfonso, the house right next to the Church of St Anastasio the Persian. At lunch that day he informed Nanette Jarre that he must go to the Embassy that afternoon for an hour or so, a statement only partly untrue. The French Embassy was in King Alfonso Square, a fashionable district, and the Avenue King Alfonso ran out of the Square.

With a good conscience and lively expectations Marcel walked from his hotel to the Embassy to see what dossiers, documents, urgent telegrams, confidential correspondence and other useless trivialities had been routed to his desk during his absence. He found a stack of impressive proportions and dumped it on to the desk of Mademoiselle Bonchance, the typist whose abilities he shared with two other colleagues, instructing her to answer all she could and file the rest.

That done, he strolled across King Alfonso Square and up the Avenue. There was a small church at the top end he had noticed before, though without paying attention to it. The entire city of Santa Sabina was full of churches, mostly in a baroque style and built by the Portuguese, and some few by the Genoese. Even in more pious times, it seemed to Marcel most improbable that so many churches could ever have been filled with penitents and worshippers.

Who St Anastasio might have been and why he was called the Persian were questions of little interest. His church was small and dilapidated, the statue in a niche over the door crumbling away, so that the face could not be made out. The house next to the church was built so close to it that it was joined on – and so was the building on the other side, Marcel saw. Perhaps once upon a time these buildings had an ecclesiastical purpose – now they were private residences, he saw.

His knock at the door of number 117 summoned an elderly Santa Sabinan man in black trousers and a clean white shirt. 'My name is Lamont,' said Marcel, knowing that Genevieve would be mortally offended if he mentioned her surname at a secret rendezvous.

'Madame is waiting for you,' said the man in solemn tones.

He led Marcel up a flight of broad wooden stairs that needed polishing and through double doors into a long room made dim by half-closed shutters at the windows.

'Monsieur is here,' said the servant, not repeating his name.

Genevieve rose from an armchair to say 'Thank you, Vasco', put down the glass she was holding and extended her hand to Marcel to be kissed. She was a tall slender woman of his own age – svelte was the word that came into his mind whenever he thought of her, narrow of face and with a long thin nose. Her hair was dark brown and worn short, swept across her forehead from left to right in a deep swag. She was dressed simply in a white blouse and white linen skirt.

At her invitation Marcel sat down in an armchair across

from her own and accepted the small glass of cognac she poured for him. With Genevieve it was sure that it was the real thing, not the local firewater imitation, for her husband imported his own supply from France in the diplomatic bag.

'This is a very pleasant room,' he said glancing about at the honey-gold wooden floor and the oriental rugs, the comfortable furniture and the well-chosen pictures on the walls.

'It belongs to friends,' said Genevieve, giving nothing away. 'They are on vacation and so I borrowed it.'

'You are looking more beautiful than ever, *chérie* – I find it impossible to resist you,' said Marcel, finished his cognac and put down the glass.

'Enough of that!' she said coldly at once. 'You know I will not let you paw me about!'

This was the way of it with Genevieve – she had no interest in the pleasures of long and tender lovemaking, she wanted to be misused. Her pleasure lay in a certain *nostalgie de la boue*, thought Marcel, a longing to be humiliated sexually. In Paris she probably picked up truck drivers and market porters to beat her and *zeqq* her, but Santa Sabina society was too limited for little antics of that type to remain a secret – her caprice would soon become known in diplomatic circles if, for example, she went to the fruit market and stood against a wall for two or three men.

'Pull your skirt up and show me your *kuft*,' Marcel commanded, his voice hard. Words were important in the preliminaries of Genevieve's love game – brutal words could arouse her more than caresses.

'You disgust me,' she retaliated, and she stood up to leave, handbag over her arm. Marcel also rose to his feet, and in two long strides was close enough to seize her round the waist and spin her round off balance, until she fell sideways back into the chair, her belly over the padded arm, her head down by the floor and her bottom in the air. Marcel forced her to remain in this awkward position by a strong hand on her back.

'You are hurting me!' she said loudly and coldly.

'But I haven't even started yet,' he said, and put his other hand up her white linen skirt to the elbow, feeling between her bare legs – for elegant as she was, even she could not bear to wear stockings in the daytime unless it was a question of duty.

She was squeezing her thighs close together to prevent him touching her, but he clenched his fist and rammed it forcefully up between her legs until he felt lace and silk against his knuckles. Genevieve writhed on her belly across the chair-arm and told him he'd be sorry if he didn't stop at once. In reply he unclenched his fist and slipped his hand into her knickers.

'You wouldn't give me a look at your *kuft*, so I'll make you,' he said, his fingers probing none too gently in the short curls and fleshy folds between her legs.

'Dirty beast!' she said, struggling against his restraining hand to get up from the chair. He held her fast while he undid the gilt-leather belt round her waist and opened the waistband of her skirt – in another moment it was down round her knees.

He stared in admiration at the ivory crepe-de-Chine knickers that covered the taut little cheeks of her bottom. Nothing more than a narrow strip of the flimsy silk passed between her legs to cover her *kuft* – and soon not even that, for he slid the knickers over her hips one-handed and down, and was rubbing his fingertips along the hairy split he had revealed.

The position was too inconvenient to continue for long – not for Genevieve, who adored being made to suffer, but for Marcel himself. He clasped her about the waist with both arms tightly and lifted her off the chair, turned around and sat down with her across his thighs, her head and feet touching the ground, her bare bottom at his disposal.

'You've seen what you wanted to,' she said, her voice muffled a little by her position. 'That's enough now!'

Marcel was fondling the smooth narrow cheeks he had exposed. He parted them and trailed the tip of his middle finger across the pouting little knot of muscle there. More than once he had violated it ruthlessly with his *zimbriq* in an act of Greek love that never failed to reduce Genevieve to hysterically shrieking ecstasy. Perhaps he would do that to her today, and perhaps not – everything depended on his mood at the critical moment.

'You can stop that!' she exclaimed in a voice of outrage and disgust. Marcel chuckled and pushed his finger a little inside, at which her body went tense over his lap. But his interest lay elsewhere just then, and he pried open the long pink lips of her split. Her knickers round her thighs made it impossible for him to push her legs wide apart, but he could reach her hidden bud with a fingertip. Genevieve began to shake and before long he felt the slippery wetness of arousal.

'It's not too worn-out a *kuft* for a woman of your age,' said he with a sneer. 'When you were seventeen it might have been worth a good *zeqqing*. What have you done to it all these years to make it so slack – played with your fingers?'

'You animal!' she cried. 'If you're going to rape me, then for God's sake get on with it and get it over!'

Marcel smiled to feel her belly palpitating on his thighs and sending little tremors of pleasure along his stiff part – which was trapped against him by her body. Her thighs were straining to move further apart against the restriction of her knickers.

'Rape you?' he answered. 'Is that what you imagine I want? When a beautiful golden-skinned girl of eighteen is waiting for me at my hotel, a girl with big soft breasts and the divinest little *kuft* in the world? You flatter yourself, Genevieve!'

She had her hands flat on the floor and she was pushing up at him in nervous little jerks. She began to whimper and writhe on his thighs, and then in a crescendo of shrill little cries to the movement of his finger inside her, she reached the point of climax and dissolved in a long wail of ecstatic release.

It was important to move quickly, before Genevieve's throes faded away. With a great effort Marcel stood up, lifting her in his arms, and crossed the room with rapid strides to drop her without delicacy on the long sofa. She drew up her knees as if to kick him with both feet and drive him away, but the movement served his purpose equally well, in that he was able to wrench her skirt and knickers down her legs and throw them behind him.

'No more!' she shouted angrily. 'You promised not to rape me – get away from me!'

Marcel jerked his trousers open and let his stiff length jut menacingly out. Before she could say any more, his hands were on her raised knees, forcing them wide enough apart for him to fall on her belly, driving the breath out of her in a sobbing gasp. She struggled with open mouth to fill her lungs again, in which time Marcel had thrust himself deep into her wet *kuft* and was *zeqqing* her furiously.

'I hate you!' were her first words when the power of speech was restored, the words jerky and broken as her body was shaken by Marcel's forceful plunging.

He said nothing, his face buried in her perfumed hair, all he had to say being conveyed by the strength of his *zimbriq* inside her body.

'Hate you, hate you, hate you!' she wailed, even at the very moment her belly heaved up under him, her head rolling to left and right on the cushions, her eyes glassy. Words failed her then, and she squirmed beneath him, moaning in her climactic spasms, her hands clutching at his shoulders. The violence of her *zeqqing* affected Marcel equally and he stabbed relentlessly into her slippery depths. Her scream of ecstasy when he poured his passion into her drove him to more frantic effort, causing her slender body to bounce on the sofa under his thrusts.

When their savage delight was finished, Marcel lay panting for breath on her belly, and she, her face shiny with perspiration, lay trembling and content beneath him.

'I hate you, Marcel, you know that,' she said affectionately. 'You always know exactly what to do to me, you beast.'

'And I adore you too,' said he, freeing himself from her and sitting up.

Now there was time for such minor considerations, he

removed his jacket and tie to make himself more comfortable. Genevieve in her white blouse, naked from the waist down, sat up on the sofa and folded her legs under her. Marcel suggested a little more cognac and filled up their glasses from the bottle she had brought.

'I haven't seen you since the birthday concert for da Cunha's mother,' he said. 'I'm very glad you telephoned me today.'

'Are you, Marcel? They say you're so occupied with Madame Jarre that you don't even go to the Embassy any more.'

'What nonsense,' he said, his smile charming. 'His Excellency gave me the task of chaperoning our distinguished visitor about the city while she studies whatever it is that she is studying for UNESCO. He relieved me of all other duties during her stay, but believe me, it is no great pleasure to escort her to the shabbier parts of the city.'

Marcel was not adhering strictly to the truth in this, for if he did, he would have to admit that their expedition to the San Simeon quarter had turned out to be extremely pleasurable.

'Is she making a study of poverty, then?' asked Genevieve. 'I had the impression from what Honore said that her interest lies in cultural differences, or something of that sort.'

Marcel shrugged and said he did not understand ethnography at all, but by the time Madame Jarre had dragged him all over the island in her researches, no doubt he would know more about it. Meanwhile, had Genevieve heard that Jacqueline was determined to return to France before the month was out?

'She has spoken of it many times,' said Genevieve, running a long thin hand through her hair to smooth it after the rumpling it had received, 'but I do not take it too seriously – not yet, for she has a new Australian friend.'

'Ah, the blond Adonius with the overdeveloped muscles she met on the reserved beach,' said Marcel with a chuckle. 'I have not seen him, but someone told me that he had been a disappointment to Jacqueline – perhaps it was you.'

160

'It was not I who told you – we haven't seen each other since she told me about him. His appearance led her to expect much of him and she was desperately disappointed at first. But it seems that a little patience has worked wonders, and she has trained him most successfully to understand her needs.'

Into Marcel's mind came a vision of a straw-haired young thug with the muscles of a wrestler lying passive with closed eyes to be manipulated by Jacqueline to the point of sexual climax.

'I am pleased for her,' he said, 'though I had always heard that Australians were untrainable in the civilised arts.'

'Perhaps, perhaps. I think it was her reluctance to be wrong about anything that made her persevere with him. And though she claims that his performance is now satisfactory, I was with her only yesterday on the beach and she struck up an acquaintance with a very pretty young man with black eyes who has recently arrived at the Indian Embassy.'

'What's his name,' Marcel enquired, 'and has she tried him out yet?'

He was by no means surprised to hear of Jacqueline's double dealing, and he wondered whether he could make any use of this information to protect himself if she carried out her threat to tell her husband he was her lover.

'Varaha Gokhale,' Genevieve informed him, 'and she was trying to arrange a meeting with him for today – in fact, they may be together at this very moment.'

'You said he was very pretty – what does that mean?'

'Black eyes, shiny black wavy hair, a face almost as delicate as a young girl's, a slender body, a smooth hairless chest, and the bulge in his swimming trunks not very impressive,' said Genevieve with a wry smile on her long narrow face. 'I thought he might be without interest in women, but Jacqueline insisted otherwise.'

'Poor Jacqueline!' said Marcel with a chuckle. 'I shall look forward to hearing what she tells you of her experience when she succeeds in getting her hands on the Indian boy.'

'From what she has told me of her adventures, *hand* is right,' Genevieve said with a shrug, starting to unbutton her blouse, 'but you know more of that than I, as you have been one of her friends for so long.'

As Marcel had taken note already, Genevieve had come to their meeting without a brassière. Her blouse fell open to reveal her small breasts, slack from maulings over the years by relays of the type of sweaty thug she had preferred. To please her it was necessary to behave like a gangster.

'My poor breasts,' she said, 'bruised and squashed flat under your weight! Thank God that's over!'

'Over? Don't be a fool – it's only just beginning,' said he, reaching over to take hold of her exposed breasts – but not to fondle them. He sank his fingers viciously into the soft flesh and squeezed mercilessly until tears shone in Genevieve's eyes and she moaned and winced.

'You're hurting me!' she said plaintively.

'What pathetic little *gublas* you have!' he retaliated. 'I've seen bigger on Santa Sabina girls of twelve!'

'Pig! Child-molester! Pederast!' she accused him. 'Don't think you can try your nasty ways with me!'

'You have nothing to say in the matter!' he said, making his tone as menacing as he could. He stood up quickly and used her cruelly abused breasts to drag her to her feet, bent forward and changed his grip to her waist, and threw her brutally over his right shoulder, so that her head hung down his back and her legs down in front of him.

She had long legs and long arms, but they were thin, and she was tall for a woman, but her body was slender, so that she was light enough for Marcel to stand upright and carry right across the drawing room without too strenuous an effort. She kicked as a matter of course, her bare toes thumping at his thighs, and he covered his upright part and his precious pompoms with his left hand to protect them from accidental injury. She beat his backside with clenched fists, but that could be safely ignored.

His intention was to carry her into the bedroom and

throw her down on her back. But he was a stranger in this apartment, and the door he chose at random led into the dining room. So be it, he thought, and he would have shrugged, but for the naked weight of Genevieve over his right shoulder. The table was of polished walnut and had eight chairs round it. With his foot he pushed aside the nearest chair and dropped Genevieve's bare bottom on to the table with a thump – and a squeal of protest from her.

Before she could make any ambitious plans of her own, he put his hands on her *gublas* again and pushed her down flat on her back on the table-top, her legs dangling over the edge.

'Stop it!' she said. 'You've raped me once – what species of criminal are you to try it again?'

Her words were chosen to provoke him to further violence, of course, as Marcel understood very well and appreciated. He slid his hands quickly under her knees and flung her legs in the air and over his shoulders.

'I'm sure you've dined often at this table,' he sneered down at her flushed face.

'Often,' she gasped, 'and my husband.'

'What a pity the owner of the table can't be here to watch me *zeqq* you on it! And perhaps your husband would find it of some interest to see you on it with your legs up above your head! I'm sure it's been years since you last gave him a look at your *kuft*! How long – five years, ten years?'

'He has his own interests, you disgusting lout!' she said at once, trying to kick him in the side of the head.

'And you have yours, is that it?'

While Marcel was taunting her he guided his throbbing *zimbriq* between her thighs and to the brown-haired split that awaited him. With a hard push he sheathed himself in her wet warmth so forcefully that she cried out in shock.

'You never expected to be the main course at this table, did you?' Marcel gasped, pounding at her soft belly with the fury that aroused her to madness. She clawed at her own breasts and squirmed on the table as if she were being tortured to death by red-hot irons. She began to shriek loudly in a sort of delirium of sexual delight, her legs thrashing on his shoulders like the beating of a drum.

The scene was a comic one, or would have been so if any other person had been present to witness it – stark-naked Genevieve writhing on her thin back on a dining-table, and Marcel standing between her upraised legs, sweating in shirt and trousers while he rammed into her. Their violence was exaggerated to the point of theatrical farce, and of its nature it could last for only a brief time – Marcel's whole body shook as the moment of truth arrived. He had barely time to gasp out 'You're being raped, you bitch! I'll split your belly open before I'm done with you!' before his loins jerked sharply and his lust spurted into her.

His words gave Genevieve the final hard push over the brink and into the chasm of wailing ecstasy. She screamed and kicked her legs about in uncontrolled paroxysms of release, her bottom lifted off the table, rising up at Marcel in tremulous jerks – and her fingernails drew angry red marks down her breasts and belly.

In all, it was a very satisfactory climax for both of them. When it was over, Marcel put his hands on the table on either side of her and rested his weight on them, panting for breath and trembling in the aftershock. Genevieve lay still and limp, breathing through her open mouth.

'My God!' she said, 'I don't know what you do to me, but you drive me crazy! I feel that I've been devoured!'

Marcel eased himself out of her clinging wetness and took her hands to draw her to her feet. She showed him where the bedroom was, and he stripped off completely and lay down to recover his strength a little, while she fetched the cognac and glasses.

They lay side by side on the bed, propped up on big square pillows, and sipped Monsieur St-Beuve's excellent cognac for a while in companionable silence. Eventually Marcel asked what he wanted to find out from Genevieve.

'The woman you pointed out at the Theatre des Beaux

Arts,' he said idly, 'Madame da Motta. Do you know of any diplomats among her admirers?'

'Ah, it's her you want, is it?' said Genevieve in a tone so desolate that Marcel almost laughed. 'We Frenchwomen are no good any more?'

'That's absolute nonsense,' said Marcel, stroking her thigh casually. 'I asked because I happened to see her with someone from the Czech Embassy, and that made me wonder. I remember you told me she had an Italian lover at one time – but the person I saw with her is so extremely unappealing that I was surprised by her taste. Unless he has hidden qualities.'

'Very often the ugliest and most uncouth men make marvellous lovers,' said Genevieve. 'Unshaven, sweaty, barrel-chested men with broken black fingernails and hairy bodies – men wearing unwashed vests and stained underpants . . .'

'Enough, *chérie*,' Marcel interrupted. 'I understand perfectly what you are saying. But for a moment think about my question – are there any rumours about Madame da Motta's boyfriends?'

'Many, but from the past, nothing recent that I know. Between you and me, dear Marcel, His Excellency Jean-Jacques Ducour was greatly taken by her and tried to start an *affaire*. But alas for his pride, she thought him much too old for her, and he had to be contented with a few smiles and a kiss on her hand.'

Genevieve's story tended to confirm what Marcel had guessed – that Svoboda was not Graziosa's lover. He was using her as a go-between and the Czech's real business was with her husband, the Minister of Industrial Developments. And since there would never be any industrial developments while Pascal da Cunha was President, it required no tremendous intellectual abilities to deduce what Svoboda's and da Motta's business together was.

'A crushing blow to His Excellency's self-esteem,' Marcel commented with a sly smile, 'and that reminds me I have a tiny item of gossip for your ear – you recall that the lights failed at the Theatre des Beaux Arts? And Monsieur Ducour employed the concealment of darkness to make advances to Madame Jarre.'

'He put his hand down the front of her frock,' said Genevieve with a knowing smile. 'I was in the box at the time – you don't think I'd miss so delicious a morsel of scandal as that. Not an Ambassador fondling the breasts of his guest in the dark – but how did you know? You weren't there at the time.'

'Madame Jarre confided in me later,' said he, trying to sound nonchalant. 'She was a little unsure how best to deal with him if he tried to continue these advances.'

'She was making a fool of you then,' Genevieve said. 'She had no uncertainty about how to deal with Jean-Jacques that night – she opened her legs and let him put his hand up her skirt. It wasn't so completely pitch dark in the theatre that I couldn't make out what they were at.'

'Really?' said Marcel thoughtfully. 'He felt her *kuft*?'

'She practically invited him to do so. Evidently she finds it exciting to be touched by a man of some importance. From what I heard, it's taken until today for him to find a reason to meet her in a secluded place to complete the *zeqqing*.'

'Today?' said Marcel, astonished. No wonder Nanette had been so casual when he informed her he was going to the Embassy that afternoon – she wanted him out of the way for her own reasons.

'He's driving her out to examine the old ruined shrine on the Vilanova road,' Genevieve explained. 'Five minutes to inspect the shrine and an hour on the back seat of his car.'

There were very few cars on Santa Sabina, other than those of the President and his Ministers, but the Ambassador had one – a fairly old but huge and comfortable Citroën de luxe. He used it mainly to make himself more impressive when he called on the Minister for the Exterior, one of President da Cunha's several cousins. Many regarded Annibal Palmella as slow to the point of mental retardation, but as Santa Sabina's relations with other countries were minimal, it made little difference.

Marcel had ridden in the Ambassador's car and knew

that there was plenty of room on the rear seat to spread Nanette out and *zeqq* her. Or any other obliging female, for that matter. Which raised a question of some interest – what women had enjoyed the comfort of the Ambassadorial car before Nanette Jarre? Marcel had never given any thought to His Excellency's amusements, but he now knew the location – after all, in a city and society as limited as Santa Sabina well-known persons like Ambassadors were not likely to slip into sidestreet hotels with women on their arm and ask for a room for the afternoon.

Marcel shared his conclusion with Genevieve.

'Yes,' she said, 'and here is another interesting thought for you, *chéri* – at this same time you and I are together here, our eminent Ambassador is parked somewhere up a country track with Madame Jarre on the back seat, and dear Jacqueline is playing with her new Indian friend. As for my own husband, heaven knows what he is getting up to!'

'What else is there to do in the afternoons but *zeqq*?' said Marcel with a shrug. He was displeased with Nanette for keeping quiet about her rendezvous with His Excellency. Naturally, he had said nothing to her about his own meeting with Genevieve, but that was different. On the other hand, after their visit to the San Simeon district, he laid claim to no rights – Nanette had shown she did what pleased her, and that he could accept. Within reason. Surely it was unreasonable of her to drive off with His Excellency without a word to her closest friend, namely, himself?

'So he failed with Madame da Motta, but he has succeeded with Madame Jarre? Who else does he *zeqq*, Genevieve?'

'Jean-Jacques is very, very discreet,' she replied. 'There is an employee at the embassy who admires him sufficiently to put herself at his service if he fails elsewhere. You must know her – a plump and rather plain woman, Mademoiselle Delacoste.'

'Well I'll be damned!' Marcel exclaimed, for he too had more than once availed himself of Gabrielle Delacoste's facilities, 'but how right you are – he is marvellously discreet to keep it secret. In fact, he is as discreet as you are, Genevieve. Which raises a fascinating possibility in my mind.'

'What possibility?'

'You and he together?'

'That's absurd,' she said instantly, her tone indicating that the matter was not to be pursued further.

'Absurd,' Marcel agreed. 'His Excellency lacks excellence in everything, according to his wife. Certainly he is somewhat too old and not strong enough to handle a woman like you. For that it is necessary to deploy a *zimbriq* like mine. Who else is his friend, then, besides the plump Mademoiselle Delacoste?'

Genevieve's denial had made him certain that she allowed the Ambassador to *zeqq* her, and this might be useful in protecting himself against Jacqueline's threat of exposure. And so would a knowledge of any other special little friends of Ducour's.

'There's a very elegant Santa Sabina lady he calls on in the avenue Empress Eugenie,' she said. 'Madame Monsarez, a widow, I believe. Her husband was a judge who had a misunderstanding of a serious nature with President da Cunha and soon after died of an accident when a mule bolted with the *barossa* he was in.'

'Interesting,' said Marcel, thinking exactly the opposite. He guessed he would learn nothing else of Jean-Jacques' amusements that would be of any real use to him, and he casually mentioned the news he wanted reported to the Ambassador as part of a plan he had devised.

'The ugly Czech at the secret rendezvous was not much younger than His Excellency,' he said, 'and so if Madame da Motta takes only young men as her lovers . . . well!'

'But what are you suggesting?' Genevieve asked, agog at the prospect of an unusual morsel of gossip to pass on to friends.

'I hardly know what I mean,' said Marcel, suitably vague now. 'It is believed that Colonel Svoboda is a KGB agent – but what could they want with Madame da Motta?'

'That's easy,' Genevieve said at once, 'to pass messages for them to her husband and back again.'

'Perhaps. But da Motta is Minister for nothing much. I do not see the point of this hugger-mugger dealing through his wife.'

Before Genevieve could pursue the discussion to the point she came to realise that he was acting deliberately, he took action to divert her thoughts into another direction.

'Stop that!' she exclaimed. 'Leave it alone!'

She had glanced down while considering the implication of his words and seen that Marcel was playing with his *zimbriq*. It was stiff already, and under his manipulation it became visibly longer and thicker.

'Look at it, Genevieve,' he said, 'see how strong it is – I'm going to put it up your *kuft* again in a minute.'

'No – oh, no, no, no!' she said sharply. 'I refuse to submit yet again to your animal lust!'

'But you have no choice but to do as you're told,' he replied equally sharply, his hand sliding faster up and down his fleshy length, 'a woman's role is to lie on her back and open her legs for me to ram *this* up her – I'm going to *zeqq* you whether you want to or not, so turn on your back and spread your legs!'

'I won't!' she cried, and with that she twisted sideways to jump off the bed and leave him. Marcel grabbed at her heel just as she passed almost beyond his reach and she swayed with one foot on the floor and her other leg bent backwards over the bed. But his grip was insecure and he felt his fingers slipping – yet even the second or two he had held on was sufficient to destroy her balance. As she jerked free from his hold, she fell over forwards on hands and knees on the floor.

Marcel hurled himself off the bed like a tiger pouncing on its prey. She heard his roar as he leaped and turned her head to look over her shoulder, her mouth wide open and her eyes round with some strong emotion – fear, perhaps, though perhaps not. A moment later Marcel was on his knees behind her, pressing down on her hips to prevent her escaping from him. There before him lay exposed the lean bare cheeks of her bottom, and her wet and hairy *kuft* beneath.

He was too aroused to waste any more time in admiration – he thrust his loins forward and slid his stiff *zimbriq* into her, without even a guiding hand. The clasp of her soft flesh was so instantly exciting that he butted at her fast and hard, like a Santa Sabina he-goat mounting a she by the roadside. Genevieve tried to slide away from his hard penetrating part by bending her elbows outward and letting herself collapse underneath him. But he wrapped his arms tightly round her belly and kept her up on her hands and knees by sheer strength.

'I told you I was going to *zeqq* you,' he gasped, 'you cannot get away from me, Genevieve – I shall keep you here till I have used your body for everything I can think of!'

'*Ah, mon Dieu!*' she moaned in despair – but something in her voice suggested that his brutal words had aroused her further. Her actions soon demonstrated the truth of that – she began to jerk her hips backwards to meet his strokes, and she was crying out inarticulately. Marcel moved faster yet, slamming fast and hard into Genevieve's slippery warmth, hearing his belly smack against her bare bottom. An instant later he cried out wildly to feel his desire spurting into her.

But for Genevieve it was not enough – she continued to shrill out her sweet torment as she struggled to achieve her climactic release, her bottom thumping back at him to drive him deeper. For Marcel it was over, but his male pride forbade him to leave her abandoned in so very desperate a plight. He jerked his wet *zimbriq* out of her, and she screamed 'No, put it back!' While it was still stiff enough, he steered it higher with his hand, up the crease of her bottom. A savage push – and the swollen head was forced into the puckered knot of muscle between her cheeks. Genevieve screamed.

A second hard push, and half of his *zimbriq* was inside, and he was thrusting with short jerks into her, knowing the time would be brief before his spent part started to droop. But Genevieve was violently affected by what he was doing to her – her screaming grew more forceful and the taut cheeks of her bottom squirmed against his belly.

'I loathe you!' she shrieked, at the very instant her body was seized by convulsive jerks that announced the onset of her climax. Marcel recognised the ecstasy in her voice and grinned to think his violation of her rear had humiliated her to this intensity of frantic pleasure.

# 10

## A Taste of Rural Pleasures

Marcel did his best to convince Nanette that there was nothing of interest on the island outside Santa Sabina city, and little enough there. But she was insistent that country people were of great interest to her studies, for their isolation from urban influences preserved unchanged over the years the early customs and traditions of ethnic groupings. In short, she meant to see the countryside for herself.

Marcel shrugged and agreed to take her. Early the next day he arranged for a *barossa* to collect them after breakfast at the Grand Hotel Orient, to transport them across the city to Vasco da Gama Square, where the buses started from. Nanette had taken his advice and wore a green safari shirt outside well-washed cotton twill trousers, and sturdy shoes suitable for walking.

Marcel too was dressed for roughing it away from the comforts of the city, in a well-worn linen suit. He had tried to explain to Nanette that uncertainties of public transport and vagaries of country people made it impossible to know for how long they might be away, and though she gave him a sceptical look, she at least packed a change of clothes and underwear in a hold-all, as he did – to be carried by a strap over one shoulder.

The bus for Vilanova was scheduled to leave at eight

o'clock, and by Santa Sabina standards it was reckoned punctual when it pulled out of the Square at twenty minutes past. As it threaded its way through city streets towards the suburbs, Marcel tried to impress upon Nanette the difficulties of communicating with Santa Sabina country people, who rarely understood more than a word or two of French.

'What then,' she asked, 'they speak Portuguese still?'

'Not even that. You must understand that none of those who in turn made Santa Sabina their colony paid very much attention to the agricultural life, so long as it produced enough for them to eat. The Arabs used the island as a slave depot, shipping in Africans and interbreeding them with the original inhabitants, whoever they were. The Portuguese gentry lived in the city while overseers managed their estates and investments – precisely as the Hundred Families – their descendants – still do today.'

'I have read the history of the island,' Nanette reminded him abruptly. 'Not one of the books I consulted in the Library here says that rural Santa Sabinans have a different language from the town people.'

'But it is unlikely that any of your books even mentioned the rural Santa Sabinans,' Marcel pointed out. 'They are regarded as a natural resource, like rivers to provide drinking water or trees to provide timber for the city. No one thinks of them as people. Did any of your books give you a total for the island's population?'

'Why no, now you mention it. What is the total?'

'It is not known. There has never been a census, because no one sees any point in spending money to count heads.'

The bus left behind the last straggle of buildings and was on the road to Vilanova at last. The first few kilometres climbed upwards, until the road was winding along the rocky coast-line, creeping round tight curves above an unfenced drop to the sea down below. At the eleventh kilometre marker-stone Marcel tried to see over the edge to his private beach – the secluded little cove where he had taken Mariana Mendez for a picnic. But it was too well concealed by the overhang of the cliff and the thorny shrubbery that clung to the descent. Nevertheless, the memory of that day made him decide to visit Mariana as soon as he got back from this harebrained expedition to the countryside.

'Anyway,' he said, turning back to Nanette with a shrug, 'the Portuguese never succeeded in five hundred years in teaching their language to more than the city folk. The Arabs had never tried, not viewing the population as human beings, only as merchandise to buy and sell. And when the island was appropriated by France in 1709, the administrators sent here by King Louis took the line of least resistance – they remained in the city, spreading their language there, but nowhere else.'

'What a fascinating place this island is,' Nanette surprised him by saying. 'What else ought I to know, Marcel?'

'You will shortly observe for yourself that another result of Europeans confining themselves to the cities is that the rural population is darker of complexion than the town people – for the obvious reason that the settlers intermarried and interbred freely with the urban population.'

'There is enough here to keep a whole team of enthnographers occupied for years,' said Nanette. 'I must revise my estimates and ask for much more funding when I deliver my preliminary report to UNESCO. I've seen some very pleasant villas along the roads leading out of the city – are they expensive to rent?'

The thought of settling in Santa Sabina evidently pleased her greatly, and Marcel added to her euphoria by informing her how cheaply a villa could be leased, and how low were the wages of local servants.

The bus was due to arrive in Vilanova by midday, but business not easily understood took the driver out of his seat at a tiny village of ten houses and a bar two-thirds of the way along the road from the capital. Marcel and Nanette sat in the bus for at least fifteen minutes, the heat growing more intense as morning advanced. The other six passengers – members of the same family, to judge by their looks – discussed the delay at length before reaching no conclusion at all, that being the Santa Sabina way.

Marcel told Nanette that it was evident they would remain in the village for some considerable time, and suggested they get off the ovenlike bus and see what the bar had to offer. It was little more than a hole in a wall, the bar, but over the door stood its improbable name – *Les Grands Routiers* – in painted letters half a metre high.

They sat at a three-legged table in the shade and were served by a twelve-year-old girl with a happy smile and bare feet. There was a choice between the vile Santa Sabina beer, *araq* and fruit juice. They favoured the palate and the liver by choosing juice and were brought two tumblers and a large earthenware jug of an oversweet liquid they decided must be mango juice.

The mystery of the missing bus driver was eventually solved. He came strolling down the road with a broad smile on his face, followed by a straggle of five villagers – two men and three women – bent almost double under the weight of sacks slung over their shoulders. Marcel and Nanette looked on in open-mouthed amusement as the sacks were loaded into the bus and the driver counted out colourful Santa Sabina banknotes into the hands of his helpers.

'I thought we were perhaps delayed while the driver went to find a woman to *zeqq*,' said Nanette, 'but it seems he had other plans.'

'If it had been only that, he would have returned in no more than a quarter of an hour,' Marcel told her. 'It has taken this long because he has been visiting a farm or two nearest to the village to bargain for what is in the sacks. He is evidently an entrepreneur, this driver of ours, who makes use of his access to public transport to buy cheap from the producers and sell at a profit in the city.'

'What do you imagine is in the sacks?'

'Almost certainly fruit of some type. Did you see how little he paid for five heavy sacks? He will double his money when he sells in the market at Vilanova.'

The driver climbed up into his seat and gave a wheezy blast of the horn to announce the imminent departure of the bus, just in case any of his passengers were missing. Marcel and Nanette got aboard with some difficulty, the sacks almost blocking the entrance. The other passengers had remained in the sweltering bus throughout the delay, passing the time pleasantly by eating the packed food they had wisely brought with them.

There was a great deal of food still left in the woven straw bags and wickerwork hampers the travelling family had spread out on the seats. The grandmother smiled at Marcel and offered him a sandwich – it was smoked swordfish slices spread thickly with peanut sauce and clamped between two slabs of rough bread. Island etiquette meant it would have been discourteous for her not to offer food to a stranger at mealtime, and even worse if he refused it. He smiled back and took the sandwich, bit into it and passed it on to Nanette, whispering quickly to her that she must eat some of it.

Another member of the family handed him a bottle of the local beer – even more atrocious when warm, as this was. He swigged a mouthful down, and managed a smile as the grandmother dipped in her bag again and passed him a cold roast rabbit's leg. In this way the next three-quarters of an hour were occupied by eating and drinking from the seemingly endless family supplies. It was with relief that Marcel welcomed the arrival of the bus at last in Vilanova, though Nanette appeared happy enough chatting with the Santa Sabinans and establishing their relationship to each other, their purpose in travelling, the occupation of the men, the number of children each of the women had, and other useless information of the sort that social scientists collect.

The bus turnaround in Vilanova was in the central square, a singularly ill-chosen site for a transport terminus. The driver parked outside the fine old Baroque church of St Dionisio and waited while his passengers disembarked by scrambling over his great pile of sacks. In accordance with the official timetable the bus was due to remain there for thirty minutes before returning to

Santa Sabina city, but the scheduled departure time was past by over an hour already, and the bus would leave only after the driver had completed arrangements to dispose of his cargo.

Across the square from St Dionisio was the best of the three café-restaurants in Vilanova. Marcel had planned to have lunch there with Nanette before continuing their journey deeper into the countryside, but their appetites had vanished after being stuffed with food on the bus. In best Santa Sabina style he had acknowledged his gratitude for the hospitality bestowed upon him and Nanette by presenting to the old woman a packet of the pungent local cheroots and a ten-*tikkoo* note.

He led Nanette across the square and took a table outside the restaurant and ordered them iced coffee and cognac. Nanette asked how long since he was last in Vilanova, and he told her he was here about two years before, on a short walking-holiday with a Dutch friend, to see the Sierra Dorada mountains. There was a village to the west of Vilanova, he explained, where the priest spoke excellent French and perhaps could be persuaded to act as interpreter for Nanette in her researches.

After they had rested from the discomforts of the bus journey they slung their carry-alls over their shoulder and Marcel led the way westwards out of St Dionisio Square. It was after three o'clock in the afternjoon and he was looking for premises that he recalled passing on his first visit to Vilanova. It was on the very edge of the town, a whitewashed single-storey building with a fenced-in paddock at the side, where six or seven mules stood idly about under the trees.

The ostler was a small and wrinkled man of indeterminate age, with a nose hooked like the beak of an eagle. He was attired in a dirty leather apron over thick black trousers, and a pair of cracked and unlaced boots. Perhaps, thought Marcel, they are to protect his toes when a more than usually awkward mule steps on his feet. When he saw his customers were foreigners, Miguel – for so he introduced himself – beamed with joy in the certain knowledge he could charge them three times the ordinary tariff for the hire of his beasts.

Marcel was well acquainted with the ways of Santa Sabina and bargained with Miguel until they agreed on a daily hire rate only twice what the locals paid. The money changed hands – two days' rent in advance, the equivalent of twenty-five francs, and a youth of perhaps twelve saddled a pair of mules and led them to the gate. Marcel gave Nanette a leg up into the saddle, mounted his own animal, and off they set at an unhurried pace.

The street from the square had turned into a lane long before it reached Miguel's house. There were a few more buildings, of a semi-agricultural type, some of them obviously deserted and falling down, and then the lane dwindled into a track. Up ahead lay the regrettably ugly Sierra Dorada mountain range, in which direction the track mostly led.

They rode side by side, letting the mules decide on the pace, along a footpath between large open fields, where green sprouts of *miltsa* were pushing up through the brown earth. Two crops a year were harvested, Marcel told his companion, and it was used for breadmaking, beer-brewing and spirit-distilling – giving a sour taste to these products – and for mule-feed, though it was not known what the mules thought of it.

The heat of the afternoon was oppressive and not conducive to haste or argument. They meandered along an ever-fainter track in amiable discourse, reins loose on the mules' necks. After an hour of this unaccustomed mode of travel Nanette wanted a rest and a drink, so they dismounted. Marcel had thought to provide himself with a two-litre bottle of spring mineral water from the restaurant, and they drank from this sitting on the grass under a wide-spreading acacia tree. The label claimed the water came from the health-giving spring of Santa Paloma in the mountains, and perhaps it did.

There was no need to hitch the mules to the tree – they stood with drooping necks, half-asleep and content to stay where they were. Nanette announced that her brassière was causing her some discomfort in the excessive heat, and Marcel suggested that she remove it. She unbuttoned her safari shirt and felt behind her back to unfasten the plain white brassière supporting her small breasts. A red mark across her body beneath them showed where the lower edge had chafed her perspiring skin with movement.

Marcel soaked a clean handkerchief in Santa Paloma water and wiped it over Nanette's exposed breasts to cool them a little. They were, as he had observed the very first time he saw them, elegantly small and round, pale-skinned and with prominent red buds. She permitted his attentions to them until he leaned over to place a tiny kiss on the nearest.

'I hope you don't think that's why I took my brassière off,' she said. 'It was because of the heat, nothing more.'

'Naturally,' he agreed, shedding his jacket, 'in a climate of this type logic would require that the people went naked at all times. But other considerations apply, apart from logic. Social and ethical considerations cause us to conceal our bodies in clothes that make us hotter than we need be. But in our private moments we are able to free ourselves of these restrictions.'

While he was speaking he unbuckled his belt and unzipped his trousers to let his *zimbriq* emerge into the light of day. The sight of Nanette's pretty breasts had stiffened it.

'The heat inside trousers becomes uncomfortable,' he said by way of explanation.

'It's not the heat at all,' she said, reaching over to prod his twitching part tentatively with her forefinger, 'it's the result of handling my breasts. Why do you find it necessary to disguise the truth – is this standard diplomatic practice?'

'Perhaps it is,' he answered, tiny spasms of pleasure running through him as Nanette's continued prodding caused his *zimbriq* to dance up and down. He edged closer to her on the grass and put his hand on her thigh, well above the knee, 'but as you are wearing trousers yourself, you must know what I said is true. It would be more comfortable for you if you allowed me to open them and let in the air.'

Nanette looked at him without expression, but the tip of her tongue appeared between her lips. He sighed as her hand closed round his eager part.

'I can't decide if you are trying to be sincerely helpful or simply want to get my knickers off and *zeqq* me,' she said with a shrug of uncertainty.

'Both, of course,' he replied, grinning at her.

Her hand began to slide gently up and down his stiff *zimbriq*, and he reached over to fondle her breasts and roll their russet red buds between his fingers. She made no move to stop him, not even when he leaned close and touched the tip of his tongue to them. He heard her sighing and put a hand between her legs and fondled her through the thin material of her trousers.

'If only you knew how many times I've been on my back wearing these old trousers in forests and savannahs around the world!' she murmured when Marcel pressed her down to lie flat.

'But I intend to have them off,' he said at once, to regain the initiative, and he undid the buckle of her belt. It was not easy to make up his mind about Madame Nanette Jarre, the famous ethnographer. It was true he appreciated her frankness and her readiness for lovemaking but, on the other hand, she behaved too frequently as if she were a man. This confused Marcel.

All the same, being confused is not the same as being refused – he had her washed-out cotton trousers wide open and his hand down inside for a moment to clasp her *kuft* through her knickers before he drew both garments down her long smooth legs. He had to remove her shoes before he could get her trousers right off, and once liberated from their restraint, and her underwear, she spread her legs wide on the grass with a long sigh of relief.

Marcel touched the tuft of dark brown curls he had uncovered and the long loose lips of dark pink under them – her *kuft* felt hot to the touch, and no wonder, after an hour on the saddle of an ambling mule. He helped her to sit up for a moment while he removed her safari jacket, then she lay back, completely naked except for short yellow socks.

'And if someone comes along and sees us?' she asked, not in the least concerned by the prospect.

'No one will bother us,' Marcel assured her. 'Santa Sabinans are used to seeing couples *zeqqing* in public places and pay no attention. Surely you remember the fruit market?'

He stripped off his own clothes until he was as naked as she was – even more naked in fact, for he took off his socks.

'Naked lovemaking on the grass under a tree,' Nanette said with a smile, 'with dumb animals looking on – can Santa Sabina be the Garden of Eden? Was the Tree of Knowledge an acacia?'

'I do not think so,' Marcel murmured, stroking the insides of her spread thighs, 'for Adam and Eve ate the fruit of the tree, but acacia pods are uneatable, except by animals.'

His fingers played lightly over her *kuft* for a while before parting the lips and sliding inside to tease her secret bud with a gentle touch. She became wet quickly, and lay with her eyes closed and her arms stretched out away from her sides, like a starfish on a rock. Marcel had a knee on the grass between her thighs and was at the very point of mounting her when her eyes opened wide and she pushed him away.

'I'm not at all sure that I want you to put it inside me in this heat,' she said. 'The thought of your hot body lying on me is not pleasant.'

'Then you can *zeqq* me Santa Sabina style,' he offered.

'Too energetic,' she countered. 'I'm sweating already, even lying still. *Zeqqing* you would be too much.'

Eventually they agreed on a compromise of a sort – with just a fingertip inside Nanette's *kuft*, Marcel raised her to a slow climax of sensation, her legs beating against the grass at the supreme moments. When she was calm again they changed roles, he lying on his back while she took the head of his stiff *zimbriq* between finger and thumb and flicked it until his essence came spurting out into her hand.

Then they looked at each other and laughed. In a little

while they dressed and rode on, and by early evening they arrived at the village Marcel was aiming for. They took a room together at what served for an inn for travellers – in effect it was an all-purpose bar and café with a room or two to let upstairs.

They sat outside in the street to drink a glass or two of the village wine, drawn straight from a gigantic wooden barrel and with no nonsensical claims to be *Chambertin St-Louis Cotes de Vosges* or other imaginary appellation. The cuisine proved to be nourishing rather than pleasing – a thick brown stew, highly spiced, which Marcel guessed to be goat meat, followed by hard brown cheese and freshly picked figs. Fortunately there was no other choice and so the problem of the proprietor not speaking French did not arise.

When the sun was down and the evening a little cooler, Marcel took his companion to meet the village priest, whose house was right next to the church at the far end of the village street. Father Isidor remembered Marcel well – as well he might, there having been no other foreign visitors in the past two years and he made Nanette very welcome. They sat in his garden with a big carafe of white wine, and Nanette asked her questions about the life of the villagers. The priest was enchanted by the thought that people in a distant part of the world could be interested in what went on among his congregation, and answered her in his provincial French.

When the carafe was empty he called out and a copper-skinned young woman of perhaps twenty-one or twenty-two came out of the house to refill it for him.

'But you remember my granddaughter Ofelia, Monsieur Marcel,' said Father Isidor.

'Of course,' he said, smiling and standing to take her hand. Ofelia had good reason to remember him, and her brown eyes were gleaming, her work-hardened hand squeezing his warmly. On his previous visit to these parts she had been his guide to the historical caves in the mountains and he had *zeqqed* her very thoroughly, and she him.

When she brought the refilled carafe the priest asked

her to sit with them, explaining that Madame Jarre was a distinguished explorer who had come to learn about the customs of the island. If Nanette had been at all surprised to hear Ofelia described as granddaughter of a celibate priest, she kept it to herself and fell into lively conversation with her when she understood that Father Isidor had taught her French.

Meanwhile, Marcel was kept occupied answering questions about the city for the priest, who looked upon Santa Sabina city as a different world, a bizarre place where incomprehensible things were done for unimaginable reasons. Marcel found himself more or less in agreement with this opinion, though his perspective and Father Isidor's were very far apart. An hour or more passed pleasantly in this way, until Nanette said she had been told by Ofelia there was a village dance that evening, and this was of considerable ethnographical interest.

Father Isidor made it plain he thought the dance unsuitable for any foreign lady, particularly one of Madame Jarre's high distinction and Parisian refinement. Marcel was amused, knowing something of the ways of Santa Sabina bucolics, and asked why the good father allowed the entertainment to take place, since evidently he regarded it as undesirable – perhaps on grounds of morality or religion?

'Alas, the Church has not yet succeeded in five hundred years to drive out the vestiges of paganism,' said the priest with a sorry smile. 'The *Shaqqaf* dance is a primitive manifestation of the spirit of my people which lingers on in the countryside. If I cannot suppress it, I must ignore it. They are good people at heart, and they will be in church on Sunday, whatever they do tonight.'

Nanette was deeply interested and enquired of Father Isidor what *Shaqqaf* meant and what went on in the dance.

'It is a name,' he said reluctantly, 'no one remembers now if it was a man or a deity. As to what is done, I regret I cannot discuss that with you, Madame.'

'Then I shall see for myself!' Nanette declared. 'This is

an opportunity not to be missed – your *Shaqqaf* dancing is the ideal example of what we ethnographers seek out and record. You have no objection, Father, if Ofelia shows me where this spectacle takes place?'

'She may do so, if you wish,' the priest agreed reluctantly. 'Most fortunately Ofelia is married and can have no part in the dancing.'

Not very long after that they thanked Father Isidor for his hospitality and set off for the dancing, which Ofelia explained took place outside the village on the threshing floor. She was obviously pleased to have escaped from her grandfather for the rest of the evening, and delighted to be in the company of two foreign visitors. There was, Marcel explained in an undertone to Nanette, a curious status attached to being acquainted with foreigners, and especially to working for them, it being common belief in Santa Sabina that foreigners were all very rich.

'Ofelia – when I was here before with my Dutch friend you had been married for a year and had a baby son two years old,' said Marcel. 'Do you have any more children now?'

'Another boy, a year ago,' she said, smiling happily.

'You spend so much time with Father Isidor, who looks after your children,' he asked, 'and your husband, does he not want you with him more often?'

She told him her mother took care of the children. As for her husband Domingo, he was a drover. He was away from home much of the time, herding goats cross-country to Selvas to be sold in the market. Father Isidor demanded most of her time, to be his companion and cook and housekeeper. Marcel gave her a 50-*tikkoo* note, using the polite local formula *for the children*.

She smiled at him and kissed his hand, which was embarrassing but he put things right by kissing her cheek. Nanette observed this byplay with interest, noting the social relationships, and how they were expressed.

'How can it be a priest has children and grandchildren?' she asked, having noted that there was no shame involved. 'In every part of the world I have visited Catholic priests are required to be celibate, even in countries where they preach Marxism and revolution from the pulpit. Is Santa Sabina so different?'

'What you say cannot be true, Madame,' said Ofelia. 'Boys are not chosen to be trained as priests until they are twenty and grown men – by then they have children, because girls who *zeqq* them forget some days to chew the *qagga* leaf.'

'I see,' said Nanette, storing away the information for later use, 'and after they are ordained priests – are they required then to give up *zeqqing*?'

'Naturally,' said Ofelia, 'and it is a sin for them when they forget and lie down for a woman. Twice a year the Bishop sends a special priest from Vilanova to visit the villages round here and listen to all the priests' confessions and forgive them.'

The threshing floor was not far outside the village and was a circle of hard-trampled bare earth on which the *miltsa* harvest was threshed by hand. Ten or twelve torches soaked in oil were set upright in the ground about the perimeter to illuminate the proceedings, and a crowd of perhaps thirty villagers were there already. They were all young, Marcel noticed, not one of them over eighteen, which one would expect if *Shaqqaf* dancing was only for the unmarried.

They paid no attention to Marcel and Nanette when they took seats on the grass close to the circular floor, though everyone in the village knew by then that two foreigners were staying at the inn. Like every other public activity in Santa Sabina, time had no important part to play – events began when they began. Half an hour passed, Nanette busily interrogating Ofelia about her life, the night hot but overcast and without moon or stars, the threshing floor lit only by the flaming torches.

Eventually a rattle of a small drum announced the start of the dance, accompanied by a rapid and staccato clapping of many hands, and the shrilling of a flute. To this miserable music a group of five youths advanced in a shuffle-shuffle-stamp step. They had removed their shirts and their sweating torsos gleamed in the torchlight. From the other side of the floor a group of girls moved out to meet them, bare feet on the trodden earth in the same shuffle-shuffle-stamp. The girls too had stripped down to the waist and their breasts swayed and rolled to the rhythm of their steps.

'*Oh la la*,' Marcel exclaimed, 'it's the Folies Bergère!'

The two groups danced towards each other, never touching, but an element of sexual braggadocio now revealed itself in the way the youths jerked their loins up at the girls, and the girls flipped their breasts at them in return. Nanette's camera came into action, though Marcel thought it unlikely even the fastest film would capture much in such poor lighting.

'Ah,' said she, her eye to the viewfinder as the camera went *click click click click*, 'do you see how these young men become aroused, Marcel?'

It was true – the front of the boys' trousers were beginning to bulge out as *zimbriqs* stiffened to the stimulus of the girls and the music. Without breaking step, the girls together gave a shrill cry sounding like *lululululu* and pointed at the boys' groins. Emboldened by this acknowledgement of their ability to produce a stiff *zimbriq*, the boys advanced threateningly toward the girls, *shuffle-shuffle-stamp*, and the girls retreated as if in modesty – an emotion which Marcel was certain none of them had ever in her life experienced.

Now the boys were beckoning to the girls to return, but they hung back still, dancing in perfect time without moving forward or backward. To persuade them, the boys flipped open the front of their trousers and Nanette echoed Marcel's '*Oh la la!*' as out leaped a line of full-sized *zimbriqs*, rising and falling as if they were metronomes beating time for the musicians. The reply to this display of masculinity was not long delayed – the line of girls turned their backs to the youths and bent over to flip their skirts up over their backs, showing off the smooth brown cheeks of their young bottoms.

*Click click click* went the camera, and Nanette complained she had brought only three more rolls of film, all the rest being with her baggage at the inn. Evidently the display of bottoms was meant as a deterrent, although Marcel personally found it a most encouraging spectacle, for the boys retreated in shuffle-shuffle-stamp time. But then the girls stood upright and turned toward them again, and maintaining the rhythmic step, let their skirts drop to the ground and stepped clear of them, displaying themselves naked.

'*Ah oui!*' said Marcel, staring in admiration at the line of moving pale brown bellies and thighs and the thickets of black curls where they joined, 'whoever this *Shaqqaf* was, god, man or demon, he knew a good night-club act when he saw one.'

'Monsieur Marcel – you should not say things like that,' said Ofelia in reproof. '*Shaqqaf* is very powerful and may be angry. He makes *zimbriqs* stand up stiff and *saksak* squirt out for the pleasure of women's *kufts*. If you laugh at him he will punish you by never letting your *zimbriq* go hard again. Then what will you do?'

'Dear *Shaqqaf*, I meant no offence,' said Marcel instantly, 'I was commenting favourably on the dance in your honour.'

'Coward!' said Nanette with a chuckle. 'I'm certain it would take a good deal more than a village deity to keep your *zimbriq* limp for long.'

'In these vital matters it is best to take no chances,' said Marcel. 'Besides, I like the sound of this *Shaqqaf* – ever since I arrived in Santa Sabina I have existed in a state of almost permanent sexual arousal, to my intense delight, since this is the easiest place in the world to find women in the same state. I used to think the cause was some unknown mineral or other chemical substance in the water or the food, but now I believe it was *Shaqqaf's* doing, and I am truly grateful.'

'Idiot!' said Nanette. 'Oh, look!'

A new development had been introduced into the dance. The row of boys were advancing toward the naked girls, *zimbriqs* jerking up and down vigorously. But a second line of girls, as naked as the first, had moved on to the threshing floor to join in the dance, and they were behind the youths. There in the middle of the floor the boys were trapped, each with a naked girl in front and a naked girl behind. The girls in front were undoing belt buckles, or untying the knots in the string that some boys used to keep up their trousers.

To try to keep the whole group of dancers in view was to miss the detail of what was happening. Marcel focused his attention on the nearest to him, where a muscular young man of perhaps sixteen was besieged by two charming young girls, one of whom displayed perfectly pear-shaped little breasts. The youth made a pretence of resisting, dropping his hands to ward off the fingers trying to divest him of his only garment. But to no avail – down went his trousers, hobbling him by the ankles, so ending at once his shuffle-shuffle-stamp.

Marcel smiled to hear the *click click click* of the camera as the youth's hands dropped lower, to protect his upstanding and jerking part from grasping fingers reaching for it. The girls still danced to the monotonous music, and pressed closer until their bare *gublas* and bellies were rubbing him front and back. The girl stationed to the rear seized his arms and dragged his hands away from his *zimbriq*, whereupon the other girl took hold of it and rubbed it between her palms as if she were rolling a cheroot.

'We shall see what we shall see,' Marcel said to Nanette with a grin, 'and very soon now! The young men here respond rapidly to stimulation.'

'That I know,' she replied, never once looking away from the drama being enacted on the threshing floor. 'It happened to the first one I tried, when I was working in the Library – he did it in my hand long before I expected.'

'The first?' said Marcel. 'Well, well!'

The girls in the dance were evidently well aware of the rapid response of Santa Sabina young men and did not allow accidents of a frustrating nature to take place. In the group Marcel was watching, the one holding the youth's arms went down quickly on her knees, her weight dragging him down backwards until he lost his balance and fell. He lay on his back, the girl's bare legs spread wide on either side of him, his head on her belly.

His reaction was to try to get up again, but immediately she pushed her legs under his arms and crossed them tightly over his chest to hold him still.

By then the other girl was kneeling between the youth's legs, still holding on to his stiff *zimbriq*, which had increased to a thickness and length most impressive in one so young. The music had reached a squealing tempo and pitch almost painful to hear, and as if this was her cue, the kneeling girl with the perfect pear-shaped breasts squatted over his loins and impaled herself neatly on his fleshy spike.

*Click click* went Nanette's camera, and then she said '*Merde*' as she ran out of film. The mounted girl writhed in pleasure, her face shining with perspiration, her mouth open and her tongue lolling out as she lurched up and down to the frantic music and hand-clapping. A series of sharp cries escaped her as the youth between her thighs jerked upwards in spasms of released desire.

The cries were repeated all along the line as the other pairs reached the culminating point. And at once the girls dismounted and left their 'mules' lying with legs splayed apart, trembling in the aftershock. With scarcely a pause the second girl of the pair – who till now had held the youth imprisoned in her legs – took her turn. She pierced herself with the still stiff *zimbriq* while her companion held the youth's head firmly in her hands to keep him still – and for a second time he was most furiously *zeqqed*. This time, Marcel noted, it was the young man who cried out in frenzy at the critical moment, as well he might!

The exhausted dancers left the floor, their muscular bodies shining with perspiration, and the drum and flute fell silent at last. Nanette said she had never seen anything to match the dance anywhere in the world, and asked Ofelia how often it was performed, so that she could perhaps return with more film next time.

'Three times,' said Ofelia, misunderstanding the question, 'when the musicians have drunk enough wine to sustain them they will play again. Five minutes, perhaps.'

'But not the same dancers,' Marcel said, grinning at her.

'No, they are finished for tonight. The boys, that is. Only the girls dance three times – they have plenty more boys.'

'Did you do the *Shaqqaf* dance before you married Domingo, or did Father Isidor forbid it?' Nanette asked her.

'He was very strict,' she replied, 'but I always crept out of the house when I heard the music begin. I think he guessed, but he said nothing.'

'I'm going over there to talk to the girls before they start dancing again,' said Nanette.

'They won't understand you,' said Marcel, but she had already got up and was on her way to the chattering group sitting down to rest on the far side of the bare earth circle.

'Neither do I understand Madame Jarre,' Ofelia said to Marcel in a puzzled tone. 'Why does she ask so many questions?'

Marcel contemplated the difficulties of devising a simple but rational explanation of ethnography and decided not to try it.

'She is a woman who wants to know everything,' he said.

Fortunately for him, before Ofelia could enquire further into the subject, the drum rattled and flute struck up, accompanied as before by rhythmic hand-clapping. Five youths stripped to the waist advanced shuffle-shuffle-stamp on to the threshing floor, and Marcel lay propped on an elbow to watch them, while Ofelia sat cross-legged on the grass beside him.

'Monsieur Marcel – look!' she exclaimed, pointing a finger.

The girls were advancing from the opposite side of the floor, still stark naked, and in the centre of their line was Nanette, her pale skin gleaming opalescent in the flickering torchlight and her feet moving expertly in the rhythmic dance-step.

'By God!' said Marcel with a grin of admiration and a

waved salute to her courage, 'is there nothing she won't try? Purely in the interests of science, of course.'

He watched the progression of the dance, the boastful display of stiff *zimbriqs* by the youths, the retreat of the girls, then the showing of their bottoms in derision, the renewed advance. He heard Nanette's voice shrilling out *lululululu* with the best of them. He turned to grin at Ofelia in shared pleasure and saw that the way she sat, with her knees up, had pulled her short frock up her thighs, revealing her smooth brown skin.

She caught the direction of his glance at once and moved her knees apart, so that Marcel was staring at her dark-haired *kuft* and realising he must have her. He put a hand between her legs to touch the curls and rub her bare belly. Without more ado she wriggled the frock from under her bottom and pulled it over her head and off.

'Ah, Monsieur Marcel,' she said, her teeth white in a smile, 'it is like old times, isn't it?'

She dropped the leg nearest him flat on the ground and he put his head on her thigh and his cheek against her belly. The hot scent of her flesh was very arousing, and he sighed in pleasure to feel her hand open his trousers and take a firm grip on his trembling *zimbriq*.

Out on the threshing floor the drama had passed the point of separating into threes and was at the pulling down of the young men. 'Bravo!' Marcel called out in encouragement as he saw Nanette squat down sharply over a helpless young man and impale herself on him. She jerked up and down furiously, in the approved Santa Sabina style.

But Ofelia was determined to have Marcel's entire attention, and she threw a leg across him to sit on his head and rub her *kuft* against his face.

'It is I who am *zeqqing* you, Monsieur Marcel,' she said, 'not Madame. She does it for *Shaqqaf*, I do it for myself.'

It was impossible for him to reply, for the moist and fleshy lips of her *kuft* were pressed tight to his mouth. Only when she thought she had his full interest did she slide backward along his body until she was above his exposed *zimbriq*. She gripped it between hard fingers and sat down on it, driving it in, and the moment she was well mounted on him she swung her body up and down in a fast and steady rhythm that soon had him gasping to the sensations throbbing through him.

Child-feeding had made her heavy *gublas* slack and loose. They flopped up and down provocatively as she bounced on Marcel and he reached up to put his open palms under them and feel their weight as it descended on each downstroke. She grinned at him and parted her legs wider still, the thick fleece between them a darker shadow against her half-lit and shiny skin. The music throbbed frantically as on the dancing floor the second girl of each pair mounted the young man to drain him of his strength.

Inspired by the tune, if a simple phrase repeated again and again could be called a tune, Ofelia slammed herself down hard on Marcel, panting loudly, her face turned skywards. He wailed in ecstasy to feel his hot spurt of passion into her slippery *kuft*, and she shrieked and squirmed in instant release.

# 11

## Politics Is Mediocrity Of The Highest Order

Almost a week passed before Marcel was able to persuade Nanette to return to Santa Sabina city. The day after the *Shaqqaf* dance she toured the entire village with Ofelia as her interpreter to talk to those who had taken part and photograph them. She asked them scores of questions – at what age did they begin first to participate in the dance? What did they regard as the benefits of doing so, physically and intellectually? Did they find any inconsistency between dancing for *Shaqqaf* in the week and then attending Mass on Sunday? Did they believe that children born as a result of the *Shaqqaf* dance were in any way special? And so on. Her questions baffled the young villagers, but they gave her good-natured answers.

Most of them were out working in the fields, of course, which made for a hot and tiring day finding them. Marcel took no part in this important research, using as an excuse his inability to speak the language. He passed the day pleasantly in chatting to Father Isidor, comfortably seated in the priest's small garden, with a carafe or two of the local wine.

Tiring day or not, Nanette wanted to see more of the country. Next day, to Marcel's dismay, the hired mules were saddled and they set off together for the next village, more than two hours' ride away. Ofelia went along with them as interpreter, pleased to be offered fifty *tikkoos* a day, and she walked barefoot beside the mules, singing tuneless local songs at Nanette's request.

That night they were guests at dinner of the village mayor, a meal of smoked goat meat and wild mushrooms – big and brown and served raw doused in lemon juice. Afterwards Nanette decided to entertain the mayor by *zeqqing* him a time or two, while Marcel retired to bed with Ofelia and showed her the foreign way. Then on they went the next day, turning south away from the Sierra Dorada mountains, in a great circle through three more villages and so back to their starting point.

Nanette was fascinated to learn that none of the villages had a name, and asked how people referred to them. Ofelia shrugged, thinking the question pointless, and said people stayed at home in their own village and didn't trouble themselves what went on elsewhere. Why should there be names for them?

Eventually the expedition came to an end, to Marcel's relief, Ofelia was paid off and the mules ridden back to Miguel. After a better meal than any of the past week Marcel at last managed to get Nanette on board the bus from Vilanova to Santa Sabina city. Even then she was making plans to return and continue her exploration of rural customs.

Six days on muleback had tired Marcel, and the afternoon was fearsomely hot. In spite of being jolted and shaken on the hard wooden seat as the bus trundled along the ill-made and worse-maintained road, he fell asleep. Nanette was occupied with her scientific notes on what she had seen, scribbling and sorting, revising and classifying – perfectly happy to be left alone to get on with her work.

Marcel woke with his head on Nanette's shoulder. He had been dreaming vividly that he was being *zeqqed* by Graziosa da Motta, the deliciously beautiful political intriguer with the *café-au-lait* skin. They were in the back seat of the Ambassador's car, he on his back with his legs sticking out of the open window, and she perched over him with her skirt up round her waist. It was a very pleasant dream, and Marcel was not surprised to feel his *zimbriq* standing stiff in his clothes.

What was also puzzling, though no less pleasant, was to feel a hand laid over the bulge in his trousers. He raised his head from Nanette's shoulder to look at her, and saw the expression of amusement on her face.

'Were you dreaming of me?' she asked. 'Your *zimbriq* has been jumping in your trousers for the past quarter of an hour.'

Marcel glanced about the bus and saw they were now the only passengers.

'But of course I was dreaming of you, *chérie*,' he said, with a complete disregard for the truth. 'In these past days we have become very well acquainted with each other.'

'I agree,' she said, 'we have become very close friends, and that is much better than becoming lovers, don't you think?'

He thought it better not to examine the philosophy of that in case it led to misunderstandings between them, and he responded only with a *Mmnn* sound that could be taken for 'Yes, I agree' or for 'I'm not sure but I'll think about it'. Not that it mattered much – Nanette unzipped his trousers and slipped a hand inside. He felt her fingertips combing through his curls, and then she had the tip of his straining part between thumb and forefinger.

'As a scientist I am convinced that your first theory was the correct one,' she said. 'There is some unidentified substance in the water or the soil of this island which provokes a state of almost permanent sexual excitation.'

'But I no longer believe that myself,' said he, 'my revised theory is that the condition is due entirely to *Shaqqaf*.'

By then she had extricated his *zimbriq* from his underwear and had it out of his trousers, her clasping hand sliding firmly up and down it. He rested his head comfortably on her shoulder and turned his body slightly towards her to put his hand up between her thighs. She parted them just enough for him to lay his palm over her warm *kuft* and hold it through the cotton twill of her trousers.

She stared as if fascinated at his hard-swollen part sticking so boldly out of his trousers and asked what were his reasons for attributing his continuing lasciviousness to *Shaqqaf* or any other imaginary being from the obscure and confused folklore of Santa Sabina's forgotten past.

'Ah, you scientists,' said he with a shrug, 'always demanding proof, even when there can be none! You have no regard for what is felt in the heart but not measured by the intellect.'

'I have become very interested in what is felt in the *zimbriq* since coming here,' she replied, sliding her clasping hand up and down his hot and hard part. She smiled to see how his legs trembled to the thrills her fingers caused.

'And in what is felt by the *kuft*,' he sighed.

'I knew that already,' she told him, 'and it does not change even when *kuft* pursues *zimbriq*, as in Santa Sabina, and not the other way about, as we arrange things at home in France.'

Where this conversation might have led is unimportant, for it was impossible to continue it – Marcel jerked spasmodically and delivered his warm tribute into her palm.

'When do you think we shall arrive in the city?' she asked when his breathing returned to normal.

'Who can say?' he answered, her question suggesting that she had not become aroused by what she had done to him. 'Timetables have no meaning here. We shall arrive when the driver pleases – and if the bus does not break down and leave us stranded by the roadside. They never bother to maintain these vehicles, as you have probably guessed.'

'What happens when a bus breaks down on a lonely road?'

'After much grumbling and cursing the driver sets off to walk to the nearest point where he can procure a team of mules – six at least – to pull the bus and passengers to its destination. A journey from Vilanova to Santa Sabina city once endured twelve hours.'

While he was explaining the vagaries of the public transport system, he put an arm about Nanette to hold her close while he opened the front of her much-travelled explorer's trousers and slipped a hand inside. She wore small and thin knickers, and it was easy to slide his hand down her belly and inside them. She parted her legs as if by reflex action when his fingers touched her *kuft*. She let him stroke it gently for a while, but as soon as he tried to press his finger inside, she grasped his wrist.

'I'm much too tired,' she said. 'All I want is to sleep in a proper bed tonight and not wake up before noon tomorrow.'

She rested her head on Marcel's shoulder, the roles reversed now, and closed her eyes. He kept his hand inside her knickers, lightly clasping her curly-haired *kuft*, and she fell asleep at once. The bus rattled on through the dark, the unfenced cliff edge and the drop to the sea below best not thought of. An hour passed before Marcel saw the first lit buildings ahead, and not long afterwards they were passing through the outer suburbs of the city. He withdrew his hand and zipped up Nanette's trousers before shaking her gently awake.

In the familiar surroundings of his room at the Grand Hotel Orient he slept very soundly that night. Coffee was brought to him at eight by Concepcion, eldest daughter of the proprietor, who sat on the side of his bed and said she was pleased to see him back after so long away in the country. Marcel was touched by this gesture of affection, and while he drank his coffee he put his hand up her short skirt to stroke the inside of her bare golden-brown thigh.

'Have you woken up with a stiff *zimbriq*, Monsieur Marcel?' she asked with a grin, and put her hand under the thin coverlet and into the pyjama trousers which were all he wore at night. A moment later she was surprised to discover his male part lying limp and small on his belly.

'Ah, you did not sleep alone last night,' she said. 'You were with Madame Jarre in her room and she has worn you out.'

'No, I slept alone,' Marcel assured her, 'all night.'

His roving hand moved higher under her skirt until he touched the thicket of heavy curls where her thighs joined. Her legs moved wider apart to encourage him, although her expression was one of disappointment.

'Then the village girls *zeqqed* you too much,' Concepcion said with a shake of her head. 'I have heard stories of what they do in the country. Is it true the women go about with their *gublas* bare?'

'Only when they work in the fields,' Marcel said, having seen this himself many times during his tour with Nanette.

While they were talking, he gently rubbed the soft warm lips of Concepcion's *kuft*. She sighed and took hold of his wrist to press his hand against her.

'Make me *zboca*, Monsieur Marcel,' she said, smiling at him.

He pressed two fingers into her, finding her wet and ready, and he massaged her secret bud. Her climax came very quickly – she gripped his slack *zimbriq* so hard he winced, and she shook furiously in her spasms, her dark brown eyes wide open and her breath rasping in her throat.

'You are very pretty, Concepcion,' he said, 'especially when you *zboca*. Was it good?'

'Always,' she replied, her fingers tickling his slack part to try to raise it, 'but it would be better if I *zeqqed* you. Lie on your back, Monsieur Marcel.'

But after so many days and nights with Ofelia in the country he was not in the mood to be ravaged in a few frantic seconds by another energetic Santa Sabinan. He kissed Concepcion's hand and escaped her further attentions by dashing for the shower, insisting that he had an important meeting at the Embassy, and must not be late.

To give a little credibility to his excuse he left the Hotel without breakfast and walked quickly across San Feliz Square as if in a great hurry. There was a café he knew on the corner of the Boulevard St-Lazare, and here he ordered *café au lait* and croissants, with guava jam, and asked the waiter to bring him a morning paper. The only newspaper published in Santa Sabina was the *Daily Chronicles*, and it was owned by President da Cunha, who inherited it from his father along with the Presidency. It was printed in Santa Sabina city and distributed to the other towns of the island by early morning bus, and was usually on sale by midday or not much later, except when the road was blocked or a bus broke down, or a driver failed to report for work – or any of a dozen other calamities.

Needless to say, Marcel had not seen a newspaper for a week, there being no distribution in the villages. Down at the bottom of the front page, as he sipped at his coffee, he found a short report on the death of Enriquez da Motta, the well-liked young Minister of Industrial Developments. The story was a follow-up from the day before, Marcel saw, and sent the waiter scurrying to the kitchen to see if yesterday's *Daily Chronicles* was still to be found, or had been torn up to use in the staff toilet. By good fortune most of it survived and was brought to him.

Marcel had been too weary to bother with newspapers when he and Nanette reached Vilanova the day before. But there it was – a page-width headline and the entire front page devoted to an account of a most tragic accident in which Monsieur da Motta's newly imported European car had collided at high speed with a mule-drawn wagonload of pomegranates. The dread occurrence had taken place seventeen kilometres from Santa Sabina city on the road to Vilanova. My God, thought Marcel, we came right past it in the dark and never knew!

After the fatal impact which killed mule and wagoneer, said the newspaper, Monsieur da Motta's car was beyond human control. It had skidded across the road and over the cliff edge, which at this point had a height of thirty metres, and had been destroyed on the rocks below before bursting into flames. The driver had been so badly burnt in the fire that the identification of the remains could be achieved only by comparison with Monsieur da Motta's dental records.

Marcel finished his breakfast in deep thought, then continued his journey to the Embassy. He found there that he had almost been speaking the truth when he told Concepcion he had a most important meeting, though by chance only. The young woman who typed for him, on the very rare occasions he had anything to be typed, informed him that His Excellency had been wanting to talk to him urgently for the past week.

If there had been any possible way of getting in touch, said she, Marcel would have been dragged back from his tour around the countryside with Madame Jarre. His Excellency had arranged for the despatch of a messenger – a Santa Sabinan employee – to Vilanova to see if Monsieur Lamont could be traced. But in the typical Santa Sabina way, this Fernando had followed them only as far as Miguel's stables before giving up.

Smiling inwardly at the Ambassador's discomposure and panic, Marcel tried to speak to him. He was diverted to the office of Monsieur St-Beuve, husband of the superbly lubricious and madly enthusiastic Genevieve. Whether St-Beuve suspected or not that his beautiful wife arranged secret meetings with other men, one of whom was Marcel, he behaved with perfect correctness towards him. His Excellency, he informed Marcel, had left for Paris the previous day, having been recalled for urgent discussions.

'But how?' Marcel asked. 'And what can be so urgent?'

'By sea to Madagascar,' said St-Beuve solemnly. 'A freighter was due to sail at eight yesterday evening. From there he will take an Air India flight to Paris.'

'The discussions cannot be so very urgent,' Marcel commented, 'it will be a week before His Excellency arrives. But why all this activity? What is happening, Monsieur St-Beuve?'

It is understood that no diplomat ever says anything so very simple and direct as 'I do not know'. St-Beuve pursed his lips in a judicious expression and pressed his fingertips together and gave every appearance of being in possession of highly secret information. But he said nothing.

'Well?' Marcel prompted him, after a long pause.

'Understand, Lamont, these are very confidential matters and must never be divulged outside this room. His Excellency formed the view that the KGB were mounting a plan to murder President da Cunha and replace him with Monsieur da Motta. The source of this information is classified and I am unable to say more.'

Which means you do not know, thought Marcel, and how shocked you would be if I told you His Excellency's source was your own dear wife, who had the information from me when I *zeqqed* her.

'Nevertheless,' St-Beuve continued, 'His Excellency believed entirely in the trustworthiness of his source. He tried to find you all week, presumably to instruct you to attempt to validate the information.'

'Presumably,' Marcel agreed. 'But how was it to be achieved, this assassination? And how could da Motta succeed da Cunha – it would be a matter for election by the entire populace.'

'Much of it must necessarily be logical deduction from what is known for certain,' said St-Beuve, selecting his words with care to make the proposition sound more credible. 'It is known that Colonel Svoboda of the Czech Embassy is in very frequent contact with Madame da Motta.'

'The lucky devil!' said Marcel with a grin. 'She's beautiful and I'd like to *zeqq* her myself.'

'Please!' said St-Beuve, flinching at the vulgarity. 'There is no place for remarks of that type. Svoboda is a known KGB agent – it must be obvious to you that the Santa Sabina Chamber of Deputies was bribed to elect da Motta. All that remained was for da Cunha to contract a mortal disease or blood poisoning or to meet a fatal accident. I need not remind you of the fearful consequences of Santa Sabina having a President favourable to USSR interests – we might even be contemplating the launching of World War Three!'

'Happily, none of it will occur,' said Marcel. 'The

newspaper reports that it was da Motta who met with a fatal accident, not the President. Perhaps there never was a plot, dear colleague.'

'Perhaps,' said St-Beuve doubtfully, 'but His Excellency was so convinced of imminent danger that he sent several reports in cipher to Paris by radio. I had the honour of assisting him in the composition of them, but he refused my advice to scale down his final report, which has brought about his recall.'

'What was it he suggested should be done?'

'His Excellency recommended a protest to the Kremlin in the sternest possible terms, and at the same time the matter raised at the United Nations. But that was not all – he also suggested that a Naval task force should be despatched immediately with a battalion of the Foreign Legion to secure Santa Sabina, if da Motta was elected President.'

*'Le bon Dieu!'* said Marcel. 'He has been too long here – the fearful heat has damaged his brain. I fear His Excellency needs rest and treatment in some suitable medical facility in France. What did he say when da Motta's car accident was reported?'

'I have never seen a man in so traumatised a condition. He hoped to bring himself to the attention of General de Gaulle by giving advance warning of a Russian plot, and so gain promotion.'

'Alas,' said Marcel with a rueful shrug, 'it is well known to all of us that there is no promotion from Santa Sabina.'

'In the excitement of the moment, Monsieur Ducour forgot that melancholy truth,' St-Beuve agreed. 'It was pitiful to see him when da Motta's death became known. Naturally, he concluded the Bureau of Public Information had uncovered the alleged KGB plot and taken steps to neutralise it by eliminating the Minister.'

The Santa Sabina secret police went by the agreeable though misleading name of the 'Bureau of Public Information'. They enjoyed a reputation for ruthlessness, even their mildest interrogations being conducted to the wrenching-off of the suspect's toenails – and if that failed to get the information they required, it was said they used kitchen scissors to amputate other and more useful parts of the unfortunate detainee's anatomy. To dispose of a government Minister in an arranged road accident was hardly a problem for them.

'If you ask me,' said Marcel with a shrug, 'the entire thing is nonsense. I do not believe there was a plot – the Ambassador was deceived. It is a pity I was not available to advise him – but he insisted that I accompany Madame Jarre. When he returns I shall make this point to him.'

'*If* he returns,' said St-Beuve, the corners of his mouth down in a grimace of doubt. There was no need to say more – he and Marcel both understood that the Ambassador had overreacted so furiously that his judgement would now be permanently in doubt. An early retirement seemed the most probable solution, when the facts had been considered fully in Paris. Jacqueline's wish to return to France would be granted.

'Did Madame Ducour go with His Excellency?' Marcel enquired.

St-Beuve gave him a very cold stare and informed him that she was still in residence in Santa Sabina. The look set Marcel to wondering if it was possible that St-Beuve himself had a secret friendship with Jacqueline. But surely not – he was too old for her, and too dignified to enjoy her caprices. Besides, she had a new friend – the slender young Indian, whatever his name was. All in all, thought Marcel, events were turning out well and he need do no more for the present.

Elated by the devastation he had achieved, he telephoned to the Portuguese Consulate and arranged to take Mariana Mendez to dinner that evening. Ten days had passed since he saw her last and there was something he found very endearing in her efforts to adopt a European outlook. A further consideration was that he wanted a change from Nanette.

He met her at eight o'clock at Paladio's, an open-air restaurant down by the harbour, with a reputation for the best food in the city. He knew she would be pleased to be seen there, and he was on hand in good time, shaved, showered and dressed in his best white suit. She looked particularly delicious when she arrived, in a knee-length frock of palest pink, cut low over her *gublas*, and a thick necklace of polished white coral.

Marcel kissed her hand to make her feel suave and important, and addressed her as Marie. Cocktails were drunk – a barbarous custom Marcel deplored, but which Marie had read of in imported magazines and therefore knew to be *comme il faut*. They chatted and laughed together, and she asked him about the trip into the country with his colleague, the distinguished ethnographer, and he answered these questions with care and evasion.

When a waiter brought the menu, Marcel, without even a glance, ordered the most expensive thing on it to impress his companion. Paladio was the only restaurateur in Santa Sabina who served this dish – giant blind crayfish, sauteed in Pernod and wild saxifrage.

It was Marcel's intention to take Marie after dinner to the Dance-Bar Rivoli for an hour, or as long as it took to drink a bottle of their so-called champagne, and then to her apartment in the rue St Caterina and stay with her for the night. Events worked out somewhat differently.

When they were ready to leave Paladio's soon after ten and he suggested a little dancing, she said it had been so long since she had seen him that she would prefer to be alone with him. This was said with an affectionate smile on her red-tinted lips and a lustful expression in her dark brown eyes, her hand upon his sleeve and her full bosom thrust well out towards him. The idea naturally appealed to him, and he handed her up into a *barossa* waiting in line outside the restaurant.

At this moment Marie had another change of plan to suggest – her mother had been in a bad mood all day, she said, because of a disagreement with her neighbour, Madame Peres, whose husband she was in the habit of *zeqqing* most days. If Monsieur Marcel agreed, it would be better to go to his hotel. The explanation made no sense to Marcel, but he had learnt that Santa Sabinan explanations almost never did. He agreed without hesitation and gave the coach driver his new directions.

It was then that the perfectly planned evening changed course abruptly. When they descended from the coach at the Hotel Grand Orient, who should be sitting alone on the terrace outside with a drink than Nanette Jarre. It was a pleasure to see her out of her safari shirt and well-used trousers and dressed in a pretty frock, Marcel thought, but it was a pleasure he could have done without that evening. Naturally, he paused to introduce the two women to each other, and to his dismay Marie was so fascinated to meet an independent, *chic*, highly educated Frenchwoman that suddenly she and he were seated at Nanette's table with drinks in front of them.

It began when Nanette complimented Marie on her frock – from that to a lengthy discussion of clothes by the two women was an inevitable step. And half an hour later Marcel found himself up in Nanette's room in the hotel, rotating his thumbs in a wicker armchair, while Nanette showed Marie the total wardrobe she had brought with her to the island.

Marie admired all she saw, and became especially interested when Nanette showed her a pair of pink and white satin pyjamas. Marcel remembered seeing her in them the day after her arrival, when he called to enquire if she felt better after the drama of her collapse from heatstroke. Nanette's little pyjamas were *très chic*, and Marie was ecstatic with admiration. She knew from magazines and movies that foreign women went to bed in stylish nightwear, as distinct from Santa Sabinans who slept naked, but she had never before seen satin pyjamas.

Nevertheless, to demonstrate she was no ordinary young woman, she lifted the skirt of her palest pink frock to show Nanette that she too wore knickers – the elegant pair in magenta silk with the black lace trim that Marcel had given her. Nanette was suitably impressed, and wondered if the colour would suit her pale skin as well as it did Marie's *café-au-lait* tint. Suddenly the women had their frocks off to try on each other's knickers.

Until now Marcel had been increasingly impatient at

the delay in getting Marie to his own room, to undress her and play with her to his heart's content. But now his *zimbriq* was stiffening pleasantly at the sight of bare bottoms and *kufts* as the women exchanged knickers and admired themselves in the long mirror on the wardrobe door. He felt the strongest urge to slide a hand up between smooth white thighs, and the other hand up between satiny gold-brown thighs. A double-feel – a delicately amusing concept!

Marie was fascinated by the brassière Nanette had taken off, but it was impossible to cram her plump round *gublas* into the little lacy cups that held Nanette's much smaller ones. It was becoming very apparent to Marcel – and to Nanette – that Marie found the delicate touch of silk on her skin highly arousing – she was running her hands slowly and luxuriously over her belly where Nanette's eau-de-Nil knickers clung to her, her dark eyes half-closed and her mouth slightly open.

Nanette and Marcel glanced at each other and grinned, then he got up to put an arm round Marie's naked waist while, with his other hand, he rubbed gently between her thighs, and smoothed the thin silk against the lips of her *kuft*.

'Ah, Monsieur Marcel,' she murmured, her smooth cheek against his, and he winked at Nanette over her shoulder. At the touch of his hand Marie's legs trembled, and soon her feet slid apart on the floor. By now Marcel's stiff part bulged uncomfortably in his trousers and, feeling its movement against her, Marie ripped open his zip and forced her hand inside.

She was already too far gone in her headlong rush to ecstasy to do more than grasp him tight before her hips were jerking at him in climactic release. As always with the island girls, her ecstasy was of brief duration – but that was by no means the end of the affair. While she stood on shaking legs, smiling at Marcel, Nanette moved in close behind her and went down on one knee to slide the knickers down Marie's legs, and then Marcel lifted her from the floor and laid her on her back on the bed.

Without a pause he was between her legs, her frock

pulled up round her waist and his belly on hers. He was still completely dressed in his best white suit and blue bow tie, only his stiff *zimbriq* protruding, but he was too aroused to concern himself with questions of dress. He pushed up into Marie's wet and open *kuft* and felt her squirm with delight under him. Then Nanette was sitting on the bed alongside, for a close view.

'Ha!' she said. 'I see you've taught Marie our way of doing it – you on top.'

'It is I who insist,' Marie replied at once from underneath him. 'A woman on top is not *chic* – it is only for Santa Sabina peasants, that.'

'Whatever pleases you best,' said Nanette, with a shrug.

Marcel moved in and out with long steady thrusts, and Marie became quickly incapable of further conversation. As he might have expected, Nanette was not content to sit idly by and watch in silence – he felt her hands touch his sides, then slip under him to find his belt buckle. While he *zeqqed* Marie, who gasped and sighed and moaned without cease, Nanette undid his trousers and pulled them off, his shoes and socks, his underwear and his bow tie, turning up his jacket and shirt to uncover his bottom.

Marcel found it most strange and yet provocative, this being undressed by a woman while he was in the very throes of *zeqqing* another woman. Undoubtedly Nanette felt something of the same for she ran her hands over his body, stroking his chest and his back, pinching his bottom, running a finger down the crease – in short, she was feeling *him*. She seemed to be much amused to observe his bare bottom bouncing rhythmically up and down – for she stroked it fondly and felt between his thighs to hold his hairy pompoms.

'Yes, yes,' she said softly, '*zeqq* her long and hard – you're good at that, Marcel.'

Marie had reached her climax three separate times since being penetrated, and she writhed on the bed, moaning and sighing in voluptuous sensations as he thrust backward and forward in her.

'Again, again!' she cried out.

Overwhelmed by her gratifying response, Marcel accelerated the thrusting of his fifteen centimetres to short and sharp strokes that ravaged her wet *kuft* with delight. But all too soon then the torrent of his desire was unleashed into her, and she cried out in rapture and clung hard to him with hooked fingers.

He kissed her and rolled off, sitting up on the bed to remove his creased and superfluous jacket and shirt.

'My turn now,' said Nanette, 'take your frock off and give me a hand, Marie.'

Between them, they arranged him on his back in the middle of the bed, his legs well apart and Nanette kneeling between them. Marie, naked at last, her pale brown skin shining lightly with the perspiration of being *zeqqed*, sat close beside him with her legs folded underneath her. The two women examined his limp and lolling part and flicked it with their fingers to make it stand hard again.

'I know he can,' said Nanette. 'I've seen him do it three or four times straight off out in the country.'

'Oh, yes,' Marie agreed, 'he *zeqqed* me four or five times the last time we met, before he went away with you.'

'Ladies,' said Marcel with a grin, 'if you will allow a moment or two of patience, all will be well, I promise it!'

He felt an agreeable stirring of his cherished possession, a slow stretching out, a pleasurable thickening, a gathering of strength. The women chirped and grinned to see the results of their handiwork, and soon brought him to full size.

'*Voila!*' said Marie. 'Monsieur Marcel is ready for you now – I am very much interested to see how a foreign lady is *zeqqed* by a foreign man. This will be new to me.'

Marcel smiled when Nanette sat astride his belly. Poor Marie would see only what she had known all her life, woman-over man-under. Nanette had taken to the Santa Sabina way as completely as Marie had to the foreign way. His *zimbriq* was held upright by Nanette's firmly clasped hand and she massaged it briskly up and down, sending thrilling little sensations through him.

'I'm going to have you,' she said, grinning down at

him, 'in the Santa Sabina way – I adore being uncivilised.'

'But this is not *chic*,' Marie objected, and then fell silent.

Nanette rose up a little to position his upright part between her open thighs, and he sighed in pleasure as she sank down slowly and he felt her slippery warm flesh swallow him. She lowered herself all the way, until his *zimbriq* was completely embedded to her satisfaction before she started to ride him.

Her rhythm was fast and twitchy, as if she was nervous or her thoughts were on something else. Marcel laid his hands on her thighs and stroked up towards her pierced *kuft* to encourage her a little, and after a while she leaned forward to put her hands on either side of his head, so that he could reach her elegant little round breasts and play with them. That seemed to assist her to reach the climax of passion – her up and down movement speeded up until it became furious.

It required not much of that to bring on her crisis. A fierce shuddering shook her body and she gave a long descending wail of joy. The contractions of her *kuft* carried Marcel right over the brink of sensuality and his hot essence spurted up into her belly in delicious spasms. It was reasonable to expect Nanette to collapse and rest after so vigorous a *zeqqing*, but nothing of the sort happened – on the contrary, she pulled herself off Marcel's wet *zimbriq* and clambered over him to sit beside Marie and put an arm round her waist.

Marie turned her head to look at her, their lips touched, and Nanette kissed her full on the mouth, as a lover would. Marcel stared in great surprise, then turned on his side and raised himself on an elbow to look on, curious and secretly amused. He noted that Marie too was at first taken aback by this approach, but she did not try to pull away and even opened her mouth for Nanette's tongue to press her between her lips.

'And why not?' Marcel asked himself softly as he moved back to lean on the headboard and drew up his legs to make more room for his charming companions. His *zimbriq* had begun to stir into renewed life, and he clasped it affectionately in his hand. He heard Nanette tell Marie that she had beautiful big breasts and saw her feel them with both hands. Marie's eyes were downcast, as if what was happening was too much to comprehend – but under Nanette's fingers her dark brown buds were noticeably prominent and erect.

It was when Nanette bowed her head to kiss them and suck them that Marie surrendered to curiosity and to pleasure. Marcel saw her eyes close and her head go back, and heard her long-drawn sighs. Then she responded, cupping Nanette's pink-flushed face between her palms to bring their mouths together and thrust her tongue into Nanette's, while Nanette stroked her with long slow touches between her parted legs.

'*Ah, mon Dieu!*' Marcel whispered in delight, his stiff part throbbing furiously in his hand.

What followed was more than he could ever have hoped for or imagined. Nanette pressed Marie down on her back with her legs hanging loosely over the side of the bed and knelt on the floor between them, her fingers playing over Marie's dark honey belly and the neatly shorn tuft of black curls. She kissed the inside of Marie's thighs and licked them with the tip of her tongue until she had the girl writhing in delicious sensation.

The impact of what was being done to her was so immense that Marie forgot her everyday French and fell into the old language of the island. '*Amasta na zeqq-zeqq,*' she gasped loudly, her hands clenched into fists and her smooth belly arching upwards. What the words meant, Marcel had no idea, nor presumably did Nanette – but the urgent plea in them was unmistakable. She forced the frantic girl's legs wider apart, ducked her head down between them and thrust her tongue into her open *kuft*.

Marie's loins bucked upwards furiously in instant climax. She shrieked in ecstasy, again and again, until Marcel wondered if the occupants of the rooms on either side of his would come to investigate a murder! But at last Marie's cries diminished and her convulsive jerking faded to a trembling of her legs and her belly. She lay with eyes closed and an expression of enormous satisfaction on her pretty face.

'I've never done that before to a woman,' Nanette said in a thoughtful tone, looking at Marcel over Marie's prostrate body, 'but she is so evidently made for *zeqqing*, your girlfriend, that I couldn't resist. Those big soft breasts – and that broad expanse of belly – I understand how you feel when you *zeqq* her. This is a rare insight and I am privileged to achieve it!'

'But in the interests of science and ethnography, of course,' said Marcel, his hard part leaping in his hand.

'Naturally,' said she, without even a glimmer of amusement he could see, 'but for you, no doubt, it is a question of pleasure and no more than that. Observing the little experiment has had the effect of stiffening you up again, I see.'

She reached out a long arm over Marie's bare breasts to take hold of his twitching *zimbriq* and slide her fingers up and down its length. Its lively movement in her grasp informed her that Marcel was highly aroused and she put her tongue out at him in impudent amusement. He smiled back at her, though vaguely, for little thrills of pleasure were darting through his body to the sliding of her hand.

'Wake up, Marie,' she said, 'look at this!'

Marie sighed and opened her eyes, then rolled over on to her side and stared at short range at Marcel's jerking *zimbriq*, her face split in a wide grin. Almost at once, under the eager and expert scrutiny of two naked young women, there came about the normal result – his pampered *zimbriq* leaped most furiously in Nanette's hand and sprayed his virile passion over Marie's face in long jets.

'Ah yes, yes, yes,' he gasped, staring at the creamy trickles down the side of her nose and her cheeks, and a final spasm of ecstasy seized him when he saw her put out her tongue sideways to where it had descended to the corner of her mouth.

'Well!' she exclaimed with a broad grin. 'Now Mademoiselle Nanette's had both of us!'

'And so she has,' Marcel agreed, leaning back in contentment, 'but now we shall both have her, Marie.'

The rest of the night was devoted pleasurably to deciding who should *zeqq* who most often. They got into bed naked, with Marie in the middle, and in spite of what Marcel had promised her, it was really a question of he and Nanette taking turns in *zeqqing* the willing girl. And she, convinced that this was the correct and usual foreign way of things, was content to let them, until she needed a respite, whereupon Marcel climbed over her and on to Nanette and *zeqqed* her.

These games continued through the night hours, with pauses to rest, until the first pale light of dawn appeared at the open windows to the balcony. Several times Marcel dozed off and was woken by the sighs and murmurs and sighs of either Nanette or Marie being pleasured by the other. He listened each time until the gasping climax was achieved, then in the darkness took hold of whichever woman had been the active partner and rolled her underneath him.

At once an unseen hand guided his ready *zimbriq* to a very wet *kuft*, which he *zeqqed* with long steady strokes. This random and unhurried delight was repeated several times during the night hours, and towards dawn, when Marcel was lazy with pleasure and ready to sleep, the women took a turn each on top of him and *zeqqed* him very thoroughly.

When he woke again it was clear daylight and very hot already in the room. His wristwatch said it was five minutes to eleven. The warm female body in front of him turned over sleepily when he touched a hip, and the soft cheeks of a bare bottom nestled into his lap. It was Marie, her long and curly black hair over his face untidily, and her fleshy *gublas* a warm delight in his hand when he reached over to feel them. Although she was half asleep, her nature was Santa Sabinan to the core, and her plump bottom wriggled against him.

The touch of her breasts had excited him to stiffness at once and he groped her bottom to steer his *zimbriq* into the smooth lips waiting for it. She gave a little *Ah* of content to be penetrated so easily and he played with her breasts fondly while he plunged in steady and unhurried tempo into her softly shaking body.

He had found it enormously arousing in the night to share the superbly proportioned young girl with Nanette in this strange comradeship that had developed between him and the celebrated ethnographer. And it had been with a renewed zest he had *zeqqed* Nanette afterwards. The memory of their games together made his *zimbriq* grow thicker and harder yet as he slid it in and out of Marie and he sighed and moaned to himself, his rhythm becoming fast and staccato.

'Ah!' he heard Marie wail as she felt the gush of his desire and her belly was seized by an ecstatic shuddering. By now the jerking in the bed had woken Nanette, who pressed herself close to Marie and threw a leg over her, their mouths touching in a hot kiss. Her groping hands shared with Marcel the possession of Marie's plump bare breasts.

'Do not be impatient, Nanette *chérie*,' he panted through his spasms of delight, 'I mean to *zeqq* you too before we go out for lunch!'

'Do not delude yourself, *cher ami*,' she murmured back, 'it is I who mean to *zeqq* you.'

# 12

## *Life Being As It Is, One Dreams Of Revenge*

Santa Sabina city lay at the extreme eastern tip of the island for the excellent reason that the only good natural harbour was to be found there. The city stretched back from the sea and the docks on gently rising ground, old, shabby and indolent. There were some fine buildings – Portuguese baroque in style and three centuries old, but neglect had dimmed their original glory and blunted their facades. To walk through the streets looking for architectural splendour was a melancholy affair – or so Marcel thought as he made his way from the provincialism of the Grand Hotel Orient to Martyrs' Square, where the church retained some of its dignity, despite accumulated grime and pigeon droppings.

It was no longer necessary to accompany Nanette Jarre all day long about the city – she was making use now of Marie as guide, it being undeniable that Marie knew her way about the city even better than he did. Naturally, if it came to another expedition into the countryside, Marie had announced in advance that she would not go, and Marcel would be called upon. He hoped that it wouldn't come to that, lacking all desire for another extended ride on muleback. In the meantime, his time was his own and he planned an afternoon at the beach.

The reserved beach was in the western outskirts of the

city, well away from the harbour and docks. It was named that because it was reserved for those prepared to pay the entrance fee and buy the cold drinks on offer, for every other beach along the coast was freely available to anyone who wanted to make use of it. In effect, the entrance fee meant that the reserved beach was patronised almost exclusively by foreigners – in the main the Diplomatic Corps. Marcel had more than once wondered why it had not been given a more grandiose name, Plage Nice-Cannes, for example, or Grand Plage Biarritz.

The bus would have taken him there for less than a *barossa*, but the day was too hot and sultry to stand about waiting in Vasco da Gama Square. And to ride along in an open carriage was pleasant. A metre-high woven fence strung along a row of palm trees divided the reserved beach from the main road to Selvas, and there was a wooden archway with the name painted on it, by way of entrance. One of the proprietor's many children lurked here with an ancient dented cash box to collect the money, and he greeted Marcel as an old friend and took his fifteen *tikkoos*.

Thirty or forty swimsuited people lay about on the sand, and perhaps another twenty stood in the shallow sea, throwing balls to each other or splashing water into each other's face. Marcel undressed in one of the shantylike huts and strolled along the fine white beach looking for Jacqueline Ducour. He had asked at the Embassy for her and was informed she was at the beach – and so perhaps she was, and perhaps she was somewhere else with her new young friend.

But no, there she was, stretched out at ease, not on a beach towel as were most of the other bathers, but more elegantly on a striped deck chair in form like a chaise longue. This was not supplied by the reserve beach, but brought from the Embassy and set up in the place of her choice by her husband's chauffeur, a much put-upon Santa Sabinan named Ercole. His task accomplished, Ercole withdrew to the furthest end of the beach with a bottle of palm wine, removed his uniform jacket and fell asleep.

Jacqueline wore a white bikini as *chic* as any to be seen that season on the Riviera. She lay gracefully on her chair, one arm folded under her head, her eyes closed, as if lightly sleeping, but in truth displaying herself to attract the interest of any handsome young stranger who passed. Marcel approached quietly and sat down on the sand close by, chin on his raised knees.

The years had been kind to Jacqueline – she had arranged that herself by diet, exercise, massage and all other known aids to maintaining a youthful figure when one's fiftieth birthday begins to loom close. Her long neck was without a wrinkle, her elegant little breasts in the skimpy bikini top not yet slack. The line of her bare belly was flat, the deep dimple in the middle clear and provocative. Marcel smiled to feel his *zimbriq* stir in his tight swimming trunks as he sat gazing at Jacqueline's body.

Under the close-fitting material of the lower half of her so stylish bikini, the mound of her *kuft* was more prominent than he expected. But then, Jacqueline's very personal manner of lovemaking tended to deny her lovers any clear sight of her charms until they were so highly aroused that nothing made much of an impression. An urgent need to discharge their desire into her put into abeyance the faculty of aesthetic appreciation. If only she could be persuaded to surrender herself to a lover and stop imposing her will . . . but *if only* was for idiots.

Her thighs were smooth-skinned and unmarked, without a trace of flabbiness. The stiff condition of Marcel's male part urged him to press his lips to those thighs and kiss up to where they joined together . . . but he well knew that if he did so she would jerk upright at once with glaring eyes and angry words, furious that a man dared to touch her without her consent and without her initiating the caress. Yet there had been an occasion, soon after their intermittent *affaire* began, when he had imposed his will on hers.

She had been visiting him in his hotel room for a month or so and was at ease with him, certain that she could use him in any way she wished for her pleasure, for he had gone along with her in everything, finding it interesting and amusing to do so. But one afternoon of dry thunder overhead and continuous lightning, Marcel decided to play a different game with her. First it was her way, the nervous shuddering of her climax at the instant he pushed into her *kuft* and spurted his pent-up desire. Then when they had recovered a little, he held her very lightly down and covered her face with pecking little kisses – and then down to her breasts, and very carefully so as not to alarm her, down on her belly, his kisses as fleeting as the touch of a butterfly's wing. All this attention charmed and flattered her, and she let him continue.

She gasped and shivered when the tip of his tongue eased into her *kuft*, but his gentleness reassured her and she made no move to halt the proceedings. And by the time she understood that he had roused her almost to the point of climax again, it was too late to stop. Her long back arched up off the bed and her legs opened wider than Marcel had ever seen. He gripped her thighs brutally tight while he ravaged her with his tongue, delighted to hear her sobbing at the intensity of her sensations.

Her climax was only half over when he flung himself flat on her bare belly and thrust his stiffness deep into her. At that she screamed and beat at him with her fists – but he was not to be stopped now, and pounded his belly on hers violently, until his triumph gushed into her and she was taken by convulsions of ecstasy so remarkable that she almost fainted when at last they ended. She was utterly devastated by the way he had *zeqqed* her and a glass of cognac was needed to revive her enough to dress and return home in a taxi.

Since that afternoon their *affaire* had been sporadic, to say the least. A succession of other young men took Marcel's place in her affections – chosen for the pliability of their nature, it is to be supposed, and their compliance. Yet whenever chance threw Marcel and Jacqueline together, she took advantage of the moment to pleasure herself with him – and he made no complaint. He wanted no permanent girlfriend, not in Santa Sabina where obliging women were to be found everywhere, golden-brown locals and pale-bodied European wives.

Marcel's meditation on the physical attractions of Jacqueline Ducour were brought to an abrupt end by the appearance of a man holding a glass of iced mint tea in one hand and a small dish of pistachio nuts in the other. He stood staring down at Marcel in some surprise, evidently wondering why he was sitting close to Jacqueline. Marcel knew who he was at once, this smooth-chested and slender-bodied young man with a dusky complexion and black wavy hair – he could only be Jacqueline's new friend from the Indian Embassy.

He asked a question, though not in any language Marcel could understand. At the sound of his voice Jacqueline's eyes opened and she acknowledged the Indian's presence with a nod and then smiled fondly at Marcel sitting on the sand.

'Marcel – this is Monsieur Gokhale,' she said, 'Varaha – this is Monsieur Lamont.'

The two men acknowledged the introduction with slight bows of the head. His back straight and his movements lithe, the Indian sank down until he was sitting on the sand close to the beach-chair, his hand so steady that not a drop spilled from the glass in the process. Jacqueline thanked him for it, but declined the nuts. He offered them to Marcel, who also refused politely.

As Genevieve St-Beuve had said, Varaha Gokhale was pretty and slender to the point almost of girlishness. Nothing easier to imagine, thought Marcel, than Jacqueline's long scarlet-nailed fingers caressing that hairless chest and teasing his flat and nut-brown nipples to stir his passions. His eyes were luminous and jet black as buttons – their limpid stare would surely melt into total surrender when Jacqueline touched his narrow belly and slid her hand down to trail deft fingertips along his hard *zimbriq*.

Yet as Genevieve had also said, the bulge that could be seen in Monsieur Gokhale's swimming trunks was not impressive – not to a French eye. Perhaps these things were different in India – Marcel tried to recall Indian pictures he had seen in galleries in Paris – mainly depicting princes at play with ladies of the harem. A gouache of the eighteenth century came to mind – a prince in a green turban and robe sitting on a flat bed with his knees up and his robe open to his belly button to reveal his stiff part. A long-haired lovely, naked but for a scarlet scarf, sat before him, her legs widely parted. She was offering the prince a cup of something or other to drink while he sat with the end of his *zimbriq* inserted in her hairless slit and toyed with her right breast.

Gymnastics aside, thought Marcel, was the princely part of an average size or not? He couldn't remember, but he knew that in the *Kama Sutra* Indian men were classified according to the size of their parts – hare-men, bull-men and horse-men. That being so, on the evidence available Monsieur Gokhale was clearly of the hare class. Whether Jacqueline had found his abilities to her satisfaction, it would be interesting to know. She had been very dismissive of her Australian acquaintance on the grounds of inadequacy, but his performance rather than the size of his offering might have been the reason for that.

Marcel's speculation on whether the young Indian had endeared himself to Jacqueline was soon answered. She sat up on her long chair to adjust her bikini top over her elegant little breasts in a manner that drew fascinated attention to them and informed Varaha Gokhale without a tremor of shame that Marcel had come to collect her, there being an important matter connected with her departure from Santa Sabina that required attention. He was disappointed, the lustrous-eyed young man, to lose her, but she was up on her feet holding out her hand, which in his confusion he shook instead of kissing.

'You will find my chauffeur asleep under the palm trees over there, Varaha,' she said grandly. 'Please tell him to pack the chair into the car and wait for me by the entrance. Marcel, you come with me to carry my beach bag.'

She set off briskly across the sand, Marcel following behind her and the Indian making for the other end of the beach on his errand. When he was out of earshot, Jacqueline slowed her pace a little and confided in Marcel.

'Thank heaven you turned up – I was going insane with boredom listening to all that nonsense of his! I hardly know him, but he says he's desperately in love with me! He wants me to leave my husband and go with him to Delhi – just when I'm going back to Paris after years of exile on this miserable island! Have you ever heard such idiocy?'

'Ah, Jacqueline, do not be cruel,' said Marcel with a smile. 'Be pleased that young men fall in love with you so easily – it shows how very desirable you are, *chérie*!'

'Will you miss me when I'm gone?' she asked with affection, her fingers touching his wrist as they walked side by side, 'or will your adoration be transferred instantly go Genevieve?'

'No one is like you,' he said, with complete truth, evading the question. 'I shall miss you very much, but I am delighted for you that you have what you wanted at last.'

'So you should be,' she replied, 'for if my husband had not brought about our repatriation through his stupidity it would have been necessary to reveal to him that you are my lover.'

'Well, we have all been spared that,' Marcel said with a grin and a shrug. 'His Excellency has solved your problem by himself and in a way no one would have guessed, least of all him.'

One of the attractions of the reserved beach was the row of changing-huts under the palm trees by the fence. Naturally they were used by patrons for changing into swimsuits and back into their clothes later, but a far more interesting use was often made of them. Wives passing idle afternoons on the beach entered freely into conversation with unattached men, and if a mutual interest was felt, the friendship could develop into a charming intimacy in the privacy of a changing-hut. Long-term liaisons began, and sometimes ended, in these humble surroundings.

Marcel handed Jacqueline her beach bag of cosmetics, tissues, cigarettes, keys, money, letters, novels, and other necessities at the door of her hut, but she took his wrist and pulled him inside with her. The door was hardly closed behind him when she threw her arms about his neck and pressed herself close to his bare chest.

'Oh, I can't tell you how pleased I was to open my eyes and see you sitting there,' she said again, surprising him by the sincerity of her tone. 'I need you, *chéri*.'

Her lips touched his in the most fleeting of kisses while her hand insinuated itself slyly down the front of his swimming trunks and took hold of his soft *zimbriq*. Marcel smiled at her and unfastened her bikini top to bare her breasts. She drew in her breath sharply to indicate her displeasure at so impudent a gesture on his part, but he merely smiled more broadly and felt her elegant little breasts. The Ambassador was gone in disgrace and her power-base went with him – Marcel was on the same terms with her now as with any other woman.

Jacqueline accepted the new situation and did not try to stop his playing with her, though her hand massaged his *zimbriq* with a vigour unusual for her, to stiffen it more quickly. He raised his hands and held her face between his palms while he kissed her mouth passionately – something she had never allowed in the ordinary course of her capricious lovemaking. She made muffled sounds of protest and tried to pull away, her grip on his stiff part fierce, but after a while she surrendered and let him have his way. Not that he believed she was vanquished so easily – it was merely a ruse on her part until she could regain control.

When the kiss ended at last, she released her hold on him and pushed her white bikini bottom down her legs and stepped out of it. When she stood straight again Marcel touched her lightly, and for only an instant, the neat little tuft of walnut-brown curls between her thighs. He was wondering how she proposed to arrange matters to her satisfaction in the confined space of a changing-hut measuring only a metre and a half each way. There was a wooden seat like a shelf that spanned the rear of the hut but it was neither long enough nor wide enough to lie on.

On the occasions when Marcel had in the past made

use of the changing-huts for this purpose with chance-met new friends from the beach, there had been no possibilities. Sometimes he would sit naked on the wooden seat and have the lady straddle his lap in a modified version of the Santa Sabina style of doing it. An alternative for a lady disinclined to be the active partner was for her to remain standing and bend over with hands on the seat to be *zeqqed* from the rear. If he had to bet money on it Marcel was reasonably sure Jacqueline would choose the first way.

He would have lost the wager, for she turned sideways to the narrow wooden seat and put one bare foot up on it, so spreading her thighs widely, and pulled him close to her by his throbbing *zimbriq*. He was still wearing his swimming trunks, though down about his knees, and they restricted his freedom of movement – a fact Jacqueline had not missed. While he stood awkwardly with a hand against the changing-hut's flimsy back wall to retain his balance, her clever hands worked their enchantment on him.

The long thin fingers of one hand teased his stiff part while holding it lightly pressed to the lips of her *kuft*, the fingers of her other hand roamed gently over his face and throat, into his ears, under the corner of his jaw, about the corners of his mouth, exciting him with a mesmeric touch. She pushed a finger deep into his mouth, making him gasp and twitch and his *zimbriq* to leap furiously in her hand.

Her cajoling fingers traced down slowly from his chin to his throat, and then to his chest, to pinch his flat nipples with a skilful gentleness that aroused him almost too far, so that his back arched and his balance became unsure. But Jacqueline knew exactly how to judge his responses – she watched his expression closely, her tongue protruding a little between her red-painted lips, her brown eyes shining with the intensity of her emotion.

'But you are so beautiful, *chéri*,' she murmured. 'Tell me you love me, or I shall die.'

'*Je t'adore*, Jacqueline,' he responded, sighing continuously as her ministrations advanced his nervous system gently towards a condition of total overload. Her left hand had descended from chest to belly, her palm resting on it, and when she felt there the first surge of his passionate discharge, she slid the head of his hard-straining part between the lips of her *kuft*. Marcel moaned in climactic release and tried to thrust right into her but she held his jerking *zimbriq* tightly and denied him entry – so that his *saksak* spurted wildly between the thin lips.

For her this was sufficient in itself. Her beautiful brown eyes opened to the very limit and she sighed out '*chéri, chéri*,' – and melted into gentle ecstasy. Marcel gasped and jerked in his violent throes of his climax, balked of his purpose at the last moment, and conscious that it was not he but Jacqueline who had achieved a form of revenge.

When she became tranquil again she gave him a pecking little kiss on the cheek as she let go of him and put her foot down on the sandy floor.

'You are adorable, Marcel,' she said. 'You are the only one who understands me – I shall miss you terribly in Paris.'

'Ah, yès, I believe I do understand you, *chérie*,' he replied, though the words had a different meaning in his mouth, 'and it is true that I admire you enormously, though not greatly liking you. For example, you have made love in these beach-huts before – that much was evident from the way you lifted your leg up on the seat. Who showed you that little trick?'

'No one showed me,' she said, her face expressionless and her voice uninvolved as she looked at him, 'it was obvious. And you are correct. I was in this hut with Varaha Gokhale less than an hour ago, which is why I was so pleased when you arrived out of the blue, *mon cher*.'

Marcel grinned wryly at this further example of Jacqueline's ability to deflate men with a seeming compliment. He had been the subject of it many times during their acquaintance, and had invariably ignored it, refusing to let her see she had scored a hit.

'My poor Jacqueline,' he said, 'was your little Indian friend as unsatisfactory as the Australian with the huge muscles and tiny *zimbriq*? But how sad for you!'

She said nothing, but turned away to wipe her *kuft* and thighs of the results of Marcel's ecstasy. By now he had his swimming trunks up again and was able to move about with confidence that he would not fall over.

'Two more days and you will be gone,' he said, reaching out a wary hand to touch her spine lightly enough to make her shiver. 'These final days ought to be happy, so that you remember Santa Sabina with pleasure. What a pity your new friend was not able to make you happy – but I am surprised that you were not warned in advance by that certain air of girlishness about him.'

'You're wrong about that,' said Jacqueline. 'Varaha's *zimbriq* – if you insist on using uncouth local words instead of our own language – may be smaller than yours, but it is quite perfectly proportioned. In fact, *elegant* would not be a bad description. And your suggestion that he does not like to make love to women is hopelessly mistaken. He is extremely active.'

'What then was the problem?' Marcel enquired with a friendly grin and raised eyebrows. 'We know each other well enough to be honest in these matters.'

'To be candid, Varaha is excessively active,' said Jacqueline with a sigh, 'he reaches his climax much too quickly – and much too often for my taste. We were here together for only a minute or two before he had done it three times in quick succession – too quickly to insert him.'

'Truly a hare-man,' said Marcel, nodding sagely as if he knew all about it. 'I can see that was very disconcerting for you.'

'I was dumbstruck with amazement! Then he collapsed all limp and useless on the seat and claimed he was in love with me! I had to bite my tongue hard to restrain myself from telling him what I thought of this so-called love of his!'

'But he was still with you when I arrived – you did not send him packing.'

'I couldn't get rid of him. You wouldn't believe it but only a minute or two after sagging down on the seat he was stiff and ready again, without even being touched! He jumped to his feet and wanted to do it all over again! He said he'd never known a woman like me and he was crazy about me and must do it with me again . . . naturally I told him I was too tired and dashed out of here and back to my beach chair before he could rape me.'

'I doubt if that is what he had in mind,' said Marcel with a shrug of his shoulders. 'He evidently enjoyed doing it the way you showed him and wanted to repeat it. But you must have been spattered from head to foot.'

'To be precise, from breasts to knees,' she said, grimacing. 'Fortunately I had removed my bikini or it would have been too stained to go out of the hut in. He pursued me back to my chair and babbled that he adored me and wanted me to live with him – I sent him to get me a cold drink to stop his chattering, and when I opened my eyes, there you were!'

'I am glad to have been of service,' said Marcel, though his insincerity was apparent in his tone, for Jacqueline glared at him and demanded to know why men were so futile.

'Dear Jacqueline, it may be years before we meet again,' said he. 'Let us not part on indifferent terms. That would be a pity after the delight and the comedy of our unique *affaire*.'

'Comedy?' she said in surprise and displeasure, shuffling round to face him as she pulled her knickers up her legs. 'What do you mean? Do you find me funny in some way?'

It had been absolutely the wrong thing to say, he realised – the comic element in lovemaking is beyond female understanding and any reference to it can cause only grave offence.

'No, no,' he assured her, 'I meant the word only in the sense opposite from tragedy. A tragic love affair is when one of the lovers dies and the other is heartbroken. Fortunately that has not happened – both our hearts remain unbroken and the ending is a happy one. That's what I meant.'

Jacqueline adjusted her pale blue silk knickers and stepped into her skirt while she considered his words.

'But perhaps *my* heart is broken, at leaving you behind here,' she said, 'perhaps after all you are not sensitive enough to understand my feelings.'

'Then all the more reason to take our leave of each other as true lovers,' said Marcel. 'Come with me to the Grand Hotel.'

She was silent for a while, and then agreed. But while Ercole the chauffeur was driving them in the Ambassador's stately old Citroën to San Feliz Square, she changed her mind. Her fingers touched Marcel's knee and traced swiftly up his thigh, and with a smile she said she had a better idea and told Ercole to take them to the Embassy.

The extensive Ambassadorial apartment occupied the entire top floor of the Embassy building in King Alfonso XI Square and was reached by means of a private entrance and staircase. The door on the landing was opened by a Santa Sabinan maid, who took the beach bag from Marcel with a broad smile. Jacqueline said she had important matters to discuss with Monsieur Lamont and was not to be disturbed, at which the maid's smile became even wider as she withdrew.

'She now knows exactly what we are going to do,' said Marcel, shrugging as he followed Jacqueline into a sitting room.

'Impossible,' Jacqueline retorted, 'I hardly know myself what we shall do. She may guess, but she cannot *know*. And even if she did – now my exile here is at an end, I don't give a damn what she or anybody else thinks.'

She glanced round the sitting room as she spoke, discarded it as an appropriate scene for her leavetaking from Marcel, and led him to a bedroom. The bed was more than ample for two, but the furnishings were so completely in the newest Parisian style that Marcel knew it was Jacqueline's own room and shared rarely with her husband. He would have taken her in his arms at this moment and kissed her warmly, that being the normal preliminary to scenes of tenderness and delight in bedrooms, but Jacqueline waved him to a chair.

He sat and watched in fascination as she took off her clothes in a way that was neither provocative nor indifferent. Not that her undressing took long, for in the horrendous island climate European women wore as little as decency and fashion permitted. Off came her pink-flowered summer frock, a wisp of a brassière and her blue silk knickers, and *voila*! Jacqueline was naked.

'Look at me, Marcel,' she said, standing in front of him, but out of reach. 'Give me your honest opinion – are the signs of age and ugliness beginning to show?'

The question was the most dangerous any woman could ask a man and only an imbecile would answer it.

'But you are beautiful, Jacqueline,' Marcel replied instantly and in a voice vibrant with sincerity.

'Liar,' she said fondly, cupping her breasts in her hands to look down at them with a critical eye. 'I was beautiful when I was young, but now I have passed my fortieth birthday it is not possible to disguise from myself the melancholy truth that time is the great enemy of women, dragging down the bosom and bottom and thickening the waist and ankles.'

She was much nearer her fiftieth than her fortieth birthday, but it would have been suicidal to mention the fact. Marcel got up from his chair before Jacqueline's self-criticism got out of hand. He put his arms round her and kissed her, declaring that she roused him to unknown heights of desire and that he knew no one like her – and similar banalities that he had found useful over the years to soothe fractious women. And at the same time he squeezed the elegant little cheeks of her bottom.

His enthusiastic *zimbriq* stood stiff in his trousers, ready for instant action, but Marcel knew it was necessary to proceed with caution if he hoped to persuade Jacqueline to surrender to him – if she was capable of surrendering herself to any man at all. He sank down to his knees, keeping his hold on her bottom, and lightly kissed her *kuft*. Her curls were rich brown, and not too thick, so that the warm lips thrust forward clear and bare.

'Jacqueline, *je t'adore*,' he murmured, that seeming to be the appropriate remark at that moment. Her hand rested on his head, ready to push him away without warning if her mood swung in the usual direction of subduing men to her caprice. Marcel held his breath as he touched the soft lips between her thighs with the very tip of his tongue. The delicacy of his position called to mind the Santa Sabina phrase 'man-under, woman-over' – and though Jacqueline would never bring herself to sit over a man and *zeqq* him in the local manner, it was certainly a clear case with her of female superiority being asserted over humble males.

The touch of his tongue gave her pleasure and her mood was to allow him more of her favour than he had ever enjoyed before – perhaps more than any man had. Her feet moved apart a little on the carpet, yielding herself more to his attentions. His hands clasped the taut bare cheeks of her bottom to hold her close to him, while he pressed the wet tip of his tongue right into her, to search out her little bud. He heard her gasp loudly and her fingers clenched in his hair, as if to pull his face away from her, but she let him continue.

'Ah, but this is atrocious,' she murmured. 'Why should I let you make use of my body for your pleasure?'

Marcel made no answer, not wishing to permit her an instant's respite from the pleasurable tremors he knew the application of his tongue was sending through her.

'Why are you doing this to me?' she sighed. 'You will break my heart, *chérie*!' and he felt her hands firm on his shoulders as her legs began to tremble with the force of the sensations his tongue was creating.

'Ah, Marcel, Marcel . . . it is too much . . . I shall die if you continue,' she murmured, her long fingernails digging into his shoulders even through his clothes. Encouraged by her response, he flicked his tongue rapturously over her swollen little bud. A long gasping sigh and a nervous spasm of her thighs and belly informed him that he had excited her to the crucial moment – an instant more and it would be too late to stop him.

'No more, no more!' she cried out, grasping his hair to pull fiercely and drag his tongue away from her *kuft*. Marcel gripped her bottom harder and resisted the pull on his hair, though the agony was intense. It took only a second or two before her body jerked convulsively to the overwhelming sensations that seized her. Marcel felt the cheeks of her bottom clench and she thrust herself hard against his mouth, crying out in her ecstasy.

This climax of Jacqueline's was so much more intense than her usual genteel little shudders of pleasure and release that her strength was drained away in rapture. Marcel rose to his feet, sliding his hands up her sides to hold her, for she was swaying on trembling knees. He lifted her in his arms and laid her down on the bed, where she covered her face with the back of a hand, her belly shaken by delicious little tremors.

He left her to recover while he made a rapid exploration of the apartment's sleeping quarters. The adjacent room could only be the missing Ambassador's – it had a single bed and the decor and furniture were in tobacco brown and shiny chrome, more of a showplace to exhibit good taste than a room made for comfort and pleasure, it seemed to Marcel. Yet it had the stamp of Ducour's personality on it, he thought as he looked about. It was formal and correct, unsympathetic and, in the end, disagreeable.

Marcel swung open the wardrobe doors and saw that most of His Excellency's suits still hung there – he had gone to Paris not realising that he would not return. It was left for Jacqueline to see to the packing and shipping of his and her belongings in two more days, and evidently she had left her husband's until the last. He pulled open drawers, and saw neatly folded shirts and socks, underwear, handkerchiefs, and the other small items of men's apparel that would be expected.

There was a book hidden under the socks and Marcel grinned to see it was a valuable eighteenth-century copy of the infamous Marquis de Sade's first novel, *Justine*. A more valuable copy than the nineteenth-century reprint in the Augusto da Cunha Library. It was bound in calfskin and inside the front cover was a note pencilled in the Ambassador's finicky handwriting: *'This first example of the genius of Donatien Alphonse, Count Sade, known as the Marquis de Sade, was composed during his imprisonment in the Bastille and published in 1791 after his release, though anonymously.*

Below that, in the same handwriting, was inscribed:

*Is it a crime
to portray the desires
that perverse nature inspires?*

At random Marcel opened the book and read a few words from the page, somewhat surprised that His Excellency was interested in this aspect of sexual pleasure. On the other hand, it went some way to explain his extraordinary friendship with Genevieve St-Beuve, who much enjoyed being a victim. Most assuredly he would not be allowed to play at being the Marquis with Jacqueline.

*Roland was a short, heavy-set man, thirty-five years old, of an incredible vigour, as hairy as a bear, with a glowering face and fierce eyes. The part of him which differentiates men from women was of such length and extreme thickness that Thérèse had never laid eyes on anything like it. She could hardly span it with hands joined, and its length matched her forearm . . .*

'Ah, these romantic novelists,' said Marcel, shrugging, 'they invent characters with equipment so excessive that no woman on earth could accept it. But why not – after all, the Marquis was composing fairytales for his own entertainment in his cell.'

*. . . about her neck he tied the rope hanging from the ceiling, made her stand on a stool, pulled the rope tight and secured it fast. To the stool he attached a string, keeping the end in his hand as he sat down on a chair facing her . . . he excited with his hand his monstrous part, intending to jerk away the stool at the critical moment and leave her dangling . . .*

'Each to his taste,' said Marcel, 'but this is not mine.' Did His Excellency the Ambassador tie a cord round the aristocratic neck of Madame St-Beuve and drag her naked about the room until she crawled to his feet and kissed them, imploring him to *zeqq* any of her openings? Doubtless it was while they rested after a bedroom romp of this type that Genevieve passed on to him in absolute confidence Marcel's account of secret meetings between Svoboda and Madame da Motta.

The Ambassador had perhaps guessed the source of the story to be Marcel, and concluded he was withholding information so that France's official representative would be taken by surprise when President da Cunha died suddenly and da Motta took charge. That would put the Ambassador in a bad light with Paris, where it would be thought he was incapable. Hence, perhaps, the great urgency of the messages summoning military assistance to stop a Communist takeover – but alas, in Paris they remembered all too well the debacle of Indo-China and fought shy of a second Dien Bien Phu.

Marcel closed the book and dropped it carelessly, making no attempt to return it to the dressing table drawer. He returned to the adjoining room, where Jacqueline lay naked, much as he had left, her hand over her eyes as if half asleep, her elegant little breasts rising and falling to her gentle breathing. Without disturbing her, Marcel removed all of his clothes first, then lifted her off the bed and carried her into the Ambassador's room. She had not been sleeping, merely resting, and she gazed wildly about the room, where the signs of Marcel's rummaging were everywhere to be seen – drawers all pulled out, wardrobe doors wide open, bedcover thrown back.

'But you are a pirate,' she said with a curious smile on her long and beautiful face, 'a brigand!'

He set her on her feet, and immediately she threw herself on her husband's bed, stretching out an arm towards Marcel to join her. He lay beside her, and she rolled face down and half over him, to take his stiff *zimbriq* in her hand. She closed her palm about the shaft and played gently up and down, an expression of concentration on her face. Marcel's emotions were complicated and intense, so much so that he could hardly breathe.

Naturally, there was the enchanting pleasure Jacqueline was causing him to feel, an enchantment to which he had surrendered many times before – but there was in addition a fierce triumph, the knowledge that he had delivered the *coup de grace* to Jean-Jacques Ducour's crippled career. And as evidence of that here he was on Ducour's bed, with Ducour's wife naked beside him.

He adjusted a pillow under his head so he could comfortably watch her fingertips slide up to the tip of his engorged part, then all the way down, then back up, her bewitchment making it swell to an enormously impressive size.

'Were you jealous of Jean-Jacques?' she murmured, her head a little on one side to look at him. 'Is that why you carried me into his room?'

'Not jealous, not that,' he sighed, entranced by the way she stroked his throbbing fifteen centimetres. She was watching him closely, her other hand gliding flat over his belly. Sensations of delirious pleasure coursed through Marcel's body, and he was jerking his loins up and down on the bed in time with her hand.

'Tell me that you adore me, Marcel?' she said. 'Tell me – or you will break my heart . . .'

He was within two heartbeats of the critical moment. Through eyes clouded with delight he looked up at Jacqueline's face and recognised her eager expression – she was the vampire battening on her victim, to drain him of his strength for her own delight and sustenance. He must break her mesmeric spell – only a stake driven through her heart would destroy her power over him.

'Ah, no,' he said under his breath, and with a supreme effort of will he seized her shoulders and rolled her over, and rolled with her, until she was on her back and he was on top, belly on belly.

'Marcel!' she gasped in protest, but his *zimbriq* was pushing at the soft lips between her thighs and a strong thrust forced it right in. Her hands came up to rake his face with her nails, but he held her wrists and forced her arms down until they lay flat on the pillow.

'Jacqueline – *je t'adore*,' he sighed, his voice shaking with passion as he *zeqqed* her fast and furiously, driving his stake not into her heart but her *kuft*. But for all practical purposes with Jacqueline, it came to the same thing.

'Not like this!' she cried, words of no significance that Marcel did not hear – he could feel his *saksak* springing in his belly and rising up his plunging *zimbriq*, and with a great cry he spurted it deep into her warm belly. She squirmed under him, and twisted left and right to get him off her, but he held her tight and ravished her wet *kuft* more furiously than anyone ever had before in her life, until suddenly she shrieked loudly and dissolved into a long and shuddering climax.

'*Je t'adore*, Jacqueline, *je t'adore*,' he was saying, over and over again, until she silenced him by pressing her mouth to his with an intensity of passion that set him wondering which of them had been revenged on the other – if either.

# 13

# They Are Confusing, Lovers' Goodbyes

After a little more than a month in Santa Sabina to survey the ethnographical potential, Nanette informed Marcel that she must return to Paris to write her preliminary report to UNESCO. The announcement surprised him, though perhaps it ought not to have done – but he had never troubled himself to contemplate the end of her research work. In consequence, her news made him unhappy – and when she informed him that her departure was planned for the very next day, that made him unhappier still. He was angry that she had not given him more notice of her intentions, even though there was no particular reason why she should.

When finally she informed him she was taking Marie with her to Paris, that made him unhappiest of all. It explained why she had kept silent about her arrangements until the day before her departure, which merely added to his resentment. They were on the terrace of the Hotel Grand Orient, having lunch together, when Nanette unfolded her plans. Evidently she had chosen the time and place to prevent him making a scene.

'But this is ridiculous!' he said. 'Why?'

'Why not, *chéri*? The dream of Marie's life is to see France and learn the ways of civilisation, to buy pretty frocks and silk knickers in the grand stores on the boulevards of Paris, and to be addressed as *Mademoiselle*. I shall make this dream of hers a reality. The fare is not excessive and she will like my apartment in Montparnasse.'

'Then I am to believe it is entirely a gesture of generosity and goodwill on your part?' Marcel asked, open disbelief in his tone.

'Naturally. There is also the thought that I thoroughly enjoy making love with her – and never did I imagine I would say that of another woman! But there it is, *mon cher*, and I cannot say otherwise. It was you who arranged for the three of us to make love together, and since that night I adore doing it to her and she adores doing it to me.'

'You are deceiving yourself,' said Marcel, who was annoyed by the suggestion that he was responsible for the *affaire* between Nanette and Marie. 'The simple truth is that she does it with you because you give her pretty presents – satin pyjamas and silk underwear. If you pay for her to go to Paris she will make herself your slave. Is that what you want?'

'Why not? It sounds delightful to me. But you sound a little jealous – surely not? You have told me so very many times that Santa Sabina is crowded with pretty young girls who will go to bed with you for the asking. You will encounter no problems in finding another one for yourself.'

It was impossible to argue with Nanette. Marcel finished the meal in near silence, while she rattled on about the shops and sights and entertainments and friends in Paris, and how she would enjoy Marie's introduction to them.

'And Monsieur Jarre – what of him?' Marcel asked. 'How will he respond to the arrival of a pretty young Santa Sabina woman in his home?'

'Monsieur Jarre?' said Nanette, looking puzzled for a moment or two. 'Oh, you mean my husband! It will be some considerable time before he becomes aware of my friendship for Marie. He is an archaeologist and for almost three years past he has been in Ecuador digging

Inca sites for the University of San Cristobal. I do not expect to see him again before the year after next.'

Later that afternoon, displeased by the new situation, Marcel strolled round to the Portuguese Consulate to find Marie – or to be precise, Mariana Mendez. He learned she was no longer there, having resigned her position some time before. It seemed clear to Marcel that Nanette's invitation to go with her to Paris had been made very soon after the night the three of them had spent together in Nanette's hotel room. Yet it was she who claimed it was better to be friends than lovers!

By now he was resigned to what was happening, but he felt he should make one final attempt to understand, if not approve. A *barossa* took him at an unhurried pace to rue St Caterina, where plump Madame Mendez let him into the apartment. Her expression on opening the door was amiable, from which he assumed that the disagreement with the neighbour had been resolved and that she was again *zeqqing* Monsieur Peres on a daily basis. But the look of amiability vanished when she recognised the visitor, and was replaced by a look of apprehension. Nevertheless, she asked him in and went to inform her daughter.

Marie had been washing her hair – she entered the sitting room with a large pink towel wrapped round her head and wearing a stylish dressing gown in shiny black and yellow stripes that Marcel recognised as Nanette's. They sat down facing each other in chairs well apart and a strained discussion began. The gist of it was simple – Marcel told her it was imprudent to go away with another woman, and Marie countered by saying she respected Madame Jarre, and why not? She told him she would prefer to go to Paris with him, if he would take her, and when he said that was impossible, she shrugged and said an opportunity like this came only once in a lifetime.

However they spun out the conversation, there was nothing to be achieved, and Marcel knew that in the first two minutes. She asked him the time, which surprised him, since in the usual way of things Santa Sabinans paid very little heed to clocks – even bus drivers and office employees. An explanation occurred to him, and he enquired if she was expecting Nanette.

'That's right, Monsieur Marcel,' she said with a big smile of innocent pleasure, 'she is coming here to dinner with me and my mother, and then she will help me pack ready to leave tomorrow. I know you and she have been very good friends, but I think it is better if you are not here when she arrives. I like you very much and I like her very much, and it would not be pleasant to see the two people I like best making each other unhappy.'

Marcel rose to leave, wishing her well. She accompanied him to the door, and he put his arms round her to kiss her goodbye. She pressed close to him, hands on his shoulders, her pretty face smiling up into his. Marcel felt her breasts big and soft against his chest, the warmth of her body through the dressing gown, and he slipped a hand inside it to cup one of her plump bare beauties. Her smile became broader and she stretched up to kiss his lips.

'*Au revoir*, Monsieur Marcel, I shall send you my address when I am in Paris so you can visit me when you come back. I hope it will be soon.'

Marcel had not touched the tie-belt of her dressing gown, nor had Marie, to the best of his knowledge, yet it hung completely open, revealing her naked *café-au-lait* body. He put both hands on her *gublas* and played with them while he promised faithfully to visit her the first day he was in Paris on leave. That alas, was not due for another year. Marie shrugged and smiled sadly, then unzipped his trousers to feel inside. Naturally, the feel of her breasts in his palms had stiffened his *zimbriq* somewhat, and when he dropped his hand down to stroke her soft *kuft*, this process accelerated itself.

'Do you want to *zeqq* me one last time?' Marie asked, knowing the answer. 'But you must be quick!'

There was no need to say why. Her bare feet moved apart on the floor, Marcel dipped down a little way, then pushed upwards strongly to slide his stiffness into her. She was already moist and ready – the normal condition of the island women – and with a strong push he slid his entire length into her hot belly.

'Marie, Marie,' he murmured as he held her by the waist and *zeqqed* strongly.

'Monsieur Marcel,' she sighed back, 'I wish you were going onto the ship with me . . .'

But no Santa Sabinan entertains regrets at such a time – she held on tight to his shoulders and returned push for push, her bare belly pressing against him. Marcel kissed her continuously and gave himself up to the complex emotions that gripped him. A pang of loss at her going, an unease at the uncertainty of her future as protegée of Nanette Jarre, the sense of delight of her *kuft* clasping him, the enthusiasm of her *zeqqing* – it was more than any man could stand. With a throaty gasp of ecstasy Marcel gushed his *saksak* up into her, and she responded with climactic little shrieks.

In some indefinable way Marcel found the act unsatisfactory – Marie had not let him *zeqq* her from desire for him, not desire at all, but simple good nature. And that was not enough. His body had gone through the motions with her body – with the normal result – but as he walked away down the rue St Caterina, in his mind he was restless and disappointed. That sort of goodbye was worse than none – perhaps it was true after all that goodbyes were not worthwhile.

The next day, whatever his private emotions, good manners and a sense of duty required him to be at the docks to see off the ladies departing on the Greek steamer *Athanasios*, a rusty hulk of doubtful age and provenance that was scheduled to depart at midday for Djibouti. Jacqueline Ducour arrived in style in the ambassadorial car driven by uniformed Ercole, her extensive belongings crated up and delivered to the ship hours before. Nanette Jarre and Mariana Mendez, now to be known only by the name of Marie, arrived in a *barossa*, with their modest baggage stacked beside the driver.

Jacqueline and Nanette greeted each other on the salt-caked steel deck in the friendliest of manners – but when Jacqueline learned Marie was travelling with Nanette, sharing her cabin, a certain frostiness became apparent in her demeanour. She glared at Marcel as if he were responsible for the arrangement, which amused him though he thought it best to conceal his amusement. His three years of experience of Jacqueline had taught him she had no sense of humour whatsoever. He hoped that she would find a presentable young sailor to relieve the tedium of the voyage, but he feared otherwise – such of the crew who were to be seen were middle-aged, small, dirty and unshaven.

Also present on the *Athanasios* to bid Jacqueline goodbye was Madame Genevieve St-Beuve, immaculately dressed in a pale green linen two-piece and a pink pearl necklace. She too ran her eye over the mariners above deck, her tastes being very unlike her friend's. Marcel thought that she displayed a mild degree of interest in Captain Thokolokolos, a thickset thug with a mouth full of gold teeth, and that too amused him.

By twelve-thirty the party of passengers and well-wishers had consumed several bottles of so-called champagne, drinking to a calm sea and a swift passage, to their reunion in Paris, and so on, and there was no sign of the ship sailing. But that was to be expected in Santa Sabina, and no one was at all surprised.

Towards two o'clock Captain Thokolokolos decided it was time and in very poor French requested those not sailing with him to go ashore. Marcel kissed all three women on the cheek warmly, Genevieve kissed Jacqueline on both cheeks briefly, shook hands with Nanette and nodded to Marie. By now the Captain was on the bridge and blew a long blast on the ship's foghorn to indicate to any who cared that the *Athanasios* was about to cast off and run the perils of the deep.

Marcel helped Genevieve down the ramshackle gangway and they stood side by side on the stone quay while the frayed and dirty ropes that held the ship were undone. Its antiquated and noisy engines went astern for some seafaring reason no landsman could hope to understand, and the ship backed away. Up on deck by the rail Jacqueline, Nanette and Marie waved, and down on the dock Marcel and Genevieve waved back. Captain Gold-Teeth reversed his ship right out of the harbour, and only when it was well clear did he turn the prow towards distant Djibouti.

There was no more waving to be done. The passengers had gone below to their cabins, and Marcel and Genevieve were strolling along the quayside, past the only other vessel tied up there, a small freighter from Goa which seemed absolutely deserted and was leaning awkwardly to one side. Further on was the Customs House, where Ercole waited with the Embassy car.

'Do you want a lift?' Genevieve asked. 'I was going to lunch with friends at Camille's, but it's too late for that now.'

'Then you shall lunch with me,' said Marcel, 'and I will take you to a little place you do not know, but which I am sure you will like. It is called Xavier's, out on the road to Selvas.'

Genevieve looked doubtful at that, for if she hadn't heard of Xavier's, it couldn't possibly be any good. Marcel settled the matter by slipping a folded fifty-*tikkoo* note into Ercole's hand and telling him to have the rest of the day off. He saluted and made off quickly, and before Genevieve could raise any further objections, Marcel had her in the front of the Citroën, himself behind the wheel. He drove out of the docks at an unreasonable speed, in case she thought of changing her mind.

The road to Selvas ran south along the shore through groves of palm trees, thickets of bougainvillaea and frangipani. It skirted the reserved beach, where they could see those lacking anything better to do lying on the white sand, or floating on the sea. Not far out of the city, just past the fifth kilometre stone, a long single-storey house with whitewashed walls and a red-tiled roof stood back from the road. Marcel stared briefly as he drove past – once it was the home of beautiful and blonde Trudi Pfaff, wife of Herr Gunther Pfaff of the Federal German Embassy. Marcel had enjoyed an *affaire* of some importance with Trudi, but it had ended in very complicated circumstances.

The road wound on, shimmering in the heat, remaining close to the shoreline, with a view of the endless sea to the left and an equally boring view of rising green slopes to the right. But beyond the sixteenth kilometre stone there was a small village, and as Marcel drove through the main and only street with care to avoid strolling goats and fluttering hens, Genevieve gave a cry of dismay – she had spotted a sign that said 'Xavier's Bar'. Naturally, it was the roughest and most makeshift of rural establishments, where it could be guaranteed that the drink was injurious to health and life, and the food barbarous.

But Marcel did not intend to stop the car there – mentioning it had been a ruse to persuade Genevieve to accompany him. He knew this part of the country, having been here before with more than one Santa Sabina girlfriend. He went on through the village and continued for several kilometres before at last he saw the rough cart-track he was looking for, and turned the car along it. The track climbed a grassy slope, and when they were well away from the road, Marcel pulled round behind a clump of mango trees and parked.

Genevieve was out of the car almost before Marcel had turned off the engine. She stood with her back to him, hands on hips, gazing into the green of the distance, and breathing deeply in a pretence of enjoying the country air – which, it is needless to say, was as thick and oppressive as the air in Santa Sabina city. A studied nonchalance was an essential part of the way in which she approached the game of love, Marcel knew well enough. He glanced over his shoulder at the rear seat, on which perhaps His Excellency the former Ambassador had *zeqqed* Nanette Jarre, but there was nothing to be seen, no marks on the faded leather and no forgotten knickers tucked down the back of the seat – it was as if nothing had happened, and perhaps nothing had. Ducour and Nanette were only memories now.

Marcel got out of the stately old Citroën with a complicated feeling of loss and relief that something had been settled, one way or the other. He stood close behind

Genevieve and put his arms round her, his hands in her chic little jacket to feel her breasts through her blouse.

'Here in the open?' she exclaimed. 'Where anyone might come along and see me! You are insane to even think of it! Either buy me lunch or take me back at once – I insist!'

She tried to pull away from him, but he held her close to his body with one arm round her waist while with the other hand he opened her fine silk blouse and dragged her brassière up to her neck so that he could feel her small bare breasts.

'Oh, I'll buy you lunch all right,' he said, making his voice rough and deep, trying to sound like a truck driver in greasy overalls. 'At Xavier's they serve fried goat's chitterlings in peanut sauce that'll put some meat on your bones.'

He slipped a hand down the front of her pale green skirt and screwed up the meagre flesh of her belly in his hand. He could remember very well how she had described to him the ideal lover – ugly and uncouth, sweaty, unshaven, with broken black fingernails, in an unclean vest and dirty underpants. In every way he was the opposite to that, but if he stayed out of sight behind her and disguised his voice, the effect might be interesting.

'You've nothing for a man to get hold of,' he said, sounding aggrieved and contemptuous at the same time. 'A belly flat as a board and thighs like broomsticks – and *gublas* no bigger than a twelve-year old! You're not worth *zeqqing*, but you've got a slit and so I'll use it.'

'Get off!' Genevieve said sharply, turning her head to glare at him over her shoulder, presenting her narrow and long-nosed face in profile. The lock of brown hair she wore brushed across her forehead had been dislodged by her struggling and hung over her nose and one eye, giving her a dissolute appearance. Marcel picked her up with both arms round her waist and carried her kicking and screaming towards the car. She thought he meant to put her into the back and have her across the seat, and she put out a leg to set her foot against the closed door and prevent him getting it open. But that was not his intention – he threw her across the bonnet of the car and dragged her tiny white knickers down her thighs.

'Not here, not here – someone will see me!' she cried out, kicking backwards to disable him with a heel between his legs. He was too close for that, ripping open his trousers to get out his stiff *zimbriq*. He held her securely with a hand flat on the small of her back while he felt the brown-haired mound between her legs and then pinched the lips sharply.

'Who cares who sees you?' Marcel growled out in his pretended workman's tone. 'What's so special about you – you've only got the same as any other trollop. Do you think it's gold-plated? Well, I've been up it a few times and you can take my word it's no better than anybody else's, and not as good as some.'

He pushed a thumb deep into her *kuft* to prepare the route for his grand entrance and she screeched loudly, perhaps from the shock of the brutal invasion, or the indignity of his insulting description of her charms, and perhaps from both.

'What you need is a good *zeqqing* three times a day to break you of these stupid stuck-up ideas,' Marcel said as coarsely as he could manage, and in another second he had his *zimbriq* tight against the soft lips he had uncovered and was pushing it in fiercely.

'Rapist! Murderer! Animal!' she groaned as he started to thrust vigorously into her. His hands touched the metal of the car bonnet and recoiled from the dull heat of it. But the touch inspired him and without missing a stroke he used both hands to open Genevieve's jacket and blouse wide and force her breasts down against the hot metal. She jerked and squealed again, but he held her, squashing her soft flesh on the polished steel.

She was squirming beneath him, moaning and sobbing in terror and delight, and her narrow bottom was jerking back to meet his thrusts. In the house next to the church of St Anastasio, even a vigorous traditional *zeqqing* had been insufficient and it had been necessary to resort to extraordinary measures, even after his own spasms of ecstasy were finished. But this time he was determined to compel her to achieve her climax at the same time as his own.

His strategy was successful – in a monotone he repeated the crude and lower-class words for various parts of the female and male anatomy and their mutual actions, and he interspersed the list with the obscenities to be heard in the grosser bars of Paris, where workmen congregated. It was to be presumed that hearing these words recalled for Genevieve memories of former pleasures with sweaty and drunken market porters, for her body convulsed in frenzy and she sobbed out her climactic delight. The effect of her furious release on Marcel was immediate and devastating – his throbbing *zimbriq* stabbed deep and spurted his passion up into her slippery depths.

She lay limp and panting on the hot bonnet of the car after his savage delight was ended and he had freed himself from her. He picked her up again, grateful for her lightness, and put her on the back seat of the car, propped up in a corner. Her entire skin was shiny with perspiration, face and neck, down between her bared breasts to the waistband of her skirt – and no doubt her belly and thighs concealed inside it.

'My God, but I despise you, Marcel,' she said wistfully. 'You do the most marvellous things to me. Where did you learn words like that? It's years since I heard them spoken.'

'In the same quarters as you did,' he said, shrugging, 'though not in the same circumstances. But explain something to me, *chérie*, for I cannot imagine our recently recalled Ambassador possessed the imagination or style to *zeqq* you like that. Then what was the secret of his attraction to you?'

'The question is indiscreet,' Genevieve said at once. She sat up a little and rearranged her brassière to contain her small slack breasts again.

'Of course it is,' said Marcel. 'Discreet questions need not be asked, and discreet answers are boring. The spice of scandal lies entirely in shameless indiscretions between dear friends. And besides, Ducour has gone from our lives, but you and I will be together for some years yet.'

'Perhaps the tiniest hint might not be entirely inadmissible in the circumstances,' Genevieve said. 'For all his icy calm of demeanour, Jean-Jacques Ducour is a most fervent admirer of the Marquis de Sade. He enjoys thrashing women's backsides with a leather strap. I shall say no more.'

There was no need, for since finding the book hidden beneath the Ambassador's socks, Marcel was certain that amusements of a vigorous type were favoured by him. Genevieve's 'tiny hint' also explained the Ambassador's secret friendship with Mademoiselle Gabrielle Delacoste, whose position as a confidential clerk at the Embassy made her an inappropriate companion for so exalted a person as Jean-Jacques Ducour.

The truth of the matter, which Marcel thought was known only to himself, but which he now realised might be known to several connoisseurs of human frailties and the amusement to be derived from them, was that Mademoiselle Delacoste suffered from a type of guilt mania. She could find relief from this only by having her bare bottom smacked very thoroughly, at which she melted in a well-concealed climax. The shame of this compounded her guilt and left her limp and unresisting. It was by the merest chance Marcel had discovered Mademoiselle Delacoste's secret – he was baffled by how the very proper Ambassador had come to know it.

'Now it is your turn to explain something to me,' Genevieve said, sounding well recovered from the overwhelming sensations she had enjoyed. 'This business of the KGB spy and the wife of the Minister for Industrial Developments – it was all a plot to discredit Jean-Jacques, wasn't it? You used me for your scheme – and like a fool I did what you guessed I would.'

'These are important matters of state, and I am forbidden by your own husband to discuss them with anyone, Genevieve.'

'What?' she exclaimed. 'Do you mean to tell me my

husband is the one behind the plot and you were carrying out his orders? But what reason could Honore possibly have for wanting to get rid of Jean-Jacques? Certainly not jealousy – even if he knew about Jean-Jacques and me, it would mean nothing to him.'

'I can tell you nothing,' said Marcel, in his best diplomatic manner, which meant confusing the issue with nuances and hints, half-truths and mild lies. 'I have my orders. You must ask your questions elsewhere, *ma chère*.'

She eyed him up and down, evidently asking herself what might be the best way to get him to talk. Noticing that his trousers were still undone, she slipped a hand inside and held his limp *zimbriq*.

'What was it you said to me a moment ago?' she asked with a wheedling smile. 'Between dear friends discretion is boring. A touch of shameless indiscretion is necessary – your very own words.'

Marcel's always-eager *zimbriq* did not remain limp in her hand for long. She eased it out of his trousers, dandling it firmly, to increase its length and stiffness. 'Be a little indiscreet,' she whispered, stroking his pride to its full fifteen centimetres.

'Ah, Genevieve,' he sighed, lying back against the car seat while she aroused him closer and closer to the critical moment. But this won't do, he thought to himself, she is trying to take over Jacqueline's role, yet she is temperamentally unsuited to it! At once he sat up and took the nape of her neck firmly in his hand – she turned her eyes to stare at him uncomprehending, and he forced her head down into his lap.

'Suck me, bitch!' he growled in his coarsest accent. 'Your slit wasn't up to much, your mouth might be better.'

Genevieve struggled, but years of accustoming herself to the brutalities of thugs in Paris backstreets and lorry parks had sapped her resolve. Marcel felt her hot mouth swallow the whole length of his straining *zimbriq* and her warm tongue pass over the unhooded head.

'More, more!' he demanded, knowing the importance

of keeping the illusion intact, and he repeated the string of obscenities that had excited her before, this time almost shouting them at her. The effect was dramatic – her tongue and mouth worked on him as if she were using a vacuum cleaner, causing his *zimbriq* to twitch in strong spasms as his climactic moments approached.

His eyes were wide open and he was staring down at the back of Genevieve's head, but his imagination was a chaotic melange of pictures and memories. Here on this same seat Nanette had taken off her knickers for Jean-Jacques Ducour – and perhaps he too had made her take the ambassadorial length into her mouth – and this was confused in Marcel's mind with a vivid memory of Marie doing this to him under the shower in her apartment . . . and both women now lost to him.

'Here's something for you, little pig,' he gasped, wracked in body and soul by a massive climax as his essence squirted halfway down Genevieve's throat. Even when he had no more to give, she retained his *zimbriq* in her mouth, trembling and sighing in her own ecstatic throes.

While she was still jerking, Marcel took her by the forelock that had fallen over her face and pulled her across his knees, bottom-up, and flipped her skirt over her hips so that he could slide a hand down the back of her tiny white knickers. His fingers felt down between the cheeks to locate the puckered little knot between them, his middle finger pressed inside, and Genevieve groaned and shuddered in the prolongation of her deep climactic thrill.

It was late afternoon when he took her to Xavier's Bar back in the village for a much-postponed lunch. His impersonation of the type of small-time criminal thug in whose sexual bullying Genevieve took such delight had been so successful that Marcel continued the game for a while. He forced her to eat a plate of fried goat's chitterlings, served cold with peanut sauce and a salad of red *frolo* leaves in vinegar. It was vile beyond words and every mouthful threatened to choke her, but he insisted she ate it, and gave her a glass of *araq* to wash it down.

*Nostalgie de la boue* was an interesting state of mind, he reflected as he watched her eating, and no doubt it would provide many hours of innocent amusement for them both.

On the drive back to Santa Sabina city he made Genevieve take off her knickers and sit with her thighs apart and her skirt up about her waist. He drove furiously along the ill-made coastal road, his foot hard down on the accelerator, a hand resting on the steering wheel and a hand resting on Genevieve's bare *kuft*. When he dropped her outside her apartment in the Avenue Racine, she was half drunk with pleasure and *araq*, and as dewy-eyed as a young bride. He promised to telephone her soon, and drove off to return the Citroën to the Embassy.

But although the afternoon had been one of great interest and comedy, it had not erased the mortifications inflicted upon him in the past two days by Nanette and Marie. His male pride had been badly wounded, and to humiliate Genevieve St-Beuve did not compensate. He sat on the terrace of the Grand Hotel Orient and tried to comfort himself with several glasses of cognac – a local concoction, of course. By eight o'clock he felt slightly more cheerful and set out on foot for Maison da Silva.

Madame da Silva's establishment was to be found on the Avenue of the Constitution, and although it was not by any means the only house of pleasure in Santa Sabina city, it was by general agreement the best. The girls were young, pretty and very amiable. The patrons of the house were equally exclusive – members of the government and higher civil service ranks, rich landowners, and the foreign diplomatic corps.

In the salon Marcel was greeted by eight or nine naked girls, offering their breasts and bottoms to be fondled. The hour was early and most of their regulars would still be at dinner with wives and families. Marcel was the only man in the salon, while the only clothed woman was Serafina da Silva, sitting on a long sofa and chatting with her girls. As if to accentuate the bare *café-au-lait* bodies around her, she was wearing a long evening gown in maroon, with a design worked on it in gold thread.

'My dear friend,' she exclaimed, holding out both hands to be kissed, 'it is so long since you were last here!'

For a Santa Sabina woman Serafina was tall and long of face, her hair tamed by years of effort from the usual black mop to a smooth and close-fitting style. The same could be said of most of her – bosom, belly, hips, bottom – smooth and close-fitting, so that she appeared to be almost tubular. She had a long nose, long thin bare arms, long and drooping breasts inside her thin frock, long thighs, and as Marcel's close acquaintance with her permitted him to know, a long thin slit between those thighs.

The naked girls on either side of her got up to make room for him and he sat beside Serafina on the sofa, asking her if she could spare the time to drink a glass or two of champagne with him. Naturally, she never refused offers of that type, and the bottle arrived in record time, well-chilled and poured for them by a broad-shouldered young waiter whose duties included escorting to the door any visitor who became annoying in drink.

Marcel raised his glass to Madame da Silva with a smile and made his excuses for long absence. He had been kept extremely busy on urgent diplomatic arrangements, he said with a certain distortion of the truth, and a lengthy tour of the countryside in the northern part of the island. One of Madame's thick black eyebrows arched upwards and she said with caution that strange and tragic events had indeed taken place, and doubtless these had demanded his attention.

It was a fixed idea of Marcel's that Serafina da Silva was in a position to know everything of importance planned or done in Santa Sabina. His reasoning for the curious and dubious belief was that everyone of importance dropped in to *zeqq* her girls and in the nature of things divulged items of information to the young women who pleasured them. By collecting and coordinating what her girls passed on, Serafina came to know all! Except that it was not certain that under President da Cunha's rule government Ministers knew anything worth divulging, even after a thorough *zeqqing*.

Nevertheless, what could be said with some assurance was that Serafina knew all the gossip, which was a type of information, perhaps. Marcel looked at her with an enigmatic expression and said 'Enriquez da Motta' in a low and confidential voice. At once she stood up and asked him if he would like to accompany her to her office. He nodded, and would have taken the champagne bottle and glasses with him but Serafina clicked her fingers for the waiter to do that.

Her office was at the back of the house, a comfortable room with a rosewood desk and a pair of eighteenth-century style chairs of an undistinguished hand. The burly waiter refilled the glasses and departed, Serafina sat down and waved a hand at the other chair in permission. Marcel sat down and crossed his elegantly trousered legs, wondering for the hundredth or more time how he had ever managed to ingratiate himself with a bordello-keeper.

'You mentioned the terrible fate of Monsieur da Motta,' said Serafina in a solemn voice. 'It was not an accident, although the *Daily Chronicles* was ordered to say so. But you must know that already, Monsieur Marcel, you who are the secret head of French Intelligence here in Santa Sabina.'

A good many people shared this belief of hers, Santa Sabinan and foreign, to Marcel's amusement. It had originated a year or two earlier in a misunderstanding with a drunken CIA agent who at that time was with the US Embassy and who was *zeqqing* the American Ambassador's blonde and brainless daughter on days when Marcel was not. There was no point in denying the rumour – that was expected of espionage agents.

'That is perfectly correct,' he said. 'It was no accident.'

'There are some who say that Monsieur da Motta was murdered by the Bureau of Public Information,' said Serafina, glancing round the room as if she suspected an employee of the notorious secret police might lurk behind the curtains or under the worn chaise longue by the wall.

Marcel saw she needed to be encouraged, or he would

sit here for hours listening to bar gossip in tiny portions. He stood up to move closer and perch one cheek of his backside on a corner of the desk. He smiled down at Serafina and pulled one strap of her maroon and gold frock off her shoulder, then felt down into it to grasp a long dangling bare breast. It was slack enough for him to lift out of her frock completely, and he murmured 'Enchanting,' to observe the gold ring that hung from its long brown bud. She was the only woman he had ever known with breast ornaments like earrings. The first time he saw them, when she came back from a vacation in Goa, had been an exciting moment for him.

'I have heard it said that da Motta was eliminated because he was plotting against President da Cunha,' he said idly, playing with her long soft breast. 'Have you heard this too?'

She nodded and undid the back of her frock and pulled it down to bare the other breast, long, pale brown-skinned, and golden-hooped.

'Monsieur Sanches comes here often,' said Marcel, fondling a *gubla* in each hand as he named the dreaded chief of the Bureau of Public Information. 'He adores *zeqqing* your pretty girls and you are his friend – perhaps he has told you what happened.'

Serafina nodded and raised both black eyebrows in a grimace.

'Why do you ask me, Monsieur Marcel, when you know Monsieur da Motta was murdered by the Russians,' she said in a voice not much above a whisper. 'The Bureau has proof of this.'

'What?' Marcel exclaimed in surprise. 'But what reason could the Russians have for that?'

'Ah, but you make a fool of me,' sighed Serafina, putting her hands over his to encourage him to squeeze her slack breasts harder. 'The Bureau has established that Monsieur da Motta was working for you French to overthrow the President and take his place. Your Ambassador has been recalled in disgrace because of the failure of your plot. Monsieur Sanches knows it all. It was a surprise when you arrived here this evening, as I thought you would have shared the responsibility and been recalled with the Ambassador.'

*Bon Dieu*! thought Marcel, hardly able to believe what he was hearing. Was Emilio Sanches and the fearsome Bureau of Public Information so insanely incompetent that they took this rubbish seriously? Or was this a story concocted to divert suspicion from their own killing of da Motta? If so, the implications of apportioning blame between the French and the Russians were too awful to think of. Armed with that fiction and bogus evidence manufactured by Sanches, President da Cunha would wring untold concessions from both Ambassadors. When the replacement arrived for Jean-Jacques Ducour, he would discover he had inherited a hornet's nest!

But what of it? Nothing of importance ever happened or would ever happen, in Santa Sabina. Nothing changed, which in its way could be thought reassuring. Now that Serafina had confided her astounding version of events, she dismissed politics from her mind, in favour of what mattered. She got up from her chair and stood between Marcel's parted legs, as he perched on her desk, to open his trousers and take out his soft *zimbriq*.

'*Amasta na zeqq-zeqq*?' she said softly, her emotions causing her to lapse into incomprehensible Santa Sabina language as she rubbed her cheek against his and stroked his *zimbriq* firmly to make it grow hard. Marcel understood only one word of what she said – *zeqq* – but he was in no doubt as to the significance of her invitation. He drew her long evening frock slowly up her legs until he could slip a hand between them to feel the smooth flesh of her thighs below her loose-legged knickers – Serafina followed the fashion of Santa Sabina high society in underwear.

At her urging they changed places, so that she sat upon the desk and he stood between her wide-parted legs. She sighed and murmured and touched her lips to his in warm little kisses, her clasped hand sliding up and down his stiff part. Marcel's hand was up the loose leg of her knickers, caressing her thin-lipped *kuft*. Soon he had two fingers inside that long moist split and was teasing her slippery bud. Her Santa Sabina nature asserted itself at once – it was almost as if he had touched a match to the fuse of a stick of dynamite! Her long thin legs wrapped themselves round him and pulled him closer between her thighs, while she drew aside her knickers with one hand and pushed the head of his distended *zimbriq* into her wet *kuft* with the other.

'*Amasta na zeqq-zeqq!*' she said again, and this time it was not a question but a demand – and one that Marcel was happy to comply with. He pressed his cheek to Serafina's and closed his eyes to avoid seeing the very large brass crucifix that hung on the wall in front of him. He pushed upwards into her moist and welcoming depths and started to *zeqq* strongly.

Her legs were tight round his waist and her belly close up to his, but her long loose *gublas* flopped up and down against his chest to his thrusts. He rolled them in the palms of his hands, played with the gold hoops through their long brown buds, then squeezed handfuls of the soft flesh, and tugged at them as if using a bell-pull to summon a servant.

Serafina gasped, and babbled in the old language, thrusting at him with her in time with his urgent rhythm. The bell he tugged was suddenly answered – the climax he had summoned now made its appearance – and Serafina moaned and throbbed furiously against him in noisy ecstasy. To Marcel it felt as if her slippery *kuft* had become a hand clasping him and massaging him in a frenzied rhythm that could have only one outcome – and an instant later he dropped his hands to her back and pulled her towards him on the polished desk to pierce her belly as deep as he could while his rapture spurted up into her.

When they were tranquil once more they separated to rearrange their clothes and sit on the chairs while they finished off the bottle of champagne.

'My dear Serafina,' said Marcel politely, 'that was perfectly marvellous. The pleasure of your company has improved my mood.'

Her dark and knowing eyes stared at his face.

'Something has disturbed you – I saw that when you

arrived,' she said. 'Is it the affair of Monsieur da Motta and the French plot being ruined by the Russians? Or something more important – a disappointment in love, perhaps?'

'As always, your intuition is correct,' Marcel admitted with a tiny shrug. 'A disappointment, yes. Love is too strong a word for the emotion concerned – a sentimental attachment is perhaps more precise.'

'The French lady I saw you with at the Gran'Caffe Camille?' Serafina enquired sympathetically.

'That one and another. Two ladies, in fact,' he said with yet another shrug. Without knowing why he did so, he explained that the two women he adored had gone away and left him, and not for other men, but for each other. Serafina listened carefully and expressed her complete amazement that any woman could think of bringing herself to abandon so handsome, elegant, educated and vigorous a lover as Monsieur Marcel! But, alas, that was the way of the world. He must restrain his natural grief, for to be sad was to die a little, and very soon there would be others to love him and *zeqq* him.

In fact, said she, there was a new girl at Maison da Silva, a charming little creature with big soft *gublas* and with a skill in *zeqqing* that delighted everyone who made her acquaintance. She had been upstairs with someone of the first importance when Marcel arrived that evening, otherwise he would have seen her. By now she would be back in the salon and what Monsieur Marcel must do was meet her and buy her a drink. After that, matters would no doubt take their destined course.

To make sure he took her advice, Serafina stood up and held a hand out to him. Marcel got up and went with her, amused by the way in which she had reverted to business. To *zeqq* Serafina was an act of friendship on both sides and cost him nothing, though he would be charged for the champagne. But friends or not, she expected him to go with a girl before he left, and she would be displeased if he did not. After all, she had her living to earn.

There were two other men in the salon now, early arrivals for the evening's entertainment. He recognised them both – one was a senior member of the Chamber of Deputies, the other Colonel Jiri Svoboda of the Czech Embassy and also, some said of the KGB. Both rose and bowed in greeting to Madame da Silva before resuming their chat. The girls clustered around them, smiling and waggling their bare *gublas*, hoping to be picked.

'There she is,' said Madame. 'Isn't she pretty?'

She beckoned to one of the girls in the throng, who smiled at being chosen by Madame for a patron, and came to be introduced to Marcel, wiggling her plump round bottom. At first he didn't recognise her. When he met her before her olive-skinned delight of a body had been clothed in a white blouse and a short skirt of bright red. That was on the quay, waiting for the ship that brought Madame Nanette Jarre, the distinguished ethnographer, to Santa Sabina. She recognised him at once, and beamed at him.

Girls like her were, in Marcel's opinion, the fruit of the island. She was sixteen or seventeen, with the characteristic Santa Sabina mop of black hair, the round and amiable face, the well-grown bosom and the delicious thighs. Madame da Silva saw the smile on his face and left them together. He drew her down to sit beside him on one of the bamboo sofas, put an arm round her waist and told the waiter to bring a bottle of champagne.

'My dear Carmelita,' he said, 'the last I saw of you was when you went on board the *St Fiacre* to meet your Captain. And now I meet you here at Madame's. Why is this?'

'Captain Bertran wasn't on his ship,' she said with regret in her voice. 'He will never come to Santa Sabina again, the poor man! It is too sad!'

'But what happened to him?'

'The new Captain told me. Captain Bertran drank too much when he was at Port Said. He fell off the dock in the night and was drowned. I shall never see him again, so I came here to Madame, to meet important people.'

'But this is tragic,' Marcel commiserated with her. 'Life is an endless tragedy where those we adore the most are taken away from us.'

'Yes, it is true, Monsieur Marcel,' said Carmelita, 'but what can we do when we lose old friends?'

'Then we make new friends,' he answered, handing her a glass of local vintage. The label had a picture of a chateau and the words *Moet Blanc de Blanc Chateau Malmaison*, a curious concept of some interest, though without foundation.

'You are right,' said Carmelita. 'Come upstairs with me.'